Death Line

Maureen Carter

D1343003

CREME DE LA CRIME

First published in 2010
by Crème de la Crime
P O Box 523, Chesterfield, S40 9AT

Typesetting by Yvette Warren
Cover design by Yvette Warren
Front cover image by Peter Roman

ISBN 978-0-9560566-3-4
A CIP catalogue reference for this book is available
from the British Library

Printed and bound in the UK by
Cox & Wyman Ltd, Reading, Berkshire

www.cremedelacrime.com

About the author:
Maureen Carter now lives in Birmingham and has worked
extensively in the media.

www.maureencarter.co.uk

As ever, I am hugely indebted to Lynne Patrick and her exceptional and inspirational team at Crème de la Crime. It's a pleasure and privilege to be with this innovative and exciting publishing house. For professional expertise, knowledge and insight, I'm more than grateful to Lead Forensic Scene Manager Robin Slater and Investigator Chris Elliott. Their input is more valuable than I can say, and goes far beyond answering my countless questions. Any errors of interpretation are mine.

As I've said before, writing would be a lonelier place without the love and support from some special people. For 'being there' even when they're sometimes miles away my love and affection go to: Sophie Shannon, Dan Rees, Veronique Shannon, Suzanne Lee, Paula and Charles Morris, Corby and Stephen Young, Helen and Alan Mackay, Frances Lally, Anne Hamilton, Jane Howell, Henrietta Lockhurst, Sheila Quigley and Bridget Wood.

Finally, my thanks to readers everywhere – as always this is for you.

For Peter

The burgundy leather cover gave no clue to the scrapbook's contents. A hand tentatively leafed through the pages, the reader's face impassive, inscrutable. Every item was cleanly cut, painstakingly positioned: news cuttings, magazine articles, family photographs, the symmetry and chronology clearly important to the collector. The first story was on the opening page, dead centre. A short item, it was clearly breaking news: detail was sparse, head and shoulder snapshot slightly blurred. *1 July 1980* and *Leicester Mercury* was handwritten: black ink, bold copperplate.

Missing child

Police are increasingly concerned about the safety of 10-year-old Scott Myers.

Scott (pictured) hasn't been seen since leaving Belle View Junior School at Highfields yesterday afternoon.

Detective Inspector Ted Adams told the *Mercury* that Scott was not in trouble at home and had not gone missing before.

The little boy was wearing a navy blue blazer, white shirt and short grey trousers.

Anyone who may have seen Scott is asked to contact Leicester police on 01533 999999.

The holder of the scrapbook stared intently at the photograph as if willing the little boy to speak, to share his secrets; exploratory fingers ran over the grainy image, tenderly traced Scott's lips captured for ever in a gap-toothed smile. Had he been self-conscious about that? Had his friends teased him? Children could be so cruel.

Either way, the gap was tiny. It would have closed naturally. Given time.

TUESDAY
1

Josh lagged behind in the stuffy classroom, desperate to be last out. He was small for his age, wore nerdy glasses, scruffy clothes and knew he smelt bad. The other kids were always on at him, giving him a hard time, calling him Stig, as in dump. Worse, Brett Sullivan's gang usually lay in wait to give him a good hiding. Josh dreaded going home time.

Not knowing where the big lads would be was the pits. Some days they crouched by the stinky wheelie bins outside the kitchens, another time they'd be sniggering round the side of the bike sheds. Once or twice they'd followed him to the house, calling him names, throwing stones, booting him up the backside, ripping his t-shirt. Just thinking about it made his stomach churn like as if he was going to throw up. It wasn't as though he had any money or a mobile. As if. The big kids got a kick out of seeing him cry, bashing him, making his life a misery.

Little legs tightly crossed, Josh paused at the main entrance, pressed his nose against the reinforced glass and peered through into the playground. Bright sun, blue sky again; the teachers were calling it a heatwave. Josh shivered, checked the shadows. Was the coast clear? Well, his mum wasn't going to be there, was she? Never had been really. Chewing his lip, casting wary glances, Josh slipped through the heavy swing door. He knew his mum drank too much, took too many drugs, didn't clean the house or cook nice food. He loved her though, loved her to bits – and she only hit him when she was really, really, mad. He worried himself sick when she passed out. What if she didn't come round one time? When she was in a good mood, had a few quid to spare, it was mint. They'd fetch fish and chips, maybe pick up a DVD – Harry Potter, something like that – then cuddle up on the settee. She'd ruffle his hair, tell him he was her big man. His sweet smile faded fast. When had they last done that?

He sniffed, caught a whiff of exhaust fumes, glanced up to see the ice cream van pull away. His mouth watered. What he wouldn't give for a 99 or a Magnum. Not that he'd turn his nose up at an ordinary ice lolly. Fat chance. He was well skint; couldn't remember the last time he'd had money in his pocket. Head down, he scoured the pavement just in case...

It was just before he reached the block of cheapo shops, beginning to drop his guard when they jumped him. Brett and one of his bully boys. Mouth dry, heart pumping, Josh darted nervous glances every which way. Why was no one there when you needed them? Strong hands grabbed his arms, spiteful fingers pinched his flesh as they frogmarched him along.

"This way, Stiggie," Brett sneered. Like Josh had a choice. His scuffed trainers barely skimmed the pavement.

"What you want? I ain't got nothing." Josh hated the whimper in his voice. Made him sound a wuss.

"Shut it, loser."

He bit his lip, tears pricked his eyes. "I'm not a los..."

"Loser, loser, Stiggie is a loser." They were both at it now, winding him up, pulling stupid ugly faces.

He'd not cry. Not give them the satisfaction. "Come on, Brett, let me go. I never done nothing to you." Brett jabbed a bony elbow into his ribs. "Stop whinging. Dumpboy."

Josh smelt dog shit, hot tarmac. They were nearly at the waste ground on Marston Road. He so didn't want to end up there; all those bricks and rubble. They'd use him as target practice again. *Please God, don't let me pee my pants.*

"Wh… where we going?"

"The pictures, not." Brett flicked his finger into the little boy's cheek. "So you won't be needing these will you, speccy?" He snatched Josh's glasses, twirling them round and round. Shit. Not another pair. His mum'd go ballistic. Josh licked his lips, tasted blood. Scared, hacked off, he lashed out but they released their grip and were already scarpering. "Give 'em back," he yelled. "Please! I need 'em."

"Come and get 'em, shit brain."

Lost without his specs, Josh could barely focus; Brett and his mate were just blurry figures in the distance. Fists clenched, eyes smarting, he thought about giving chase, but even if he could catch them, what was he going to do? He sighed heavily, in no hurry to get home now; his mum'd kill him. Dashing away angry shameful tears, he dragged his feet, vaguely registered a red car idling at the kerb just up ahead. As he approached, the driver wound down the window. "Want to go after them? Teach them a lesson?"

Josh squinted. Did he know the man? The face looked vaguely familiar but without glasses the little boy couldn't be sure. He remembered what his mum said about getting into strangers' cars. Best not. "It's OK, thanks, mister."

"Your call. I'm surprised you're happy to let them get away with it though, Josh."

Josh? He must know the bloke. As for letting gobbie Brett get away with it – like hell. Face screwed, he peered closer. "What you mean, mister? Teach 'em a lesson?"

"Hop in, Josh. You'll see."

2

Detective Sergeant Bev Morriss glared at the pewter sky over a tatty council house on the Quarry Bank estate and told God to get her act together. The clock was ticking: the kid who lived here was missing, all hell was let loose. It was a category A incident, every available officer on the case. Bev had been landed with mother-watch – not a pretty sight. She'd just slipped out to make a call. Or that's what she'd told the family liaison officer who'd more than earn her whack with this one.

Leaning on the wall, a Doc Marten against the brickwork, Bev lit a Silk Cut, inhaled deeply, blamed the smoke when her eyes stung. Yeah right. Except it was more the image of a little boy with red hair, Bill Gates glasses and a cheeky grin – William Brown meets the Milky Bar kid. Her weak unwitting smile lasted only seconds. Ten-year-old Josh Banks had vanished into emaciated air and even out here, even over the intermittent drone of the police helicopter, the low-level buzz of traffic, Bev could hear the mother wailing.

And the cop in her was questioning if the grief was genuine. Josh had been missing for three hours before Stacey Banks raised the alarm, since when she'd shown wall-to-wall hostility. Bev hadn't even taken the brunt of it. The woman's foul-mouthed abuse had been targeted at the initial search team, even though she'd been told the family home's the first place cops look for a missing child. Home Sweet Home? Not always.

Cynical? Damn right. Bev had seen it all and then some. Either way, Josh had not been hiding and his body had not been hidden. Though filthy and rank, in the legal sense the house was clean. Ish.

Light spilled on the narrow path as the front door opened and her partner DC Mac Tyler emerged. She budged along a gnat's so he could join her, watched him wipe an already moist hankie round his clammy neck. Mac was mid-fifties and not so much running as ambling to fat; she doubted either was responsible for the heat under his open collar.

"OK, mate?" Her enquiry was casual, the glance concerned.

"Sure." The response was knee-jerk. His tense features reflected his real thoughts. With two lads of his own, he had more idea than Bev what the impact would be if one went AWOL. In what little spare time the job left, Mac did stand-up comedy; right now he wasn't cracking a smile, let alone a joke.

"Give us a drag, sarge." He held out two podgy fingers, a gesture that would normally have sparked an irreverent one-liner; she passed the baccy on autopilot. Mac took a quick draw then, grimacing, ground the stub under a scuffed desert boot. She wasn't surprised: he usually equated smoking with a one-way ticket to Switzerland. Their deep sighs were synchronised, both lost in speculation, both vaguely aware of the urban ambience – such as it was.

A snatch of Lily Allen's *Smile* drifted from a passing soft top; a scrawny Alsatian-cross piddled down a black bin liner; eau de curry and Ambre Solaire wafted in the still warm air. And an irritating TV ad from within signalled the end of *News at Ten*. Because you're worth it. Bev sniffed. Says who?

"That's another thing," she muttered. "I wish she'd turn that sodding telly off." The widescreen plasma had been blaring since their arrival: *The Bill* and *Big Brother* were bad enough, but the coverage of Josh's disappearance was neither use nor ornament.

"Helps, maybe," Mac offered. "Seeing what we're doing."

"Helps?" The voice was inadvertently high; volume lower,

6

she continued, "Banging on about the 'golden hour of a police investigation'. That's all we need." The sneer was over the top, but her fear was still there. Cops know if an abducted child's not found sharpish, odds are a body will turn up. The hanging around not knowing either way was, for Bev, the worst time. Except when... She closed her eyes, banished never completely buried flashbacks of small broken bodies. Dear God, please let us find him.

She swallowed hard, told herself it was still just possible Josh hadn't been snatched; though for seven hours he'd certainly not been seen. He'd walked out of Hyde Lea junior school in Jubilee Row that afternoon – and that was it. Nada. Thank God it was July and they'd still had a few hours' daylight to play with.

Highgate's new boy Detective Chief Inspector Lance Knight was co-ordinating the inquiry; Bev hoped it didn't turn into a baptism of fire. DCI Knight – dubbed Lancelot, natch – had called the right shots so far. Not difficult: police procedures were well established. After searching the immediate area, a mix of uniforms and detectives had visited Josh's school friends, called on relatives, canvassed passers-by and questioned drivers. No leads had been uncovered, so special-ist search trained officers had been called in.

The hastily-assembled Police Search Advisors – known as POLSA – had made a start on tracing Josh's footsteps; the half-mile route covered a row of seedy shops, rundown terraces and a scrubby patch of wasteland. Despite the police activity and as yet limited media coverage, not so much as a dodgy sighting had been reported. Light was fading now and the hunt would be winding down, but at dawn the search grid would be extended, tooth combs made finer.

"Think we'll find him, boss?" Mac hitched baggy denims over a button-straining paunch. She glanced along the street: drizzle danced like fake diamonds in the muted glow of the few street lamps that weren't faulty or fused.

"Not out here we won't." She peeled herself off the wall, nodded at the door. "Let's have another crack at Madonna."

3

Stacey Banks resembled a bleached whale with attitude. Her coarse over-dyed hair looked like wee-coloured straw with ginger roots. Under the blubber and pasty face it was just conceivable a slim pretty woman was not struggling to get out. Currently her backside was wodged into the shabby depths of a sludge-green settee. The skimpy yellow sun dress was a brave choice: the dimpled thighs were too fat to close let alone cross. At twenty-six, she looked forty-plus. The over-heated under-ventilated room stank of body odour, chips and cheesy feet.

When Bev and Mac re-entered, Stacey lifted a lazy-eyed glance. She'd been staring morosely at a school photograph of Josh that lay quivering on her lap. Taken two years ago, it was the only picture in the house of her first-born. Copies had been circulated to other forces and the media, missing posters would be printed and posted first thing. If need be.

"'Ave yer found 'im?" Her Birmingham accent was broad, the delivery still slightly slurred. Bev's blank expression was answer enough. Stacey Banks's porcine eyes creased in contempt. "Fuckin' useless. The lot on yer."

And you'd know, sister. Bev bit back the barb; a spat with the mother wouldn't help relations with the FLO. Cathy Reynolds would likely be here all night and on hand to take the flak. Besides, whatever Bev's opinion of Stacey, this was about Josh. But, boy, had she struggled to find common ground. She was now short on benefit, big on doubt. Unlike the colleagues she knew who'd cut a withering glance and dismiss Stacey Banks as white trash, Bev didn't do stereotypes, but she'd seen the

9

statements taken from neighbours and they read like scripts from *Shameless*.

Word on Mill Street had it that Stacey Banks was an anti-social slob who lived on benefits and booze, supplementing handouts with thieving and blowjobs. Police cautions for shoplifting and soliciting confirmed some of the hearsay. Worst sin in most neighbours' eyes? When there was a man around, she didn't give a toss about her kids. There was no current partner, according to Stacey.

"Where is he?" The heavy-weather wailing set Bev's teeth on edge. "Where's my little boy?" A dry-eyed Stacey buried the picture in mounds of cleavage.

Bev un-balled her fists and perched on the threadbare arm of a health hazard chair. If the woman hadn't been off her face it might've occurred to her earlier that Josh hadn't arrived home.

Still, Mother Earth knew where her other kids were. She'd offloaded the year-old twins at her mum's place round the corner. Back in January. It was either that or – according to social services – Jordan and Joel would be in care now. As for the six-year-old, he lived with his father. Tracing Josh's was more difficult. Bobby Wells was less one-night stand, more lunchtime shag. If Stacey was to be believed, his name was no more pukka than the address he'd fobbed her off with. If.

Bev had another stab. "You're sure he's never had any contact with his dad?" It was one of the first questions they'd asked. Same when any child went missing. Stranger-danger is always drummed into kids – even though stats prove it's parents some should fear most.

"How many times you need telling? He buggered off years back. Josh wouldn't know him from Adam. Nor give him the time of day if he did."

"And you say Josh has never gone off before, love?" Mac

tried the paternal approach; again it wasn't the first time of asking. But if Josh made a habit of bolting, they could maybe tone down the urgency level. Stacey rolled her eyes, she'd already answered. Mac persisted. "I know what kids are like… They get an idea in their head, lose track of time…"

"Read my lips, granddad." Bev read: go fuck yourself.

After you, sunshine. "Not helpful, Ms Banks."

"And you are?" she shrieked. "Why aren't you out there looking for him instead of sitting there on your arse, talking to me like I'm a piece of shit on your shoe?"

"Maybe if you…"

"Tea anyone?" Cathy half rose, more in peace-keeping mode than to make a brew. With a warm smile never far from regular features, she looked and played the Oxo-mum to perfection. In reality, Cathy Reynolds was Highgate nick's most experienced and ablest liaison officer.

Stacey swallowed a burp as she waved her down. "You ain't leeching off me. If you want tea, buy your own."

"I already did," Cathy said. "Don't you remember, Stacey?" The subtle implication eventually hit home, and Stacey's slack-jawed confusion morphed into sulky pout.

"More important things on me mind." Thrusting Josh's picture in Cathy's face. "Case you hadn't noticed."

Calm, unmoving, Cathy waited until the waving stopped. "We all have, Stacey. That's the only reason we're here."

"Yeah, and you're doing my head in." Snarling, she jabbed a thumb in Bev's direction. "'Specially that toffee-nosed bint."

Bev nodded at Mac. Enough already. They'd asked the biggies and were getting nowhere slow; further questioning now would be counter-productive. "I know it's a difficult time, Ms Banks." She rose, hoisted her bag. "But trust me, we're doing everything we can to find Josh. Try and get some rest, eh?" If nothing broke overnight they'd be back first thing.

"If I want your advice, I'll ask for it." The curled lip didn't do her any favours: Stacey's teeth were never going to sell toothpaste. The aggression was overt; Bev should've let it go but she was fighting for Josh.

At the door she glanced back. "There'd not been a row? Some reason Josh might not want to come home?" She could see a fair few but kids weren't bothered about living in a hovel.

For a fat woman, she sure could shift. Before she knew it, Bev's back was against the door, her head dodging Stacey's fist and baccy breath. Mac grabbed the woman's arm, pulled her off. "That's enough, love."

"Stuck up patronising cow," Stacey hissed. There was a lot of saliva flying around. "Think what yer like, but I'll tell yer this: Joshie's a good kid. He'd never do nothing to hurt me. Looks out for his mum, does Josh."

"Yeah?" Bev asked. "And who looks out for Josh?"

"That seemed to go well." Mac broke the in-car silence. They were heading for the nick, Mac driving, Bev scanning near empty streets on the off-chance of spotting a little boy who by rights should be tucked up in bed. Balsall Heath being part of the Balti triangle, its brightly-lit restaurants were still playing to packed houses; some, she noted, even had queues outside. Come to think of it, she'd not had a bite since a sausage sandwich at lunch. No sweat. Once she'd collected the Midget, she'd drop by Spice Delight and grab a take-out on the way home.

"I said that seemed to go well."

Yeah, and it wasn't funny the first time. "Big ho," she drawled. "Stick to the day job if I was you."

"Come on, boss. That's all you were doing. Your job. She'd no call to give you a hard time. You're a lot of things, sarge, but patronising's not one of them." Bev would've asked for elaboration but – novel experience – couldn't get a word in. "If I'd not dragged her off, the fat cow would've landed one on you. What was her problem?" Harsh words from Uncle Mac. He usually left the plain speaking to Bev. Then again, Stacey-people-skills Banks could rub a pumice stone the wrong way.

"Where to stop?" She stifled a yawn. The woman's truculence could be down to a bunch of factors: guilt, the need to blame someone, sheer grief at the terrifying prospect of losing Josh permanently. But Bev was too knackered to think straight. One thing stuck out though. "Know what got me? I didn't see her shed a single tear."

"I'd noticed." He hung fire while she checked in with the incident room. The call didn't last long, her monosyllables and fringe-lifting sigh said it all: nothing doing.

"Reckon she's pulling a Matthews, boss?" A few years back, Karen Matthews had colluded in the kidnap and concealment of her own daughter, then taken West Yorkshire police on a public and humiliating three-week ride. Caper like that damages trust: for a lot of cops, the name's now synonymous with conniving bastard.

Bev shrugged. A hoax so cruel needed animal cunning. She reckoned only one of those words applied in this instance. She thought it more likely the woman was still stoned, that Josh's disappearance hadn't hit her yet. Or arsey was her default mode when it came to dealing with authority. Either way, Stacey Banks was a big girl. It was a little boy with over-sized glasses who was giving Bev grief. She slipped Josh's picture out of her pocket, was still studying it when they turned into the car park at the back of the nick. Shoving it in her bag, she grabbed her bits, gave Mac a wan smile. "Don't forget Lancelot's brought the brief forward." Seven. Early birds catching wor... No. Best not go there.

"What you make of Knightsie, boss?"

The new gaffer. Not guv. Not to Bev. Only one of them at Highgate. "Seems decent enough." Time would tell; the new DCI had only been in post a couple of weeks.

Her hand was on the door when Mac reached his towards her. "Bev?" At the last second, he pulled back, didn't actually touch. She'd obviously taught him well. "The... er... guv... Any... word?" But not that well. She didn't have a problem with the 'Bev'; they were more or less off-duty and he'd been her DC for nigh on three years. Given the age gap and gender divide, she suspected his perpetual use of 'boss' held a hint of irony anyway. It was no big deal: respect between them was two-way, most of the time. But sniffing round her for news of Bill Byford was verboten any time.

"Back off, Tyler." Like she'd know anyway? The detective superintendent barely acknowledged her these days. Which was rich considering her erstwhile almost lover had saved her life a few months back. In the process, the mad git who'd tried to kill her had lost his. Now Byford – and everyone else at Highgate – was gagging for the outcome of the internal inquiry into his actions that night. Far as Bev was concerned, it boiled down to this: did her attacker fall or was he pushed? On to a handy rock.

"No offence... I just thought..." Mac raised an eyebrow.

"Well, don't." Back turned, she swung her legs out of the car. Other people's thoughts she could do without. Three weeks she'd spent in hospital recovering, and re-playing the scene over and over and... In evidence, she'd stated categorically that her assailant had slipped, that it was an accident. In truth, she didn't know, she'd not witnessed the fatal moves. With the guv's professional neck on the line, she didn't care. A damn fine cop stood to lose a sight more than his job. Like that was the only reason. Coming close to death had sorted Bev's emotional wheat from the crap. She'd finally admitted – if only to herself

– that she wanted Byford. Badly. And now, for whatever pig-headed reasons, he could barely look her in the eye.

Story of her sodding life. And Mac was sharp enough to pick up on it.

"You want something to think about?" Unlocking the Midget, she pointed to the night owls on the second floor; half-eleven and the incident room was lit like an operating theatre. There'd be no let up till the boy was found, one way or the other. "Think about finding Josh." She regretted the dig soon as it was out of her mouth. Mac of all people didn't deserve it.

Stern, straight-faced, he said: "Are you patronising me?" Dead serious. Except for the twinkle in his wise old eye.

The curve of her lips was involuntary. "Sod off home."

"Anything you say… boss."

Still smiling, she followed Mac out of the car park, flashed the Midget's lights as they wended their separate ways. Right now she wanted nothing more than to get back to her Baldwin Street pad, sling off the Docs, sluice under a hot shower, sink a vat of Grigio. She hit the gas, reckoned if she looked sharp, best friend and house mate Frankie might still be pottering round downstairs. She shook an indulgent head: Frankie had done a Sinatra, made yet another comeback as lodger, the bust-up that sent her packing in the first place paling into insignificance after the attack closer to home. Over the months since, Sister Frankie had tended Bev's wounds, physical and mental. Yeah. It'd be good to chew the cud with the old girl over a cup of cocoa. Or calvados.

Two hours later, eyes peeled, she was still in the MG cruising the dark streets of the Quarry Bank estate.

Just in case.

Eyes narrowed, Byford scanned a building site in Northfield. A child was missing: baby Fay. The cops had received a tip-off, an anonymous call. He caught a slight movement, a flapping, in his peripheral vision. He advanced slowly, then crouching he lifted some filthy sacking, dodged a concrete dust cloud that flew into the suddenly fetid air. Gazing down, he recoiled in horror; his stomach lurched in wave after wave of nausea. He tasted bile in the back of his throat, fought to keep it down. He wanted to tear his gaze away, but couldn't; more than that, he wished to God he'd never seen it. Baby Fay's tiny lifeless body reminded him of a miniaturised mummy, milky blue eyes stared sightlessly into his face. Unlike in the other dreams, the face wasn't Fay's. It was Josh Banks.

Screams woke the detective: his own. He flung off the duvet, perched on the edge of the bed, held his spinning head between naked knees, staving off genuine nausea. Calmed a touch by several deep breaths, Byford rose slowly, walked to the window, opened it even further, inhaled the slightly cooler, fresher air.

How long since the last nightmare? Two, three years? They'd recurred, albeit less frequently, since the early 1980s when Byford, a young sergeant on his first murder inquiry, had found Fay's body. He shook his head, not that the gesture affected the image. It would be with him until the day he died.

And watching coverage of Josh's disappearance had resurrected it.

Byford strolled back, drained the water glass on the bedside table. He craved a Scotch, but had already exceeded the daily limit he'd felt forced to impose a couple of months ago. The late news wasn't the only reason Josh had been playing on the detective's mind. Back at Highgate, he'd surreptitiously skimmed witness statements, kept a quiet eye on the printouts. His copper's instinct was in overdrive, part of him itched to be involved in the case. He knew it wasn't going to happen. Not with the internal inquiry hanging over his head. Maybe just as well. Fay's killer had never been caught. And the big man didn't think he could face failing another child.

Leicestershire police are extending the search for missing schoolboy Scott Myers. 10-year-old Scott disappeared two days ago on the way home from Belle View junior school in Highfields. The family's detached house is less than one mile away in Hill Top View.

Despite an extensive search of the immediate area, no trace of the boy has yet been found. Police are asking members of the public to join officers in a specially extended search this weekend. Surrounding fields and farmland will now be covered. Anyone who can help should meet at Highfields village hall at 8am tomorrow.

The man leading the operation, DI Ted Adams, has repeated his appeal for witnesses. "Someone may have seen something without realising its importance. Please don't be afraid of coming forward. Scott is out there somewhere. We all want to bring him home."

Scott's father, 35-year-old building company boss Noel Myers, said it was the first time his son had been allowed to make the journey from school alone. Mrs Amy Myers, Scott's mother, 29, was too distressed to talk.

By now the news story was splashed across the front page. Scott's photograph was sharper this time. His hair had that just-combed look and his clothes that semblance of Sunday best. What looked like a forced smile didn't quite reach the little boy's eyes. The formal pose suggested it was a studio portrait. The holder of the scrapbook wondered how the newspaper had acquired it. No pictures of the parents accompanied the article, which suggested they didn't want the press exposure. Not then anyway. The photographer had made do with a shot of the family home: white, detached, double-fronted. It looked smart, neat, well cared for.

Like Scott.

As the man stared, the little boy's image became blurred. His eyes brimmed, the angry tears taking him by surprise. He blinked hard, brushed his cheek. A damp spot appeared on the page of the scrapbook. As he watched it darkened and spread.

WEDNESDAY
4

"Morning, Mike." DCI Lance Knight's head appeared round the door of Mike Powell's office. DI Powell, a sheaf of print-outs in one hand, swung his legs off the desk, straightened a perfectly aligned grey silk tie and flashed a fake smile. One of his pet hates was people who waltzed in without knocking, an aversion he'd picked up over the years from Byford. Mind Knight could have rapped out the Blue Danube before entering, Powell still wouldn't be joining the new boss's fan club. Why drop by anyway? The brief was in ten minutes.

"What can I do you for, sir?" Powell ran ostensibly casual fingers through perfectly coiffed blond hair. The mateyness sounded forced even to his ears, but he'd rather eat shit than show he was rankled. Powell had also been up for the DCI job, reckoned he'd been robbed. Assumed his name was written all over it, hadn't figured on the board being illiterate. Was he hacked off? Hell yes. As if being pipped wasn't bad enough, Knight was three years younger, three inches taller and the best looking bald bloke Powell had ever set eyes on. Not that he was gay or anything.

"I hear you're good with the press, Mike?" Cool hand-in-pocket pose, the DCI exuded effortless confidence. Powell thought he looked more diplomat than detective, or a sort of James Bond special agent. Dressed the part too; his suits were almost as classy as Powell's own. Almost.

The DI gave a modest shrug. "I've done the odd turn." Media tart was how Bev Morriss put it. Got a way with words, had Morriss. Mind, Powell had realised recently just how tough it must've been for her a few years back when he got the

DI post over her. Maybe they could compare notes, lick wounds. Or something.

"Anyway…" Knight's full lips gave an almost imperceptible twitch. "The media's going ballistic over the Josh Banks story. The news bureau's got a list of interview requests long as your arm. Think you can manage the telly stuff today?"

"Piece of cake." Like hell. Powell saw a Damoclean sword. Or poison chalice. With Knight's sticky fingers on it. Being a talking head for the cameras was no problem, except the DI knew how these things worked. If there were no developments, there'd be naff all to say and muggins here would be the one getting it in the neck from the pack. Of course, if there was a half decent police press officer around to take… share… the flak: "Who's looking after it upstairs?" News bureau boss Bernie Flowers would be the obvious choice but the lucky bastard was on a sabbatical.

"I've asked Paul Curran to co-ordinate for the duration. Case like this needs continuity." Long fingers picked a speck of white from a charcoal sleeve. Powell spotted nails that were bitten to the quick; his childish smirk was subliminal, replaced by a knowing frown. Curran seemed a nice enough bloke but he was another new guy.

Maybe Knight sensed the DI's reservation. "Paul knows what he's doing. He was a reporter, knows what they want, how their brains work." Mindset of a vampiric vulture then. "Either way, Mike, with a kid missing, we need them on side." He lifted a cuff, checked a slim gold watch. Subtle. "Liaise with Paul after the brief, OK?"

Like there was an option. Powell seethed inwardly. Far as he knew, Curran had come from some cushy public relations berth in a sleepy Hereford backwater. Cutting edge media supremo he wasn't. It wasn't so much that, though; at least the guy would be malleable. It was the way Knight dished out orders that stuck in Powell's craw. Like he'd ever show it. "On it, boss. Good call."

"Yeah." Three, four second pause then: "I knew I could count on you, Mike." Powell looked away first, but not before he'd clocked the glint in Lancelot's eye. As the DCI headed for the door, Powell nonchalantly gathered a few files, pocketed pen and mobile. Close run thing, but he saw the skirmish as one-all.

When he glanced up the DCI was still in the doorway. "Don't play heavy with him, Mike. I know he's young, but he's enthusiastic, bursting with ideas. Give him a fair hearing. From what I've seen these past few weeks, this place needs a bit of new blood."

Powell's knuckles went white. That score-line? Maybe a tad premature.

5

"Somebody saw something. Somebody out there knows where the boy is." DCI Knight ran his cool gaze over a tense squad packed tight into a too-cramped space. Through the windows, an azure sky was at odds with the communal dark mood. With no small step let alone giant leap in the hunt for Josh, extra man- and womanpower had been drafted in. A bigger incident-stroke-briefing room was currently being fitted out along the corridor to cope with the scale of the inquiry now codenamed Operation Swift. Everyone hoped it would live up to its billing.

Bev carried out a quick scan, head-counting, clocking faces: a fair few she'd not seen before. Among them, maybe, would be members of the eight-strong POLSA team plucked from stations across the city. Wherever they worked the moveable feast of specialist trained officers tended to stick close, as in super-glued jam. Among new recruits were old hands: Powell, ankles crossed, leant against a side wall sucking a lemon; Mac, seated alongside, surreptitiously wiped canteen fallout from his shirt front; DCs Darren New, Sumitra Gosh and Carol Pemberton sat at a desk near the door. Propped against a printer was Jack-Mr-Nice-Guy-Not-Hainsworth, the incident room co-ordinator. New DC Danny Rees was on the front row, hanging on Lancelot's every hackneyed word.

Hackneyed. Bev pursed her lips. Was that fair? There were only so many ways to say what Knight was getting at. Police need witnesses. And in Josh's case, the squad needed quality intelligence now. As he paused to let the import sink in, Bev subtly scrutinised the new guy.

Until yesterday, their paths had barely crossed, but with any Category A enquiry it was a given it'd be headed by a DCI. After perfunctory intros, he'd kicked off the brief by naming Powell as deputy senior investigating officer which could explain the current citrus-sucking.

Brushing a shaggy shade-of-Guinness fringe out of strikingly blue eyes, Bev wondered idly if the follically-challenged Knight shaved his head. Lot of blokes did, cutting their losses and hoping the look was more macho. Not Knight. He was way too pretty to be a goon; the bald scalp only accentuated the chiselled bone structure, full lips, sexy eyes that were a tad bluer than grey. He was fit and knew it. One of the reasons she didn't fancy him.

Had a certain amount of sympathy though, must be well hard for any gaffer to come to an enclave like Highgate and lead a squad that took no prisoners. She gave a wry smile. Well, no prisoners far as bosses go. Bev knew the odd colleague was gunning for him, others would suck up like heavy duty Dysons. Which was worse? Close call, because behind the scenes they'd all hold back to see if he was any cop. Only then would he be admitted to the pack. Human nature, wasn't it?

Sharp cookie like Knight would be aware of all this peripheral stuff. He also had to contend with the professional pressure of the current case. A missing child didn't just give parents nightmares. Not that you'd know it to look at Knight. Casual, hands in pockets, he stood in front of one of the whiteboards like some trendy university don.

"The boy didn't just disappear in a puff of smoke." The smooth vowels would grate on some people round these parts. "We're not in the Bermuda triangle – and I don't believe in little green men." If he was waiting for a laugh it didn't come.

Ironically his head obscured the most important exhibit on the board: Josh's photograph. Bev didn't need to see it; the boy's likeness was fixed in her mind's eye. Like most officers here she'd worked on missing minors inquiries before, but something about little Josh touched her heart. Last night's trawl of the Quarry Bank estate had netted nothing. Back home, tossing and turning in bed, she was hard pushed to explain the nocturnal wanderings. Except a deep need to do *something* for a kid she fervently hoped to see in the flesh.

Knight stepped to one side revealing an enlarged street map, used a pointer to indicate key locations. "This is his school. This is where he lives." A thick red line had been added in shaky felt tip; Knight's pointer traced it. "This is the route he'd most likely take. It's not the Kalahari Desert."

Got that right. It was a half-mile strip surrounded by a maze of back streets that in New York would be called mean. It ran from Josh's squat redbrick school in Jubilee Row to the only concrete and steel high-rise still standing on the council estate. Dotted around were two-up-two-down terraces, a seedy block of shops, grafitto-ed lock-ups and a patch of waste ground. As for residents, it was ethnic all-sorts land, pavements clogged with burquas and crop tops, saris and shell suits, hoodies and hijabs. Cultures clashed, sure, street crime was rife, but people mostly rubbed along. Bottom line was this: it was riddled with places to hole up or be forcibly held.

"Anything on CCTV, sir?" Brown eyes earnestly creased, DC Rees leaned forward slightly. Out of uniform, tall, dark, smooth-cheeked Danny looked even more like a member of a boy band. And clearly keen to make his voice heard. It was a fair question – if you hadn't done your homework. This was Balsall Heath, not Belgravia. Low-rent dirt-poor areas aren't flooded with security cameras. Four, if Bev recalled correctly.

"Do you not read the reports, lad?" Two cameras had no tape, one wasn't working, the fourth was in that favourite haunt of small boys, a cut-price nail salon. Knight chewed a piece of loose skin from his thumb. "Try and keep up, eh?"

Not unreasonable. Masses of paperwork would accrue over the course of the inquiry. Keeping on top of it was essential and expected. There was too much at stake for left hands not to know what right hands were doing. Rees would learn.

"OK." Knight faced the troops. "We hit the streets, knock doors. Question shop keepers, householders, landlords, dossers, dustmen, dog owners. Anything with a pulse." Interpreters were already on standby. "We talk to taxi drivers, bus drivers, delivery drivers. Closer to home, we interview relatives, family friends, teachers, anyone who's had contact with the boy. Who's looking at sex offenders?" Abrupt change of tack. Meant to keep them on their toes? Bev wondered if he made a habit of it. He nodded as a couple of hands went up: Darren's and Sumi's. They'd have made a start yesterday. The register was always high on the checklist when a child was missing. "OK. Carry on, and if you need help – ask. That goes for anyone who can't cope with the workload."

The second whiteboard displayed the search grid. Knight talked as he walked. "As you know, it's a difficult terrain. Fortunately we have the top team. Joe Gregson leads it. Anyone with ideas, input, talk to him." All six-six of him, Bev gauged as a gym-trim guy with a grey buzz-cut rose to put face to name.

"OK, listen up." Heads turned back to Knight. "The POLSA guys will turn every stone, go through every outhouse, garden shed, lock-up. Check every drain, manhole, gutter and roof top. We walk the area, drive it, cover every centimetre. We find the boy. Failure is not an option."

That's OK then. Bev wasn't big on bluff. She sat back, arms folded, legs crossed. "Assuming he's still in the area," she said. "He could be anywhere by now."

Three, four second pause, then: "Detective Morriss, isn't it?"

26

Fingers slowly traced his jaw-line. As poses go it was classic. It cut no ice with Bev.

"Sergeant." She sniffed.

"Until we know otherwise, sergeant, it's where we concentrate resources."

She raised a palm. "Open mind is all I'm saying." It was one of Byford's mantras: eggs, baskets and all that. "Doesn't do to…"

They'd never know. Knight wasn't listening. "Ports and airports have obviously been alerted. And there'll be national media coverage." The stress on national was presumably for Bev's benefit. She opened her mouth for a comeback, but Knight was moving on. "Perhaps you could pick up on that, Paul? And for Christ's sake will someone get that bloody phone."

Carol Pemberton was nearest. The diversion was probably no bad thing. It was early days to cross verbal swords. Especially with a guy the troops called Lancelot.

This time joint focus switched to the fair-skinned sandy-haired man, early thirties perhaps, perched on a radiator. Not that the heat was on, only the metaphorical kind going by the unbecoming flush spreading up from his neck. Bev watched, fascinated. Poor Paul. Thrust into the limelight. And a ginger.

"No sweat, sir." Really? Denim shirts come with damp patches nowadays, do they? "For those of you who don't know, I'm Paul Curran." Bev had liaised with the press officer on a knife crime story a few weeks back. Knife crime, news? Given the number of blades out there, it was an oxymoron if you asked her. Curran had made a decent job of selling it to the media though. She had him filed him under DD, as in doting dad: his missus had not long had a baby.

Head down, she jotted a few thoughts, half-listening, as Curran ran through media interest: newspapers, radio and telly clamouring for access, interviews, pictures. Nice voice. She reckoned Curran could make a car manual read like the Kama Sutra.

"… course, they all want the mother." Bev's pen stilled: the media were after Stacey Banks? Already?

Curran held out empty palms. "Until the boy shows up she's the big story."

She was certainly big. Stop it, Bev. Curran was dead right of course. The media would want the full waterworks, close-ups on the tears, the hands wringing a damp hankie, the sobbed out appeal. Was Stacey up to it?

"What do you think, sergeant?" Knight had read the interview notes; Bev reckoned her thinking should've been pretty obvious. "Will she go for it?" Knight pushed.

"She may not need to." Every head turned as Carol Pemberton slammed the phone on the desktop. The ensuing silence lasted seconds, seemed longer. Carol, an experienced DC, mother of two school-age kids, swallowed hard then bit her top lip. Her classic features appeared calm, glacial almost. Bev knew her well, sensed she was only just keeping it together. "There's a body… a little boy…"

6

Blue and white police tape had been hastily slung round the wasteland's entire perimeter. The plot had housed five Edwardian villas until a few months back when they reached their dwell-by date and were demolished to make way for starter homes. Developers had second thoughts or faltering cash flow. Either way, the site was now an urban eyesore: weed-infested, fly-tipped, dog-shat. Among dust-coated nettles, crumbling house bricks, rusting bike wheels and stinking rubbish, clumps of poppies provided incongruous splashes of colour.

As did the white forensic tent erected over a little boy's body.

Though the entire Marston Road site was now ring-taped, an inner cordon marked out a forensically safe corridor to the main action. Or temporary lack of. A subdued five-strong Forensic Science Investigation team stood anything but at ease within the circle, waiting on the gaffer's nod. Elsewhere on the streets of the estate Operation Swift was in full swing; the inquiry's tactics had already been thrashed out and its tasks assigned at the brief.

Difference now? The squad was hunting a killer not looking for a missing minor.

DCI Knight was under the sterile canvas talking to police pathologist Gillian Overdale. Bev had heard enough and emerged head down, struggling to hold back the tears. When she'd prayed to see Josh in the flesh, she should have specified live. Thanks, God. Irony – and heartbreak – was that the little lad with mussed hair looked as if he was just asleep. Apart from what Overdale thought could be chocolate round his mouth there wasn't a mark on him. Not to the naked eye. Probing further was the pathologist's baby. She'd readily agreed with Knight's request to prioritise the post mortem.

Shielding her eyes from the sun, Bev strode down the pathway and headed for the Astra, metaphorically holding the shortest straw in straw land. Far as she was concerned, the DCI had passed the buck. Big time.

Tight-lipped, staring ahead, she ignored shouted questions from half a dozen reporters and five times as many onlookers keen to get in on the act. Great entertainment, wasn't it? Nearly as good as the telly: *FSI Balsall Heath*. What the…? Eyes screwed, she thought for a second she was seeing things. But, no. Pitched up at the end of a slew of badly parked police vehicles was a Mr Whippy van. For fuck's sake. Anyone'd think it was a fairground.

At the motor she stripped off the white suit and overshoes, chucked them in the boot. Glowering, she sank into the passenger seat, slammed the door. Mac had the nous to keep shtum. He'd been holding the phone-call fort in the car, plus the forensic guys were antsy about cross-contamination; the fewer people on site the less chance of evidence being compromised. He took one look at her rigid profile, fumbled in his pocket for a crumpled tissue. "Here y'go."

Out of the corner of her eye she caught his stubby fingers flicking through a dog-eared notebook, knew it was his version of a diplomatic silence. As her DC he'd suffered enough ear-bashings to know she hated sympathy and soft words. Josh's death had hit her hard; she needed a bit of space to get her head round it. Crimes against kids were always emotionally difficult to handle. Was the death two years ago of her unborn twins at the hand of a crazy making it even harder?

Making the job impossible? She closed her eyes, took a deep breath.

Mac opened the window, started the motor. Summer in the city and the temperature was rising. "Where to, boss?"

She raised a palm. "Give us a min, mate." The ice cream van's jingle blared, a tinny *Teddy Bears' Picnic*. Tasteful. Not. She shook her head. "Ever wish for a nine to five easy number? No shit-sticks. No psychos."

"No. And neither do you." He switched off the engine, half-turned to face her. "Come on, boss. We're the good guys. We'll get the bastard. Do we know how the lad was killed yet?"

"Should have it later today." She pinched the bridge of her nose. "Christ, Mac, what sort of scum kills a little kid and dumps his body like it's a pile of trash?" The vision of Josh in his makeshift shroud wasn't going any time soon.

The question was rhetorical. Mac's knuckles tightened round the wheel as she relayed how the lifeless body had been left a stone's throw from a busy pavement. Inside a filthy sleeping bag, fingers clutching a one-armed Power Ranger. Her hands shook with rage and frustration. Partly shock. She couldn't remember the last time a crime scene had come so close to making her throw up.

"Time of death?" Mac asked.

"Overdale reckons four, five hours maybe." The pathologist had hedged her bets: a warm night, insulation from the sleeping bag and Josh's tender years were all factors that could muddy what was by no means a precise science. But it was coming up to nine-thirty now, and with partial lividity and early rigor, the signs pointed to Josh dying between four and five a m.

Mac voiced a thought she'd already wrestled with. "So he could have been lying there some time?"

"Yep." She tapped a beat on her thigh. How many people had passed by? Dismissed the bag along with the other crap?

Imagined a wino in there catching his zeds? "Pensioner who lives round the corner found him." Showing a bit of community spirit, the old dear thought she'd do the decent thing and get rid of the sleeping bag in a skip up the road. That's what she'd told the attending officers. Course, she may have intended it as an extra blanket. Who knew round here? Skid marks showed she'd dragged it a few feet before the pitiful contents spilled out. A passing milkman had found the old woman in a quivering heap on the ground. When she was up to it, they'd question her again.

Bev fastened her seat belt, slipped on a pair of Raybans. And froze. Josh's specs? He'd not been wearing them. Had they fallen off, had the killer taken them? Were they missing or on site? Knight needed to know. She reached for her mobile, punched in a number.

"Cool sunglasses, boss." Winking, Mac turned the engine, checked the mirror. "Dead posh."

"Just hit the road, eh?" Quips she could do without right now.

"Where we going?"

"Where d'you think?" she said. "His mum doesn't know yet."

"Try and eat something, Stacey." The family liaison officer Cathy Reynolds pushed a plate of toast across a rickety kitchen table.

"Ain't hungry just now." Stacey lit another Embassy, traced her finger round an old burn mark on the bright red Formica top; cracked tacky lino was dotted with similar scars. Her face looked grey, the frizzy hair was pulled back in a tight ponytail, and she'd swapped the sun dress for black trackie bottoms and a hoodie. It wasn't just the gear that was more sober. Gentle, non-judgemental Cathy had sat up talking with the woman for much of the night. Stacey had become more reflective, more reasonable. There'd been no sudden transition into Mother Theresa, but she'd gradually dropped at least some of her defences. The FLO had gained glimpses of, perhaps, the real Stacey. Under the brash exterior, she'd sensed a woman who was bright, vulnerable and in despair.

"Switch the radio on, shall I?" Cathy smiled. Hoped the pop channel would drown the sound of truanting kids whooping it up on skateboards in the street.

Flicking ash and missing, Stacey shrugged a *suit yourself*. Michael Jackson's *Thriller* did the trick. "Any tea in the pot, Cath?"

She lifted the lid, peered in. Stewed and tepid. "I'll make another." Grabbing a piece of toast, she sorted the fixings while Stacey stared at the wall, smoking incessantly. Sunlight barely made it through the grime on the windows. When the bell rang Stacey bolted upright, cut Cathy a frightened glance.

"I'll get it." She was on the case already. Answering doors was part of a FLO's remit: two short rings meant Bev was likely out there – and the news could go either way. As it happened, Stacey heard it first. The story led Heart FM's ten o'clock bulletin.

A body's been found on wasteland in Balsall Heath. It's believed to be that of missing child…

Stacey gagged, staggered to the sink. Didn't make it.

7

"I thought her heart had given out, but she'd fainted." Bev drained half a bitter shandy, ran the back of her hand across her mouth. "Course, cracking her head open on the way down didn't help." Grimacing, she recalled the pool of vomit she'd slipped in rushing to Stacey's aid. She'd driven the woman to casualty to get the cut stitched, then opened a weeping emotional wound by taking her to the mortuary to identify Josh's body. It would be lying to say the shared experiences had drawn them closer, but the Wales-size wedge was gradually shrinking. Bev shook her head: must be easier ways to forge a connection. Whole sodding day had been crap: hot, sticky, soul-destroying. Ditto evening. No wonder a few of the squad had wandered over to The Prince. Knight had declined the invite.

"How is she now?" Paul Curran asked. The press officer had latched on to the party, though looking round the table it was more of a wake. Mac was dead on his feet, slumped against the bench, legs sprawled; Powell had barely opened his mouth. Danny and Darren were at the bar talking balls. Cricket, mostly.

"Her boy's dead, how'd you think?" The redhead flush again. Bev half-regretted the barb. Curran probably blamed himself for the news leak, or at least not staunching its flow. Mind, who's to say it *was* a leak? Enough reporters had been sniffing round Marston Road to put two and two together. One had probably taken a premature punt. It was a shit way for Stacey to find out Josh had died, but shortly after they'd all jumped on deck and there'd been saturation coverage: radio, telly, papers, web. With police blessing. DI Powell had done more turns than a Phillips screwdriver. And the inquiry still wasn't pointing in the right direction.

"I meant the injury, actually," Curran said, polite but standing his ground. "I can't begin to imagine how she feels emotionally."

Corrected, she stood. "No offence, Paul. Bark, bite and all that."

"None taken, sergeant." Nice smile, white teeth. And she had to admit, after the initial boob, he'd certainly known how to tame the pack. Almost had them eating out of his hand.

"Tell you this for sure." She tapped a soggy beer mat on the edge of the table. "Stacey'll feel a damn sight better when we nail the bastard." Then again, won't we all?

"I'll drink to…" He noticed her glass. "Can I get you another?"

Intravenous Pinot please. "Diet coke, ta." She was driving and there wasn't a bunch to celebrate. Though Overdale had been as good as her word and prioritised the post mortem, they still didn't know the precise cause of death. DCI Knight, who'd been in attendance, told the late brief there were no visible injuries, no signs of molestation, and clothing was intact apart from missing Mickey Mouse socks. Asphyxiation was Overdale's best guess, but given that means anything that cuts off oxygen, the term covers a multitude of sins. The absence of pressure marks, skin discolouration and tiny pinpricks of blood in the eyes known as ocular haemorrhages suggested some sort of toxic substance had had a hand in the death. Bev's sigh lifted her fringe. With the best will in the world, it'd be a while before the results were back from the lab.

Same with scores of bag-and-tags FSIs had lifted from the crime scene. Wide open site like that was a forensic nightmare, shedloads of potential but how much of it actual evidence? She pictured the sweet wrappers, cigarette butts, beer cans, bus tickets, soil samples, hoped there'd be gold dust among the dross. Hopes they might have come across Josh's glasses had already been dashed. Neither the forensic team nor uniforms searching the ground outside the cordon had had any joy.

As for the plod work, it was ongoing: house-to-house inquiries, street interviews, sex offenders' register, snout checks. Slow and ponderous, but it had to be done. Had people genuinely not seen anything? Or were they just not saying? She ditched the beer mat before it gave up the ghost. Difficult to believe witnesses wouldn't come forward when the victim was a kid.

"There's another reason I ask, sarge." Curran sat down, placed the glass in front of her. Miles away, Bev frowned. He'd lost her. "About Stacey?" A clue. "How she is?" He downed an inch of Guinness, looked a tad cagey.

"Go on." She sucked an ice cube.

"The media appeals." He held out flat empty palms. "I'm not slagging off Mike Powell, he's perfectly competent in front of the cameras, but the boy's mother would have a lot more impact."

Bev puffed out her cheeks. She'd already sounded Stacey out: the woman would do anything to see her son's killer rot, not necessarily behind bars. God help the bastard if she got her hands on him before the cops did. Even so, the media en masse at a mega news conference? It was a hell of an ordeal for anyone to go through. Maybe with some psyching up, a little coaching...

"Can it wait a couple of days, see how things pan out?"

Curran made eye contact. "You tell me."

He already knew, just as every member of the squad knew. Until they discovered a motive for Josh's death, they were dealing with a random killing.

And the same went for the killer.

Detectives are baffled by the disappearance of a 10-year-old boy from Leicester. Despite a massive police operation, there are still no clues to the whereabouts of Scott Myers. The year five pupil hasn't been seen since leaving Belle View junior school six days ago. Over the weekend, more than a hundred volunteers joined police officers and dog handlers in scouring fields and farmland near the family's detached home in the village of Highfields.

Police plan a reconstruction on Wednesday of Scott's last known journey, a week to the day since he vanished. Asked if other parents in the area should be concerned, the man leading the inquiry, DI Ted Adams, said: "Parents should always know where their children are.

We've no reason to believe there's a need to take extra precautions."

Visibly shaken, Scott's father, 35-year-old building company boss Noel Myers, pleaded with the public for help in tracing his son. "We miss Scott so much. If anyone knows where he is, for God's sake ring the police. If anyone's holding him against his will, I beg you to let him go." It's understood Scott's mother, Mrs Amy Myers, is in hospital after collapsing yesterday. The couple's other two children are staying with relatives.

Belle View school's head teacher Mr Sol Danvers described Scott as friendly, well-behaved and popular with both staff and pupils. He said everyone at the school was praying for Scott's safe return.

The man with the scrapbook studied the picture of Scott's father. Visibly shaken? He thought there were better descriptions: gaunt, haggard, eyes that looked almost haunted. Maybe that was the man's imagination, or the benefit – no, not benefit – of hindsight. The photo was one of several featured in the Mail's inside pages. Visible round the father's neck was a steel whistle on a piece of string. The man frowned but quickly realised that Noel Myers would have been involved in the hunt for his son. There was a picture of the boy, of course. The newspaper had used what the man thought of as Scott in his Sunday best. He gave a sad smile before moving his gaze to the next photograph, a long line of volunteers spread out across the Leicestershire landscape. All had whistles, all carried sticks to beat the grass, separate the undergrowth. Most wore shorts, t-shirts, wide-brimmed hats. The man imagined an unforgiving sun blazing down on a tired and desperate search party.

Party? Sighing, he shook his head. Yet at a quick glance and without context the shot was vaguely reminiscent of some sort of quaint country ritual, folk dancers, Morris men, harvesters. Instead of villagers searching for one of their own. The man ran his gaze along the people, but the image had been taken at some distance and it was impossible to discern features let alone recognise faces. He wondered if Sol Danvers had taken part in the search. He'd been quoted and could have turned up on the day. It was difficult to judge from the head-and-shoulders picture. He looked the part, short back and sides haircut, horn-rimmed glasses, sombre expression.

The man closed the scrapbook, traced a finger along his eyebrow. Would the outcome have differed had the story made the national press earlier? It was impossible to tell. Did it really matter after all these years? Staring into the distance, he pictured the past, found it almost impossible to contemplate the future.

THURSDAY
8

"... obviously you'll get it in writing, Bill, and the board'll have to ratify it. Just thought I'd tip you the wink, old man." Breezy. Dismissive. Condescending. The voice on the line was Harry Astwood's, Assistant Chief Constable, citizen focus. Detective Superintendent Bill Byford, tight-lipped, gouged a hole with his Waterman on the report he'd been writing. Astwood was more into politics than policing, a graduate tosser and ten years younger. Byford had no time for the creep and wasn't in the mood to pretend otherwise.

"Thanks for letting..." Whoops. A slip of the digit. Was ending the call prematurely the same as hanging up? Who cared? Byford slung the pen on his desk, sat back, loosened his tie. Six months of dark clouds on the horizon lifted in one fell swoop phone call. The internal inquiry had put Byford's personal and professional life more or less on hold since January. And now it was all over bar the rubber-stamping. So why wasn't he cracking open the Scotch, dancing a jig round the office? He rose, hands in pockets, paced an already well-worn carpet.

Richard Cooper was dead, nothing was going to change that. As to how he died, the inquiry had finally made up its split mind that it wasn't Byford's fault. Just like that. He turned his mouth down, wished he could be so sure. Christ, he'd been there that night and still had doubts, still had nightmares: Bev semi-conscious on the ground, her life blood leeching into the snow, Cooper looming over her with a baseball bat ready to strike the death blow. Byford dragging him off. Cooper dead with his head in the gutter, Byford kneeling beside him.

The detective had been on paper-shuffling since the incident. Now he was free to resume operational duties. Clean sheet. Stainless character. To coin a Bev Morriss phrase: Yeah right.

Wandering to the window, he avoided his reflection in the glass. If he didn't register the now permanent stress lines, the hair that was more grey than black, the slight stoop to his six-five frame, he could kid himself they weren't there, at the same time fully aware they'd worsened lately. That'd be the endless partying, the loose women. Ironic snort. Or was it the pressure, the soul searching sleepless nights? What if he didn't want the hassle any more? At fifty-more-years-than-he-cared-to-remember-plus, he'd served his time. The job wasn't what it used to be anyway what with all the hoop-jumping, the Forth-bridge paperwork, the mindless political correctness.

He sighed then narrowed his eyes. Something was kicking off in the car park below. Half a dozen uniforms running to motors, doors banging, tyres squealing. Was a time action like that would have sent his adrenalin into overdrive. He turned away, pulled a ten pence piece from his trouser pocket, tossed it in the air. Tails. He shrugged. To coin another Bev-ism: the suits could stick it where the sun don't rise.

First things first: grabbing his jacket from the back of a chair he headed for the door. Bags of time to make it official.

Josh's Joe 90 glasses were burning a metaphorical hole in Brett Sullivan's combats pocket. Couldn't be a real hole 'cause Brett had off-loaded the bins soon as he'd grabbed them, chucked them in a stinky dustcart and waved bye-bye. No naffin' use to him, were they? Nothing wrong with Brett's eyes, except for the last two days everywhere he looked Josh Banks's ugly mush stared back. And not just on the telly. When Brett had nipped in Select and Save to nick some fags this morning, the kid's pic had been all over the papers. Stupid git getting himself killed. And the cops wanting witnesses.

Brett was in McDonald's now, wagging it. School was no place to be. He needed to think. He polished off a big Mac then slumped against a cracked orange banquette. What the feck was he meant to do? Slurping the dregs of a chocolate milkshake, he gave the bird to an old geezer who'd glanced up, glowering. Granddad shook out a copy of the *Sun*, hid his grizzled face behind it. Stone me. Brett curled a lip. Stig was there again. Was it a sign from on high? Was it buggery.

He watched an ugly slag and her two screaming brats leave the next table then leaned across and dragged over a carton with a few chips in it and stuffed his face. Brett hated the filth. His older brother was banged up in the Scrubs, his old man had done more time than Big Ben, Brett himself could open a police caution shop. He owed the Bill squat. He burped then dragged a sleeve across his mouth. OK, Stig'd had it tough, but if Brett 'fessed up about the glasses, the cops wouldn't let it go. They'd needle him till he couldn't think straight. Then stitch him up. Sod that for a game of *Star Wars*. It wasn't down to Brett. Stig should've known better, stupid kid had been asking for it getting into that sodding car.

Bev stood at a desk, leafing through a pile of paper, glanced up when the door opened. Her widest smile was in situ before she could stop it. "Guv! How you doing?" She tucked a strand of hair behind her ear. It was ages since Byford last showed his face in the squad room. Scrub that. It was five months, two weeks, three days.

"Not bad, thanks." Brisk nod. She gave him a subtle once-over. Looked as if he was putting on a bit of beef, hitting the booze, maybe? Couldn't live without her, eh? Yeah. And I'm the Pope's daughter-in-law.

"DCI Knight around?" he asked.

Only if he was the Invisible Man. The place was comparatively deserted since the turnout first thing, just Hainsworth and a handful of DCs phone-bashing and taking incomings. Most detectives were in the field... detecting. And keeping the peace. A couple of officers thought a spot of bother could be brewing on the Quarry Bank estate, angry residents scared about their kids' safety, demanding police protection. Powell had asked her and Mac to suss it out, nip it in the bud. Mac was waiting for her in the car with a pair of secateurs.

Smile dropped, she matched Byford's delivery. "Not seen him since the brief." Jotted a number on a post-it note, shoved it in the pocket of her navy linen pants.

"He said something about a strategy meeting?" Partial enlightenment came from a rookie DC nestling a phone under his chin. "Policy review? Something like th..." He raised a finger, returned to the call.

"Cheers, mate." Bag hoisted, she was about to hit the road, took a call on the way out. Just some routine query from admin. Byford was now chewing the cud with Hainsworth over by the printers. Call ended, she headed out again, take two. Byford held the door.

"Ta, guv." He looked well pleased with the proximity. Not. Like she was? "You back with us, then?" The question was more to fill an uneasy silence than in any real expectation. If he'd heard from the brass, surely he'd have said? It wasn't as if it didn't involve her. She cut him a glance, couldn't read his expression as he worked on a reply.

"Maybe."

Was equally enigmatic. She frowned. "How's that work then?"

"Later, Bev. How about...?"

"Sarge!" Shit. Fire broke out? Bomb gone off? Both spun round, made brief body contact, side on. She felt warm flesh, smelt the soap he used, the mint tea on his breath. Had no time to consider what the effects were having on her heart rate. The detective constable who'd been on the phone was waving frantically from the squad room doorway. Even from here she could see he was wired.

"Sarge. The killer?" As she neared, his trembling hand held out a scrap of paper. "Looks like we've got a name."

And address.

9

Roland Haines. It had a familiar ring. Bev ran it through her memory bank. Where'd she heard it before? Byford was quicker off the mark. "He's known to us. Bristol police, if I remember right." He creased his eyes, clearly trying to recall the detail. "Case was in the news a few years back..." Not quick enough.

Waving the note, Bev glanced at the DC. "What you done with this?" True what they said. Cops were getting younger these days: floppy fringe, bum fluff, pimple cluster under a retroussé nose. This guy could've been on work experience.

"I passed it on to Inspector Hainsworth? He's getting a squad car there? Someone else is on to the gaffer?" Answers sounded like questions. Either way it was three out of three. Least he was learning. Textbook stuff.

They were back in the squad room now, Jack Hainsworth shouting down the phone, Byford heading for a computer. Sun streaming through the windows. Light on the case as well?

"What's your name?" Bev asked.

"DC Freeman. Tony." He was bouncing on the balls of his feet. Either the excitement was too much or he needed a piss.

Perching on the edge of a desk, she kept her voice calm. "You took the call?" It'd be dead easy to get infected by Freeman's excited conviction. Everyone wanted a collar but there was a load of nutters out there. Hoaxers. Axe grinders. Stirrers.

Eager nod. "Yeah. A woman." He smoothed already impeccable hair with a still fluttering hand. "Wouldn't say who she was. But she lives in one of the flats in Marston Road?"

Good. Should be easy to trace if need be. "Go on."

"Says she saw a motor pull up in the early hours on Thursday, and this bloke take something out of the boot. She thought it was a roll of carpet or something." Or something? Bev shuddered. Hold on, though. Unless Mrs X had X-ray vision...

Freeman must've read her thoughts. "Street lights were on, and she saw his face in the courtesy light."

Better. "How come she knew it was Roland – " Bev glanced at the note again. " – Haines?"

He shrugged. "Maybe she saw him in the papers like that guy." Freeman nodded over at Byford who was tapping a keyboard. Christ, Bev thought, the rookie didn't even know the big man. "Either way, sarge, she says she recognised the face, realised she'd seen him around."

Even better, but: "How come she didn't...?"

"What've we got?" The door took a hammering, Knight came hurtling in, tie over his shoulder, Powell on his tail.

"Take a look." Byford swivelled the screen. As one, they moved closer. He'd pulled up a court report from the *Guardian*. And a picture of Mr Nobody, the sort of guy you'd pass in the street, not think twice. Roland Haines still gave Bev the shivers. He'd stood trial for murdering a child in Bristol in 2005.

And been acquitted.

Haines hadn't changed much over the years. Apart from the lavish damson eye shadow. Clumsy. Head-banged a door according to Hawkins and Gibson, the uniforms who'd brought him in. Their word against his, and he'd been yelling blue murder. Had he not been so tired and emotional, someone might have given a shit. Haines was currently cooling off in a holding cell before helping with inquiries. The search team taking his Balsall Heath pad apart had already found a couple of heroin baggies. Leverage as they were known in the trade.

Elsewhere in the nick, feelings were also running high. To some cops Haines was already 'that murdering bastard'. Quite a few had dropped by to have a butcher's through the peephole. Not that it was a freak show. Roland Haines was middle-aged, mousy-haired, average height, average weight, average looks. Call me Norm, as Bev had just told Mac on the phone.

She was in the canteen, multi-tasking, scoffing a pasty and cramming for an interview: Haines's. Knight wanted her in on it. Mac was calling from Balsall Heath where, in lieu of Bev, he'd taken Carol Pemberton to cast an eye on the Quarry Bank's troubled waters. Sounded to Bev like they needed a little oil drizzled. According to Mac, a dozen or so hotheads were calling for a visible police presence 24/7 on the estate until Josh's killer was arrested. If not, Mac reckoned the ringleaders would likely take to the streets themselves.

"Any chance I can drop a hint we're holding a suspect, boss? Make clear it's off the record, obviously."

"Nah." She blew on a steaming mug of builder's tea. "Knight wants a lid on it. See how it pans out." Lancelot was adamant. The latest development was on a need-to-know basis. Not a peep to anyone, especially the press.

"Nice."

He'd lost her. "What?"

"Pan. Lid. Nice one."

"Hey, mate!" Three second pause. "Hear that?"

"What?"

"The sound of eyes rolling."

A mock guffaw down the line. "God, I love a woman who makes me laugh."

"Sod off, Tyler." Smiling wryly she ended the call, went back to her homework studying Roland Haines's criminal record. For an inoffensive looking bloke, he'd pulled some nasty stunts: flashing, lewd behaviour, child pornography, indecent assault, sex with a minor. He'd spent twelve of his forty-two sleazy years doing time. She checked her watch; Lancelot should've got his act together by now. He'd been liaising long enough with Bristol cops, hopefully he'd have something to pull out of the interview hat.

She drained her mug, blew pastry off the paperwork. No doubt about it: Roly had been a very naughty boy.

But was he a murderer?

10

"I. Did. Not. Do. It." The stint in the holding cell had sobered Haines. He wasn't going to make the judge's bench any time soon, but ramrod straight, arms crossed tight, he sat in a hardback chair in Interview Room One, skewering Lancelot with an unblinking stare. Bev clocked the ill-fitting, well-worn navy suit, the narrow tie that was in situ despite the sauna heat, the neat side-parting. Yep. Mr Conventional just about covered it. She cut the DCI a glance; though Knight was a sight more aesthetic than the tired surroundings, she doubted that was why Haines was giving him the dubious benefit of his undivided focus. The unwavering eye contact was more likely aimed at relaying what appeared to be the absolute conviction of his innocence. *I didn't do it* was pretty unequivocal, wasn't it? But then he would say that, wouldn't he? And apart from initially furnishing them with what sounded like a frankly flimsy alibi, the flat denial was all he'd uttered, albeit half a dozen times. As for turning down a brief prior to the interview kicking off? Cocky? Confident? Could go either way.

Bev crossed her legs, flicked a loose thread of cotton from her trousers. Just about the only sound in the deliberate police silence was the swishing of tapes, audio and video. The chewed biro in her hand was superfluous, other than giving itchy fingers something to do apart from close round Haines's scrawny neck. She sat at the DCI's right, observing, assessing, mainly Haines, to a lesser extent the DCI. Not being au fait with his interview technique, she needed to pick up subtle signs, intuit when he wanted her to jump in, or not. So far he'd been politeness on legs. Well, bum.

Swishing tapes, ticking clock, gurgling pipe. Stares that could be called hard. Or defiant. The silence wasn't working. Haines was playing the same game. Bev pictured a little boy's body on a slab in the morgue. This was no game. Why didn't the gaffer go for it?

"You were seen, Mr Haines." Knight rose, made a slow circuit of the metal table, came to rest against a pea green wall, hands in pockets, ankles crossed. "As you're aware, we have a witness."

"Maybe so." Casual shrug. "But they didn't see me."

Hoo-flipping-ray. Bev tapped the pen on her thigh. Haines had changed the record, if not his tune. They waited. Waited some more. Haines fidgeted in his seat, all shifty-eyed. Fact that Knight had positioned himself just out of Haines's eye-line was deliberate far as Bev could see. Since the get-go the suspect had barely acknowledged her presence; now he wouldn't even look at her. Could be telling. Though Christ knew what. Issues with women? Scared? Revolted? Certainly uncomfortable.

Knight upped the ante. Maybe anti. "Sergeant?" The anonymous call placing Haines at the crime scene had been transcribed. Knight nodded at Bev's copy on the desk, lobbed the ball in her court. "For Mr Haines's benefit?"

Haines was already familiar with its contents. Knight had read out the key points. Still, once more with feeling. She reached for the paper. Haines's corresponding backward movement was slight. He'd recoiled. Or had she imagined it? One way to find out. Chair legs screeched against floor tiles as she moved in. Any nearer and she'd be sitting in his lap. And it was no figment of her imagination. Beads of sweat oozed in a line above his thin top lip, buckets of it elsewhere must account for the smell now assaulting her nostrils.

She gave an ostentatious sniff, opened her mouth to start reading.

"Save it, love." He flapped a hand. "I'm not deaf."

Soon sodding will be. "Musta heard then. Name's Morriss. Detective Sergeant to you." She edged in an inch or two, didn't want the tape to pick up her next words. "Don't 'love' me – you worthless gobshite." The endearment had the undesired effect. For the first time Haines looked her in the eye. His tiny irises were pale blue, the palest she'd seen, the whites were flecked with red and the lashes sparse enough to count. Not that she stuck round long enough to take a tally. She glanced away first, then backed out of his face. Taken aback. What she'd registered was naked hatred. Pure evil, if she was given to oxymoron and cliché. And if the saying was true that the eyes are windows on the soul, then somebody close the curtains. Get a blackout. Haines was latest in a long line of crims who'd tried freaking her out. Fact he'd succeeded briefly was a first. Must be the contrast between the everyman look and those creepy peepers. God forbid she was getting soft in her not so old age. A cop couldn't afford that.

Haines gave a knowing smirk, cocked his head at the nearest tape. "Need to speak up a bit, love."

"Loser," she mouthed, then told herself to cool it. Haines wasn't worth the aggro. They were here to nail not nettle him.

Clearly Knight sensed the frisson. He pushed himself off the wall, casually strolled back to his seat. "Let's run through it again, Mr Haines. Where were you between the hours of midday Tuesday and five a m? Wednesday." Still scrupulously polite.

"Told you before." Haines stuck a nicotine-stained finger in his ear, examined the colour co-ordinating wax. "Why don't you check it out, Mr Knight?" He wasn't being polite. Less uptight now, he was taking the piss.

Like they weren't checking his alibi. Two DC teams were on the case as they spoke. For part of the time, Haines claimed he'd been doing business with one of the working girls operating out of two or three streets off the Hagley Road in Edgbaston. Officers were out there touting Haines's mug shot, armed with a description of the prostitute. Timing wasn't brilliant given the girls spent most of the day in bed, sleeping. And given what Knight had gleaned from the cops in Bristol, it was out of character for Haines to pay for sex. On past record, he usually took what he wanted. And not always from women.

Wasn't the only thing Knight had picked up. The child murder charge against Haines hadn't been heard let alone proved: the case had been dropped.

"Answer the question, Mr Haines." Knight tightened his lips a fraction. Patience running out? Gobsmacking it had lasted so long, considering what he'd learned from his opposite number.

The dead kid Robbie Sachs had lived with his single mum in the same rundown multi-occupancy property in the Saint Paul's district as Haines. 'Uncle' Roly was a soft touch when it came to providing sweets, soft drinks, somewhere for the kids to hang out. Robbie and a few of his mates used to gather in Haines's place to play computer games, net surf, that kind of thing. Until Robbie was found battered to death in Haines's bathroom.

Should've been an open and shut case. Then the judge threw it out. Contaminated evidence, DNA secondary transfer. Big time cock-up. Haines had been let off the hook.

Maybe he could read her thoughts. The slimeball had a smug smile on his face, probably regarded himself as fire-proof.

Knight smiled too as he leant across the desk. "You still a

kiddie-fiddler, Haines?"

Bev struggled to keep a straight face. Nice one, boss. Kiddie-fiddler was a term she hated, but it had done the trick. Haines was seething, the ears were getting a steam-clean now.

"You charging me?" he snarled.

Palms out, Knight asked: "What's the rush?"

"That's it." In his haste, Haines toppled the chair, headed for the door. "I'm out of here."

"Sit the fuck down." The DCI's bellow made Bev's bum prickle. "We haven't started yet."

Late afternoon, the search team had nearly finished. At that stage, Roland Haines's seedy bedsit wasn't a crime scene so two uniforms got the initial glory. Doug Wallace and Andy Pound had gone through all the rooms bar one. Saved the best till last, Dougie quipped back at the nick. Best or worst, depending how you looked on it. Either way the sock had been rolled up and hidden in the cistern: a child's sock, Mickey Mouse. Chances of lifting DNA were infinitesimal, but even then a damn sight bigger than it not belonging to Josh Banks.

11

The briefing room buzzed like an apiary on ecstasy; the squad had just been brought up to speed by Knight. The murder of a child was the worst crime in the book, and to have collared the killer so quickly was equivalent to winning the lottery. It was breezy smiles, matey winks all round, doubtless The Prince would be humming tonight, too. In contrast, a slightly subdued Bev had taken a seat at the back, hadn't even bucked up when Byford slipped in five minutes after the six p m start and adopted his once customary perch on the window sill. No matter how hard she tried, she couldn't shake off the image of Roland Haines's face when he'd been told what they'd found.

Knight sat on the edge of a table, swinging a leg. He'd witnessed it, too, but she'd describe his current mood as jubilant. "Course, Haines claims we planted it."

What he had actually said was *you stinking lying filth have stitched me up*. And that's about all he said. The rest of his comments, mostly four-lettered, were yelled at the top of his voice. The clam-like silence came only after a truculent demand for a lawyer. They'd had to suspend the interview. Pending the unforeseen, it'd resume first thing.

"Yeah, sure. General issue, isn't it? Kids' socks. Dead handy when a cop's fitting some poor sod up." Hainsworth's observation elicited a chorus of sniggers from the stalls. Bev would've joined in but for that image. Haines's reaction to the discovery was utter incredulity. The shocked expression so total and spontaneous, she didn't think it possible to fake. Jesus, for a second she thought he was going into cardiac arrest, clutching his chest, colour draining from pinched features. The scared-witless panic that ensued appeared equally genuine. Then it seemed to her as though, to Haines's way of thinking, the penny had dropped, a bent copper penny. Whatever other doubts Bev held, she was damn sure her reading of that, and Haines's searing contempt, was on the money. Didn't mean he was right, but...

"Can I let the press have a whisper, Mr Knight?" Tie askew, glasses slipped down nose, Paul Curran propped up a side wall. He'd been jotting notes on an A4 pad, looking gung-ho as the rest of the troops.

Knight considered it briefly. "Yeah. Man helping with inquiries. Usual line." Made sense. She clocked Mac's nod of approval. He'd been pushing for it to be made public since returning with Carol Pemberton from the Quarry Bank estate. A few tempers there were high as the temperature, he reckoned. Hopefully a suspect in the frame would assuage the hothead contingent.

"Aren't we naming him?" Curran asked. Did she detect a hint of disapproval?

Knight shook his head. "Not yet."

"How come?" Powell wanted to know.

"Loose ends. Time enough tomorrow." The tone said *end of*.

Decision wasn't down to the DCI sharing Bev's doubts; he wasn't privy to them. She knew he'd issue Haines's inside leg measurement once he thought the case was watertight. They were waiting on sealant, primarily the informant from Balsall Heath. Once they'd tracked her down an ID parade would be organised with Haines starring in the line-up. As to the prostitute he claimed could alibi him, teams were still in Edgbaston trying to trace her. Going through the motions? The girl was proving elusive. Or non-existent?

"Something on your mind, sergeant?" Knight asked.

She had neither time nor sympathy for Roland Haines. Guy was a sleazy turd who'd probably already got away with murder. But if he wasn't responsible for the sock found on his property, someone else was. She pictured that ashen face again, those freaky eyes, the spittle round cracked lips. Haines deserved to go down for how ever many years of his waste-of-space life were left.

But not for a murder he might not have committed. Not if the real killer went Scot free.

"Sergeant Morriss." Knight's hand was in his pocket, jingling coins. "Is something on your mind?"

She must've been staring into space. She focused on the DCI, shook her head. Haines wasn't going anywhere. It could wait.

Byford was waiting by the Midget when Bev knocked off just gone seven. The early out was as unexpected as it was welcome. Given the hours clocked up lately, she'd almost forgotten what her best mate Frankie looked like. La Perlagio – star that she was – had offered to have pasta and Pinot on the go for a girlie night in. Bev had declined. Not. She'd snatched Frankie's hand off. Perlagio. Pasta. Go figure.

Head down, still slightly preoccupied, she didn't spot the guv until they were at arm's length. Shame, that. She might have surged forward accidentally on purpose. Or beaten a hasty retreat. He was fiddling with his trademark fedora, so he didn't see her approach either. When he did, the smile that tugged his lips didn't quite reach the sexy grey eyes. "Bev."

How deep and meaningful could one word sound? Bugger. She wasn't ready for this, not in the mood. "Evenin' all." She gave a mock salute. Then mental cringe. As an attempt to lighten what could turn into a heavy exchange, it was piss-poor.

Must be the blue lamp on the wall. Thought association and all that bollocks.

Byford cottoned on, loosened up. "Wasn't he a bit before your time?" *Dixon of Dock Green*. Daddy of all TV cops.

She flapped a hand. "Don't ask." A few of the old shows were on DVD. It was forced viewing at her mum's house. "I blame the parents."

It was the full treatment now, his George Clooney smile. "So did Larkin." Philip. The big man was quick, but how quick?

"Pa Larkin?" Feigned furrowed brow. "David Jason played him, didn't he? *Darling Buds of May*?"

"He was better in Inspector Frost."

"Nah. *Fools and Horses* any day... why the fuck are we doing this, Bill?" Silence. Except a pair of pigeons, billing and cooing on the perimeter wall.

The 'Bill' was rare as hen's dentures, rarer than Mac calling her Bev. Byford held her gaze. She swallowed, reckoned the big man was a damn sight easier on the eye than Haines. And admonishing the guy was a bit rich considering she'd set the tone. But he was the one who'd put distance between them, nigh on six months of it. There'd been times she ached, not even to jump him, just to talk, have a quick jar after work, a cuppa in the canteen. Way he was studying her now, you'd think he wanted to paint her from memory.

"I don't know, Bev. You tell me."

She shook her head, toed the tarmac with a Doc Marten. Yeah, she was royally pissed off with him, but it wasn't just that. She was crap at letting people get close. Been badly burned over the years, best not to chance it at all. So, naff banter was easier than opening your heart; being in denial beat being in too deep. And wordplay was less risky than foreplay. The snort was loud and unwitting. Yeah right. She should be so fucking lucky. Morriss duvet action meant changing the sheets. Bev… the born again virgin.

The big man ran his fingers round the hat's brim. "Just that… you've been distant, Bev. I thought I'd give you some space…"

Space? More like a black hole.

"*I've* been distant? *I've* been…" She jerked her head round. The rising volume had startled the pigeons. They were winging it, scared shitless judging by the brickwork. Hands on hips, she lowered her voice. "*You* accuse *me* of…" Footsteps approaching. She held fire. Two uniforms sauntered past, synchronised smirks on their faces. Across the way, Powell gave them a cheery wave as he got into his car. Grenadier Guards'd give them a march past next. Place made Piccadilly station look like a mausoleum.

"Why don't we go for a drink? Bite to eat? Somewhere quiet." Byford asked.

Tempted. Torn. Teetering. "No ta." He'd just given her food for thought, and she'd not let Frankie down. Again.

He cocked his head. "We could… talk."

Her raised eyebrow was pretty voluble. He'd not even told her the outcome of the inquiry, the fact he was back on operational duties. She only found out 'cause it was all over the nick by the time she came out of the Haines interview. Word was that Knight would stay on as SIO with Byford acting in an advisory capacity. Like that was going to happen. Knowing Byford if he was back in harness he'd be chomping at the bit for a taste of the action. Either way he could've had the decency to give her a heads-up. She'd e-mailed to say great, thanks for telling me, big of you. OK, maybe not those exact words.

"Fair enough." He dug in a pocket for car keys. "Knowing how arsey you can be…."

"Arsey? Me?" Damn cheek. Uncharacteristic use of slang there, though. Must be feeling a tad prickly too.

"… I just want you to be the first to know…"

"First?" It was a night for snorting. "Do me a favour, guv."

"… that I've resigned. I'm jacking it in."

"So what did you say, my friend?"

Frankie and Bev, glass in hand, were slumped in opposite corners of a chocolate leather two-seater like a mismatched pair of slightly wonky book ends. Even without the candlelight glow La Perlagio would look impossibly glam, raven-haired, long-limbed, Nigella only less obvious. No mean cook either. She'd learned at her father's knee and when she wasn't working in his restaurant, sang semi-pro: blues, a little jazz, local joints mostly. They'd met on the first day of primary school, closer than some sisters. Even so, it had taken Bev three hours before she could open up enough to spill Byford's beans, make that bombshell. Actually, Bev mused, it had taken three hours, two bottles of Pinot and a couple of Calvados snifters. Between them. Bev wasn't greedy. The fettuccini Alfredo with scallops and garlic bread was good. But she'd forced that third portion down. Like hell. Smiling, she swirled the shot glass, feeling surprisingly mellow. Wonder why…?

"Earth to Major Bev." Frankie gave her almost full wine glass a flamboyant wave. "Is there anybody there, please?"

"Watch it!" Flying vino. She ducked but failed to dodge the fallout, sucked a few drops off her arm.

"Open another bottle if you're that desperate, Bevy."

"Funny girl." Tight smile.

Amy Winehouse was saying no to rehab in the background. Bev was toying with the idea of a nightcap. Frankie straightened, tossed back the pre-Raph locks, turned face-on. "Put me out my misery here. Boss man says he's slinging his hook – what's your next line?" The tone was glib, but Bev wasn't so squiffy she couldn't read the concern in her mate's dark eyes. She'd confided only in Frankie about her on-off relationship with the guv. Frankie was well aware it had a darn sight more ups and downs than in and outs; also knew just how much Byford meant to her.

"Got on my knees. Begged him. Don't do it, guv. Stay here, I..."

"Yeah yeah yeah. And you said?"

"Tricky saying anything when your jaw's on the floor, Frankie." Bev's sigh lifted her fringe.

She nodded. "Needs trimming, that."

"I know."

Few seconds' silence then: "Musta said something, Bevy?"

Got that right. *Start a collection shall, I?* Bev closed her eyes, pictured him storming off, driving away without a backward glance. Start a sodding collection. Foot. Herself. Shot. Talk about kneejerk reaction. But the shock announcement had felt like a slap in the face. And she'd lashed back without thinking. Even now she didn't know how the guv's news would affect a future they might or might not have. Either way, the subject was too raw, she could live without Frankie's two penn'orth, however well-meaning. "Nah, mate. Not a dickie. By the time I'd got my head round it..."

"Hey, Bev." Frankie knew her too well, didn't buy it. "When you're ready. Tell me."

"Sure." Reckoned she'd have three months to work on it. That's how much notice he'd have to serve. She knew he loved the Lakes, had a son up there. He'd joked once about retiring there. At least she'd thought it a joke.

What she didn't know was this: when the time came, would Byford take off up north? And would he leave behind more than the job?

Start a collection, shall I? Byford shook his head, gave a wry smile. Bev's comeback was almost funny. Or it was by the time he'd driven home, picked at the leftovers of a shepherd's pie and downed a dram or two of malt in front of *Newsnight*. Relaxing now in his beloved recliner, Byford took in the city nightscape from an upstairs window, his mind's eye still on the exchange in the car park. The stroppy posture, the pithy putdown were archetypal Morriss: mouth in gear, blue eyes flashing, toe tapping. Prickly? Oh yes. Infuriating, exasperating, stubborn as a mule farm. You got it. But underneath? He still wasn't sure. Maybe that's why his smile was tinged with sadness this time.

The news had caught her on the hop, of course. If there'd been more time to think, he could probably have predicted her reaction. But then he'd not long put his resignation in writing. The decision when to go had rested on finding Josh Banks's killer. Based on what he'd heard at the brief Byford thought: job done. Haines hadn't been charged, and even though Byford had jumped the gun, it had only been by a few hours.

Either way, it was time to move on. The letter would be waiting on personnel's desk first thing. The big man drained the tumbler, ran the malt round his tongue. Regrets? Sure. After thirty odd years, he'd miss the job, miss Birmingham, miss one or two old friends. And he'd miss Bev even more.

If he couldn't persuade her to go with him.

The man with the scrapbook studied the photograph first, held a magnifying glass over the face. Unwittingly, he caught his breath at the likeness. The little boy so resembled Scott they could have been twins. The lookalike wore identical clothes, carried a similar satchel, and had been captured mid-stride, one sock half-mast, walking through the gates of Scott's school. The man took in the brick walls, high railings and a barely discernible chalked hopscotch grid.

His hand no longer shaking, he moved the glass back to the little boy's image. He wondered if the substitute Scott also had a gap-tooth. The child took his walk-on role too seriously to tell, cognisant of why he was there, and who was not. Unaware he'd been holding his breath, the man exhaled deeply. Sighing, he laid the magnifier on the table. He didn't need it to see the cutting; he'd read it so often, he knew the words almost by heart.

Leicester Mercury, 8 July 1980

A week to the day since Leicester schoolboy Scott Myers disappeared police staged a reconstruction of the 10-year-old's last known movements. Despite a massive police operation and extensive searches involving scores of volunteers, there've been no sightings of Scott since he left school last Wednesday. Detectives hope the reconstruction will jog memories and prompt witnesses to contact the police.

The man leading the hunt, DI Ted Adams, said: "It's unusual at this stage of the inquiry for no one to have come forward. I'd ask everyone around Highfields to think about where they were on the afternoon in question. Did they see Scott? Did they notice anything odd, anyone acting suspiciously? For Scott's sake and his family's, it's vital we receive help from the public."

Speculation among villagers near the Myers home in Highfields is growing. A source close to the family told this newspaper that Scott's mother is under sedation in hospital. The source, who wants to remain anonymous, said Mrs Myers was particularly close to her son and feared the worst.

When asked if he thought Scott was still alive, DI Adams refused to comment.

Still alive? The man swallowed. His gaze returned to the little boy in the reconstruction. The reporter had described the scene as dramatic. Idiot. He slumped back in the chair, squeezed the bridge of his nose. The man was aware by now that even as Scott's last known steps were being staged, they'd already been taken.

FRIDAY
12

Still a news junkie on the sly, Paul Curran had most of the dailies and all the regional mornings delivered to the house, a bog-standard Bartley Green semi that would do for the three of them for the time being. Half seven now and the front pages were laid out on the kitchen table, all singing from the same hymn sheet. Curran scowled. Maybe that should read him sheet. Hair still damp from the shower, he played a preoccupied fork through rapidly cooling scrambled eggs. The press coverage hadn't come as a surprise. He'd heard the story on the bathroom radio and there'd been a brief mention on Breakfast TV. But seeing the photo splashed all over the papers was a gut-wrencher. Somehow the eggs had lost their appeal.

Grimacing, he shoved the plate away, deliberately obscuring the nearest picture. He'd need a dinner service to do a proper job: eight identical images of Roland Haines's face remained, all giving the same glassy-eyed stare. Haines looked as hacked off as Curran felt. DCI Knight hadn't even wanted the suspect's identity released. And here he was getting more column inches than Katie Price. OK, the leak could've come from just about anyone in the squad, but Curran reckoned it'd be his neck on the block. Or would it?

He felt the stirrings of a smile as he reached for his coffee. It wasn't all bad news. Truth be told, the journo in him had a sneaky admiration for what the pack had done. They'd no choice but to rush the story out, 'cause soon as Haines appeared in court reporting restrictions would come down like a ton of the proverbial. He'd have done the same in their shoes.

Hearing muffled footsteps overhead, he rose to pop the kettle on. Rachel would be down any minute gasping for a cup of tea. He knew she'd been up in the night feeding a fractious Rory. Curran glanced at the baby's picture, one of a zillion stuck to the fridge. Smiling, he traced the baby's cheek with a tender finger.

Yes. If there was any justice in this world, it wouldn't be long before Haines was remanded in custody, up to his neck in charges. It'd be back slaps and high-fives all round. And the leak would be water under the news bridge.

Bev tapped her fingers on the wheel waiting for a green on the main drag through Moseley. Like the rest of the world and its aunt. She was a tad later than planned and was hitting rush hour metaphorically head-on. Despite or because of the booze, sleep had been log-like. That's if logs are prone to weird dreams and immune to wake-up calls. She could sue both alarm clocks under the Trades Description Act. Neither had lived up to its name; her awakening had been down to Frankie belting out the lyrics to *Summer Time* before slamming the front door and clacking down the pavement on her Eiffels.

The tune was damn catchy; Bev was humming it even now. Had been while grabbing a shower, slipping on a sky blue shift dress, slapping on some lippie and snatching breakfast, the virtual variety, again. Scooping up the post on the way out, she'd briefly questioned why Oz Khan had bothered putting pen to paper when she couldn't even be arsed to read his e-mails. Far as she was concerned, soon as her former lover started shacking up with someone else, he'd written himself out of her love life. Now detective sergeant with the Met, her one-time DC could go screw. Which he undoubtedly did. Bothered? Fuming. She blamed it on the traffic. Wished she could get rid of the damn lyrics in her head, all that 'don't you cry' bollocks.

Mind, the song title was in tune with the day. A quick scan of the streets showed shorts, skimpiness and shades all round; sky so flawlessly blue it looked fake. Bev was an expert on blue, wore nothing but for work. As this morning proved, it saved dithering.

And the traffic was moving; 'bout time too. Inching down the window, she wrinkled her nose at waves of eau de exhaust. Thank God she'd resisted the temptation to go topless, soft top, that is. Yeah, those dreams had been dead kinky. Haines, buff naked but for a mortar board, had been switching a cane across the gaffer's buttocks. Cut to Byford in Hawaiian shirt and hammock, necking pina coladas, DI Powell handing over peeled grapes. She sniffed. Couldn't imagine where that came from.

Sod. Go-mode didn't last long. Handbrake was taking a fair few hits this morning. She glanced at her watch. The brief would be kicking off in twenty minutes, at this rate she'd be luck… *What the 'kin' hell?* Nah. Must've imagined it. What with the night visions and all. Out of the corner of her eye, for one split second she could've sworn she'd caught a glimpse of Roland Haines on the telly. Not one telly, a whole bank of the buggers in the showroom next to the bookies. No way. She turned, peered over her shoulder. Yes way. Haines in all his opposite of glory. What were the odds on that?

A slaphead in the white van behind papped his horn. She gave him the bird in the mirror, touched the gas. Thank God they were moving. She'd hate to miss anything, and there were bound to be fireworks.

And the livin' is easy? She raised an eyebrow. Course it is.

There'd been no stomping in slamming doors, striding up front. Early arrivals to the brief didn't even notice the gaffer's low-profile presence glowering at the back. Bev, ferrying a mug of builder's tea, cut him a glance as she passed, knew exactly where he was coming from. The positioning and pose were deliberate tactics: Lancelot wanted an unwitting squad filing in like naughty kids under the headmaster's disapproving glare. Paul Curran had definitely clocked him. As Bev squeezed into the pew next to Mac, she spotted the press officer's Adam's apple do a double-take.

The g-as-in-gaffer word spread, banter gave way to wary silence. Maximum impact.

Strolling to pole position, Knight slipped a casual hand in pocket, swept a slow gaze over the audience and kicked-off high decibel. "Total fucking disgrace."

Bev stifled a yawn. It was all a bit stagey for her. If the guv was up there, they'd be straining to hear. Message would get through loud and clear, though. Byford was no ham. She glanced round. Curious the big man hadn't showed.

Knight had his props ready; he grabbed a stack of news-papers from the desk behind. "How the fuck did this get out?" Bums shuffled, eyes shifted, most of the thirty-strong team developed a fascination with footwear. Curran raised an uncertain hand. Knight dismissed it with tetchy flap. Right now, he said, the source of the leak was secondary, his main concern was its consequences. Waving the local rag in their faces, he upped the volume: "Have you any idea how much damage this could do?"

Not in the same league as the harm Haines inflicted, Bev reckoned. She sensed Mac bristling, noticed Powell purse dubious lips. But it wasn't the point, not the way Knight was spelling it out. With each salvo, he slung another paper back across the desk. Bev kept a close eye on his skin tone. The pink tinge had been on the rise and now came close to the colour of the Sun's masthead, the paper he brandished briefly before it too hit the deck. "It's not trial by tabloid." Knight loosened his tie, snatched at the top button of his shirt. "They've hung drawn and bloody quartered the man."

Haines's bleeding body parts flashed before Bev's eyes. Shuddering, she perished the thought. It was difficult to work up pity for predatory creeps like Haines when the yuman rights brigade did such a good job. She'd save her sympathy for the victims.

While Knight continued reading the riot act, she peered at the papers on the desk. Haines hadn't just been named, his back story had been resurrected. Reporters had written up as much of it as they dared, or their editors-stroke-lawyers thought they could get away with. Among a rash of quote marks, stories were scattered with: 'it's believeds', 'sources say', 'it's understoods', and that great catch-all: allegedly. Most damning of all, perhaps, were references to the Bristol court case that never was.

"His lawyer's out there – " Knight jabbed a finger over their heads "– banging on about his client's rights." *Never?* Bev sat back, legs crossed, knew the words fair and trial would get an airing next. "Tell me this." Knight folded his arms. "How the hell is Haines going to get a fair hearing now?"

Close. She sniffed, circled an ankle. Knight left a few seconds' gap that no one rushed to fill, shook his head, then took his time walking to the water cooler. From the corridor came the sound of running footsteps. That stopped at the door. Heads swivelled as the wood took a chunk of plaster off the wall. For a sec Bev expected to see Haines's brief storm in arguing the toss. They should be so lucky. It was DC Darren New who entered, glancing nervy darts round until he located Knight.

"You need to see this, guv." A none too steady hand raised a video. Given Dazza had been tracking down sex workers

Bev doubted it'd be family viewing. "Haines is on here. And I don't think he's our killer."

13

Roland Haines had not dumped Josh Banks's body. His alibi for even longer than the time in question was tighter than highly strung piano wire, considerably tauter than the spotty white buttocks spread across the stained stripy mattress now showing at a cinema near you. Not. Darren had treated Knight to a private viewing prior to the home movie being screened to a packed house in one of the nick's video suites. The gaffer had come out with that haunted look, like he'd seen a ghost. Bev's verdict? It left a nasty taste…

Back in the office now, she nibbled a sausage roll, shoved the greasy remains across her cluttered desk. "Sorry, mate. Yours if you want it."

The cholesterol-fest had been Mac's shout; he'd nipped across to Gregg's for a bite to keep them going. Even though breakfast had gone by the board, Bev had lost her appetite. The recurring vision of Haines's pasty flesh was only part of the reason.

"Un-fucking believable, eh?" Sour-faced, she slumped back in the chair, hands behind her head. It was a brief respite before heading out to the Quarry Bank estate.

Mac examined his bacon bap. "You can say that again." She'd rather not.

Either the Balsall Heath informant had lied, made a genuine mistake, didn't exist – or Haines had a double. While allegedly offloading the boy's body, Haines had been caught on film dead to the world in a rented room in Hogarth Row just off the Hagley Road. If there'd been a rent book, the name on it would be Carrie Spinks. But it was cash – among other things – in hand. Known on the street as Cash and Carrie, Ms Spinks was a working girl.

She also happened to be Haines's step-sister.

"Darren did good finding her." Mac's bap was history; he made inroads on the sausage roll while Bev swigged Red Bull. Daz, she mused, had had a damn sight more joy than the two-strong team tasked with tracing the mystery caller.

Modesty unbounded, Daz had chalked the success down to his Tom Cruise looks. Another sex worker had tipped him the wink and the address. He'd knocked several times last night but the place had been empty. Turned out Spinks had been playing away. Daz had given it another whirl en route to work. Leery at first, he'd told Bev, Carrie nearly wet herself when he asked if Haines was a regular john. She'd soon put Daz straight about the relationship. Course they'd not been doing the bizz, she said.

Bev curled a lip. Yuck. The very thought…

"Bet I know what you're thinking, boss." Lechy waggle of bushy eyebrows.

She nodded at his diet coke. "Get that down your neck, mate. Some of us have got work to do." Sooner they were done, sooner they could hit the road. First preference for Bev would've been the follow-up interview with Haines, but that wasn't to be. Knight was in there now. He'd just sent word via a uniform, wanted more checks on Haines's movements on the afternoon Josh disappeared. The creep had added detail to the earlier version.

Pensive, she wandered to the window, looking for loop-holes in Carrie's story, knowing there weren't any. She turned her mouth down. Plenty of press guys out there though, wouldn't be long before they sniffed out the latest twist.

As Daz had reported it to the squad: Carrie had let her half-brother bed down after he'd turned up at the place three sheets to the wind around midnight on Wednesday. That he came bearing a few lines of Charlie in his back pocket helped his case. But nowhere near as much as the street camera that had clocked Haines's arrival and subsequent departure six hours later. Even if Carrie had been tight with the truth, the closed circuit footage was timed and dated, proof irrefutable. Unless Haines was a member of the magic circle he'd not been in two places at once.

As for Carrie filming him in the buff? A laff, wannit?

Cracked Bev up. Sighing, she shook her head. It was dead funny except it loosened their grip on a collar for a little boy's murder. Knight had reconvened the brief, assigned catch-up tasks to the squad like there was no tomorrow. In a sense, there wasn't. The Haines cock-up didn't just mean Operation Swift was back to square one: a day could've been lost.

"Why are we waiting, why-eye are we waiting...?" The crooning was crap. She turned to find Mac tongue through cheek, doing a Benny Hill salute and holding the door. "Chop, chop, some of us have got work to."

She grabbed her bag, keys, shades. "Lippie git."

"Takes one to..."

"Enough already." She raised a palm as she passed. Her lip twitched though. Go mad in this job without a bit of joshing.

And looking on the bright side, they still had a child's Mickey Mouse sock in with the forensics guys. Assuming the creep couldn't wriggle out of that one.

"Ask one of your fit-up merchants, Mr Knight." Roland Haines wasn't having a laugh, the face was deadpan, the tone dripped conviction. Like a sink estate Sunday school teacher, he sat all prim and pious, next to a pin-striped brief who could've been a night club bouncer in fancy dress. Knight looked to be the one having doubts.

"He's asking you, Haines." Powell snarled, leaned menacingly across the metal desk. The DI was doing his bad cop act. He had it down to a fine art. Maybe that's why the gaffer had asked him to sit in on the session. Tactics had been worked out before Haines walked in: Knight would play it cool. The tapes had been running fifteen minutes. Looking at the gaffer, Powell reckoned Knight needed an ice pack.

"Back off, detective." Haines stared. Powell stayed where he was. The creep didn't faze him, but Morriss had been right about the eyes. Knight played a pen through his fingers, sign he was happy for Powell to take over.

"What you scared of, Haines?" Dying of boredom if his expression was anything to go by. "Just answer the question. How did the sock get there? Quit stalling." He'd been happy enough to relate his movements Wednesday afternoon, almost thrown in his bowel movements. But nothing on the sock. Genuine? Ingenuous? Powell couldn't call it. For a few seconds more, he maintained eye contact before moving casually to reach a jug of water.

Haines gave a theatrical sigh. "What part of 'I don't know' do you not get?"

Smug tosser. Powell took his time drinking, then: "See, I wouldn't have a problem if it was a few bulbs... pack of seeds, maybe."

The laugh was more of a bark. "Pardon me while I piss my pants." He didn't crack a smile. "The sock was planted. You know that well as I do..."

"Alan Titchmarsh a mate, is he?"

"Tut, tut, tut. Really, Mr Powell..." The brief, bald as Knight but butch with it, wasn't struggling for words. The condescending tone implied he'd not stoop so low.

Haines had no such qualms. "Do me a favour, Mr Detective, do I really look dense enough to leave incriminating evidence lying round?"

"Now you come to mention it…" Powell squinted, scrutinised the guy's face. "Yeah."

"Well you're wrong, dickhead." Deliberately, Haines stroked what looked still-tender bruising round his eyes. He'd already dropped dark threats about suing, police brutality, unfair arrest, prejudicial reporting. All that cobblers. "And soon as the facts are straight, you'll be paying for that, too."

Powell balled his fists; Knight's lips were already tight. No one reacted to a tap on the door. Co-ordinator guru Jack Hainsworth came in with a slip of paper. "Guv. Just come in. Something you should know."

"Why in God's name didn't he say so before?"

Good work, sergeant. Well done. "Best ask him, gaffer." Hell should I know? Silence on the line suggested DCI Knight was running through what she'd just relayed. When Josh Banks walked out of Hyde Lea junior school at three-fifteen on Wednesday afternoon, Haines had been losing several shirts on the three o'clock at Doncaster, the three-thirty from Aintree and the three forty-five from Goodwood. No wonder he'd junked the betting slips. Not all bad luck though. Ladbrokes still had the tape from its surveillance cameras: Haines watching all three races with a couple of cronies.

Winner was clear. How long did Lancelot need to work it out? "Means he couldn't have done it, boss." Mac tapped her on the elbow with a dark chocolate Magnum. She mouthed a Ta, mate, watched him amble off sucking an ice lolly. They were outside the bookies on George Road along with a passing parade of shopping trolleys, baby buggies, buses and bikes. High noon; blazing saddles. Bev could feel the cotton dress sticking to her bum.

"It's my fault," Knight said. Not what she'd expected.

"Come again, gaffer." She was struggling to pull off the wrapper.

"Blinkered vision. I got fixated on the intelligence about Haines being seen dumping the body."

She shrugged. "We all did." But then Lancelot was the boss, the buck stopper.

"Yes, sergeant, but I'm the one supposed to have an overview. We got sidetracked. If we'd run a more thorough check on his movements earlier..." She narrowed her eyes, cast her mind back to the interview room, recalled Haines's knowing smirk.

"Yeah, but..." Hold that thought. She frowned. Sodding Magnum was a distraction she could do without, a load of gunge was leaking out the paper.

"What?"

She spotted a bin, wandered over, got shot of the mess. "Way I see it, soon as we picked him up, he could've put himself in the clear... if he wanted to."

Knight was speeding up. "You think he was playing us?"

Like the Royal Philharmonic. They ought to do the bugger for obstruction. "He was enjoying it, gaffer. Knew he hadn't done it. Knew we couldn't touch him. Maybe thought he could screw a few quid out of us for the injuries." A bob or two for the black eyes. "The only time he got antsy was when we told him about the sock." Because if its presence wasn't down to him it meant someone else had joined the game. On the opposite team. "It was news to him, gaffer, I'd stake my pension on that." Knight was rubbing his chin, she heard the rasp.

"He claimed it was a plant all along." The DCI sounded pensive. "Christ, this is all we need. You know what it means...?"

Bent cops, rotten apples, bad press. He could be right. But Bev was thinking about the duff tip-off that had led them to Haines's door in the first place. Who, where, and more importantly why, had an anonymous informant pointed the finger in the wrong direction? She was about to share, but the question must've been rhetorical.

"Right, OK." Brief, businesslike, the DCI cutting losses. "He gets a bollocking for withholding information but we'll have to release him. We need to review, refocus, redirect the inquiry. Get back soon as you can. Well done, sergeant."

Better late than never.

"'Kay, boss?" Mac sounding chipper.

She turned to see what he was up to, arched an eyebrow. "Where'd you get that, mate?"

He didn't even look sheepish as he waved half a Magnum at the nearby bin. "Shame to see it go to waste."

Still pensive, Knight hung up, picturing a basket bulging with venomous snakes. Bad enough a child murderer was still at large, but it looked as if someone had deliberately tried to implicate an innocent man.

The DCI rose, walked to the window, thought it through. Photographic evidence made it clear Roland Haines could neither have abducted Josh Banks nor dumped the boy's body. But someone – and it could be a police officer – wanted Haines to go down for it. The sock hadn't appeared in the guy's bedsit by magic. But wasn't a bent copper too obvious an explanation? And the original intelligence placing Haines at the Marston Road crime scene had come from a woman.

Knight chewed his bottom lip. On top of all that, it looked as if the nick had a leak the size of Wales. Floundering wasn't quite the right word for the DCI's current state, he wasn't out of his depth yet. But he wouldn't say no to a lifebelt.

He strode back to the desk, picked up the phone, hesitated only briefly before hitting Byford's internal extension. "Bill…?"

14

"I wanna see him? Where is the bastard?" High-pitched screeches punctuated by what sounded like a fist pounding wood.

"Hell's that?" Back at Highgate, Bev was halfway up the first flight of stairs heading for the squad room, Mac bringing up the rear. The fracas was kicking off at the front desk. And getting louder. Bev cast a wry glance over her shoulder. "Reckon Vince needs a hand?"

"Nah, Vinnie's no wuss." Well true. Vince Hanlon was fifteen stone of rippling... lard, longest serving front line sergeant in the nick, and safer pair of hands than a micro-surgeon. "Nothing he can't..."

Smashing glass. Jagged screams. Hurled obscenities. "Yeah right," Bev murmured. "Let's have a shufti."

The sight pulled them up sharp. A dishevelled Stacey Banks waved a broken beer bottle perilously close to Vince's air space. The blood could be coming from either of them, difficult to tell from this distance.

Bev edged forward, voice low and soft. "Hey, Stacey, calm it, shall..."

"...'kin' tell me to back off, you fat fucker." Her own vast bulk swaying, she took more wild lunges with the bottle. Vince stepped back, palms raised. "Look, love..."

"Bastard killed my boy. Got a right to see him." Slurred words, staggered steps. Spectators were gathering, a couple of uniforms, two other men Bev didn't know, punters probably. Mac wandered over presumably to keep them well back, protect and serve in police-speak. Stacey was drunk enough to be dangerous. "Hey, Stacey?" Bev's traffic-stopping voice had the desired effect. The woman swirled, clearly finding it difficult to focus, almost lost her footing in a pool of beer and blood spill. It was apparent now that Stacey had a hand wound. Casual stance, senses alert, Bev slowly approached the action. "What kinda good's this doing?"

"Good?" A defiant toss of the head dislodged the ginger beehive. "I ain't 'ere to do good. It's the evil shit as killed Josh I'm interested in. Gimme five minutes with him."

"Come on, Stacey. It isn't going to happen." The woman didn't need telling, her face fell into resigned features.

"Have to know *why* he done it, Bev." The bottom lip quivered as she stifled a sob. Poor cow. Bev's heart went out to her. Stacey's parenting skills mightn't be up there with Penelope Leach's, but Josh's death was a hell of a wake-up call. "Need to see the bloke… it's not a lot to ask is it?"

"Course not." She let a few seconds lapse then: "But Haines isn't here, Stacey." Technically he was, but she didn't need to know that.

"That's a lie." Puzzled face. "Said in the…"

"Papers got it wrong, Stacey. We're still looking for the killer. And we'll find him, I promise. We want justice for Josh much as you do." She sensed some sort of confab going on behind, kept her gaze on Stacey. Maybe it was Bev's conviction, the look that passed between them. Stacey seemed to crumple, the fight gone. Tears welled in her eyes, dripped slowly down fat cheeks already slick with sweat. She barely reacted when Vince took her wrist, gently removed the bottle from her grasp. Clearly, she'd been weighing up what Bev had said. And found it wanting.

"Wasn't just the papers cocked it, was it?"

"How's she feeling?" Two podgy fingers poised over the keyboard, Mac glanced up as Bev entered the squad room; any distraction from paperwork was welcome. Judging by his pile of notes, she reckoned RSI was on the cards. He wasn't the only lucky boy; eight or nine other officers were hunched over desks, tapping out reports, bashing phones.

"Ish." Bev waggled her hand. She'd not long slipped Stacey a tenner for cab fare, promising to keep her up to speed on any developments. I'll not hold me breath then, was the tart reply. Way the inquiry was going Bev couldn't blame her.

Sighing, she ran her fingers through her hair. "Know what we need, mate?"

"Where shall I start?" He gave a lopsided smile.

"We need a decent break. Somethin' solid to get the teeth in." Maybe they should stock up on KitKats because at the moment they were all backtracking, making up lost ground, checking nothing had been overlooked. It meant most of the team was trawling through old witness statements, cross-referencing police reports, plugging the gaps on the house-to-house, re-interviewing residents where even the slightest chance existed that further probing might hit a richer seam.

Mac slumped in the chair. "Not like the last break then?" The one that fingered Roland Haines.

Which reminded her…"Did you get the tape?"

"Cued and raring to go." He gave a helpful nod.

"Ta, mate." She wandered to a desk by the window, dumped her bag, rifled the drawers for a set of headphones. It was curiosity more than anything, wanting to hear the voice of the woman who'd called in. The informant had led rookie DC Tony Freeman to believe she lived in a block of flats in Marston Road. As they now knew, the only property that even vaguely fitted the description was the four-storey Heathfield House. The team detailed with tracing her had been knocking on doors, questioning everyone who lived there. They'd only completed the task in the last half hour, and drawn a blank. Roland Haines's movements on the night Josh's body was dumped were clearly not the only lying line the caller had spun. Bev scowled. Sodding timewaster could audition for Spiderwoman.

Headphones on, she hit play. The voice was definitely female, the right side of middle-aged, no trace of an accent. Listening to it, Bev wasn't surprised it had sent Freeman's boxer shorts in a twist. Unlike the loony tunes who usually rang in after a media appeal, the woman came across as precise, matter of fact, straight as a dye.

"… *oh, yes, I saw his face quite clearly, officer…*"

Bev cocked her head. Was that something in the background or just static? She rewound, played it again, eyes closed. Not sure. Maybe if it was enhanced? She'd get the techie boys on the case, couldn't do any harm. Slipping off the cans, she narrowed her eyes. Something else was bugging her as well. Was the woman too precise? Could she be reading from a script? Or was there a prompt standing by in the wings?

"Hey, mate…?" She spun round. Mac was on the phone, lifting a finger for hush. She strolled across, craned over his shoulder trying to read his scrawl. It could have been the footwork of an inebriated millipede.

"And?" she asked as the phone hit the cradle.

"Said you wanted a break? How 'bout a small crack?" He told her the caller was young, male and either local or a damn good mimic. The lad claimed he'd seen Josh Banks get in a car outside a newsagent's on Marston Road around half-three on Wednesday afternoon.

Obviously the caller hadn't given his name. She turned her mouth down. "Model? Reg? Colour?"

"Red. No number. Male driver. And that's it." He held out

empty palms. "We got cut off or..."

"1471?" She'd no need to ask. He was already tapping it out. It'd likely be a case of going through the motions. Everyone these days was a telecom smart arse; withholding a number was child's play. Eyebrow raised, she stood corrected. Mac's pen was moving and he sure wasn't writing his shopping list.

Beaming, he called the number. "Gone to voicemail."

"No worries." They'd keep trying and if they had no joy it should be easy enough to get a trace. Without realising, the informant might know more than he was saying. Witnesses don't generally suppress information, but first time round the full picture doesn't always emerge. Surprising what further questioning can sometimes elicit.

"What you reckon, boss? As breaks go, will that do you?"

Time being it would. "That'll do nicely." Turning, she grabbed her bag. "Best give the gaffer a bell."

Mac was already on the phone.

The minute Knight heard about the red motor, he wanted the intelligence released as in yesterday. Paul Curran had alerted the media to a hastily arranged news conference at Highgate. Expecting a big turn-out, a first floor room had been set aside. Curran and DI Powell were in there now kicking their heels waiting for the pack to show.

The DI checked his watch, strolled to the window. "Eh, Paul? Seen this?" The media were in a frenzy all right, but they were in the wrong place. It was all kicking off on the pavement out front. Cameras thrust, mics pointed, bodies jostled, questions were fired. Focus was on a bloke in the middle waving his arms, shaking the odd fist. Powell narrowed his eyes. "That who I think it is?"

Curran craned his neck for a better angle. "Roland Haines, how the...?"

"As I live and breathe." Powell had known the gaffer would be authorising Haines's release. They'd no option but to let the guy walk. No evidence, more to the point. The heroin found by the search team was neither here nor there. Small beer. Not worth the paper effort. But... "Talk about bad timing." Running slap bang into the press gang. Powell blew out his cheeks. Or was it perfect timing? Had the encounter been stage-managed? Had the media been tipped off as to when Haines would emerge?

"Revelling in it, isn't he?" Curran observed. Hearing the exchange wasn't necessary to get the gist but the press officer inched the window open anyway.

Powell rolled his eyes as combustible phrases rose in the hot air: police state, fascist thugs, slapping in compensation claim, several more in the same vein. "Tosspot."

They turned in synch at the sound of a throat being cleared. Toby Priest the *Birmingham News* crime correspondent. Powell raised an eyebrow. The newshound wasn't exactly on the ball. Maybe he'd come in round the back, missed all the fun. "This gonna take all day?" Priest drawled. "I've got a deadline to meet."

Beggars choosers. Powell straightened his tie, mentally ran through his lines. The rest of the pack wasn't going to pull out for a sideshow.

Standing in reception, Byford cast a jaded gaze over the main attraction, too. Roland Haines was certainly enjoying his fifteen minutes of infamy. Ironic, really. The detective was bowing out partly on the strength of believing Josh's killer was banged up. Now Haines was free as a bird. And looked to be singing like a canary. Did Byford regret handing in the resignation letter? No. And now it was out in the open, he'd heard one or two comments doing the Highgate rounds that convinced him the choice had been right.

"OK, sir?" A smiling DCI Knight headed towards him. Then pulled up sharp at the glass doors. "What the hell's going on?"

Byford shrugged. The scene spoke for itself. Haines centre stage, shooting his mouth off to an excitable media. The superintendent had suffered enough bad press on his own account to last a lifetime, he almost felt sorry for the DCI. The big man could read the headlines now. He shook his head. "God knows how they found out he was being released."

"Not sure about God." Knight's jaw tightened. "Source is closer to home if I'm not mistaken."

"Any ideas?"

"I wish. Working on it though. Hoping you might have a few thoughts, Bill."

Byford nodded. Wished him well. He'd come across officers in the past who made a packet slipping the press snippets, knew it was usually the police who ended up footing the bill. "Go out the back, shall we?"

He'd agreed to Knight's suggestion of a quiet session in the café round the corner. Tactics, strategy, brainstorming, the DCI had called it. Byford suspected there might be a bit of brain-picking going on as well. He had an inkling Knight was one of quite a few officers who'd be after his job.

15

DI Powell, bearing laden tray and wide smile, headed towards Bev across an almost deserted canteen. Her heart sank. Alone with her thoughts, she could do without company. The solitary supper in the nick was because she couldn't be arsed to cook and resident chef Frankie was having a night on the tiles. Oh yeah, and Sumi Gosh had cried off a trip to the flicks at the last minute, Mac was on a hot date with The Squeeze, Pembers was babysitting and... now she came to think of it maybe idling a few minutes with Powell wasn't such a bad idea. Light relief and all that, given how the inquiry was going. And that she'd finally got round to reading Oz's letter.

Toothy smile still in place, Powell slipped into the opposite seat. "So Morriss, reckon I'll get it?" His raised eyebrow was in better shape than hers.

"What's that then? Swine flu?" Masking a sly grin, she prodded a fork into a piece of kidney. She knew exactly where the blond was coming from. Powell was as subtle as Dracula in a blood bank. With the guv's departure imminent, the DI had his eye on the greasy pole. When he suddenly reached out with a napkin, she shot back. "Hey! What you doing?"

"That was so sharp, Morriss, I thought you'd cut yourself." Ingenuous wink. "Pass us the salt." She curled a lip. The fish on his plate was already swimming in vinegar. "Anyway, petal, you know what I mean. Way I see it, Knight'll go for the guv's job which means..."

Petal? "Yeah yeah. There'll be a DCI post going begging." The feigned indifference concealed deep anger. The ink was barely dry on the big man's resignation letter, already the pygmies were eyeing his office. The more she felt, the less she'd show.

"So... what you reckon?" Head down, he was shovelling in chips like there was a potato famine.

She pushed her empty plate away. Bit back a barb about the odds being higher of finding a chain of McDonald's on Mars. Powell's current studied indifference meant he badly wanted the leg up and, she supposed, must value her opinion for what it was worth. Pursed lips, she rated his chances. Whatever their past run-ins, Powell wasn't a bad bloke. They'd grown close over the years. OK, not close, that was going too far. But at least they knew where they stood.

"You're a fine cop, Mike." Fine and dandy. Never a hair out of place. All that high maintenance.

Frowning, he glanced up. "You taking the piss?"

"As if. Give us a chip." She returned the wink. "Straight up. You're a pro. Got to be a front runner." Good looking, personable, Powell was everything she wasn't. Unlike her, he played all the games by the books, minded his PCs and Qs when the thought police were in earshot, and 'cause he was a plodder, rarely stepped out of line.

Two or three second stare then: "Thanks, Bev."

She sniffed. "Mind, you might have to sleep with the boss."

There was a gleam in his eye. God, she'd handed him that on a plate. He opened his mouth then, like her perhaps, thought better of it. "Miss Byford, will you?" It wasn't a snipe. Question was sincere though she didn't much care for his obvious concern.

"Easy come easy go." She gave a one-shoulder shrug, knew it'd be like losing a right arm. And leg. So why was she treating the guv like he was in the latter stages of the plague?

"Yeah right. Y'know, Bev, there's no harm saying how you feel." Pull the other one; it hurt like shit.

"Drop it, mate." Non-negotiable. She turned her head, gazed through the window at a couple of jets crossing the wide blue sky. Eight o'clock on a Friday night. God, was this the high life or what? Eat your heart out, Paris Hilton. Still, Powell wasn't exactly clubbing it.

Blowing on his tea, he asked: "You in tomorrow?"

"Yeah. First thing." She'd offered after the late brief. Knight wanted a review team to take apart the inquiry so far, plus a couple of potential leads needed chasing on the motor seen in Marston Road. Nothing else had emerged during the session. Except for the rockets Lancelot had launched at forensics and toxicology who still hadn't reported findings and at the, quote: 'bastard with a sieve that was jeopardising the entire operation'. Knight was so desperate, he'd actually called on whoever was responsible to put their hand up to it.

"I'm in over the weekend as well," Powell said. "Show willing, eh?" Looking for Brownie points more likely. "Wouldn't do you any harm, you know."

"What's that?"

"Concentrate on your career for a change."

Had the guy got a death wish? "You cheeky sod." Eyes flashing, she scraped back the chair. Even with a hand tied behind her back, she reckoned she was a better detective than Powell would ever be. Glaring, she grabbed her bag. Knew if she was honest, he'd also hit a nerve. What the hell else had she to focus on? Johnny Depp was hardly beating a path to her door. Byford was beating a retreat. Oz was getting spliced. Why the hell he'd invited her to the wedding beat Bev, though. The bastard. Oz, that is. No, make that Powell, too. She cut him a lethal glance. "When I want adv…"

"Cool it, Morriss. I only meant if I get made up…"

"…it'll be at a counter in Boots, mate."

"…there'll be a DI post going. Maybe time you tried again?"

Wind. Sails. But only momentarily. She reckoned if she made inspector, they'd be doing happy meals at McMartians.

Quick whiz round Tesco later, Bev was putting her key in the door at Baldwin Street. She hated going home to an empty house. The guv always said the same. Slinging the fob on the hall table, she kicked off the Docs, toted the bags into the kitchen. Booze mostly, bread, bacon, baccy. She sighed. At least Byford had had a taste of marriage, had kids who'd find him a berth in an old folks' home come the time. Fuck's sake, Beverley. Get a grip. She opened the fridge, poured a glass of Pinot, placed the bottle against her forehead, gave a wry smile. Maybe she should have taken Powell up on his offer of a quickie. In The Prince.

Cheeky bastard.

Still smiling, she shook her head. Admittedly Powell was quite tasty since he'd started going to the gym, let his hair grow a little longer, but blonds had never been her cup of PG. He'd given her food for thought, though. Raising the glass, she toasted the future, pictured absent friends.

DI Bev Morriss? Who knows? When hell freezes over? Or when she started playing the games? She snorted. That'd be the Winter Olympics then?

The courting couple thought they were seeing a shop dummy, dumped by kids having a laugh. Monica and Ron had been to the village pub and were strolling amiably arm in arm back to her place. Full moon, balmy night, love was in the air. Neither was in the first flush, but they lingered for a kiss and cuddle on the bridge over the railway line at Foxton, just outside Birmingham. Relaxed, merry, maybe they'd had a drop too much because the unexpected sight gave Monica the giggles: the odd angle, legs askew.

Squinting, Ron leaned over the bridge to get a better look. "I don't reckon it is a dummy, Monica. Look at the clothes. Must be a guy."

Frowning, she leaned over, too. "Don't be daft, love. It's July."

They were both easy mistakes to make.

"You don't think…?" Curiosity piqued, Ron peered further down the line. "Hell fire." And froze. His whisper somehow had more impact than Monica's whimper. Both so wanted the object to be a red ball. Both dismissed the thought instantly. This time neither was mistaken.

Though shiny and slightly deflated, it was still recognisable as a head.

SATURDAY
16

The intercity had been travelling at just shy of a ton, the body on the line unnoticed by the poor sodding driver though services were halted now. Wasn't uncommon. There were around a hundred similar instances a year, according to some stats. Luck really that a British Transport police officer rifling the dead man's pockets for ID recognised the name and had the nous to call Highgate CID. By the time Bev and Mac arrived, the embankment was lit like a movie set, special effects provided by nature. Moonlight cast a silvery grey sheen through a row of sycamores, and skimmed slopes overgrown with weeds and grasses. From a field across the way, a bunch of Jerseys gazed on dolefully, chewing the cud, looked as if they were commenting on the action. It was more film noir than *Brief Encounter*. Though for Roland Haines it had been that too.

Roland Haines. The early shout had come as a shock. Though Bev reckoned DC Danny Rees who made it was more shaken. Even old hands don't come across headless stiffs every day. Rookie Rees and Darren New were the first non-uniform officers attending, and given the dead trainspotter was Haines, they'd wanted senior back up. Powell had buckpassed. Again. It was now down to Bev and Mac, or more accurately the FSI guys, to pick up the pieces – actually, make that body parts. It was a toss-up who was most pissed off.

Blowing her cheeks out, Bev locked the motor, glanced along a line of parked police vehicles that further narrowed the already tight country lane. The meat wagon was standing by, but it looked as if the pathologist was running late. Though suicide had been the natural initial assumption, discovering Haines's identity had turned that idea on its head. Bev grimaced; the phrase was unfortunate given the circs. Either way, until it was established whether Haines had indeed taken his own life, the Foxton cutting was being treated as a crime scene.

Still fairly subdued, Bev and Mac watched from the bridge, elbows on rail. Cooks, broth, spoil and all that. It looked almost surreal down there. Moonlight glistened off steel tracks and metal cases as a white-suited and overshoed FSI team carefully picked its way through undergrowth, dead branches, and rotting or rusting detritus. Each investigator's gaze was focused on the rough terrain, except when one or more of the four knelt for a closer look, deciding whether to bag and tag. Crime scene manager Chris Baxter's gait and stance were distinctive. Bev raised a palm acknowledging his nod. Further down the line, stills and video cameras were capturing everything that didn't move. Including Haines whose mangled corpse could give Humpty Dumpty a metaphorical run for his money.

"Shit way to go," Mac murmured.

"Likely didn't know what hit him."

"Other than the 23.10 to Euston?" She heard the humour in his voice.

"Funny boy. Y'know what I mean." Daft as it sounded it was probably true. Anyone opting for death by diesel train would have to be well tanked up. And if the choice wasn't theirs, they'd hardly lie down and take what was coming. They'd need to be unconscious or at least restrained, rope, cable, whatever.

"Think he had a sudden fit of remorse, boss?"

"Dunno, mate." She couldn't really see it. Those eyes of Haines still gave her the creeps. Maybe he'd made one enemy too many. No point jumping the gun though. Not till they knew the score. For that they needed Doctor Death.

Mac must've been thinking along the same lines. "Wonder what rubbish excuse Overdale'll come up with this time?" Home Office pathologist Gillian Overdale. Bev preferred the nickname. Bloody woman always kept the cops hanging round. If anyone mentioned it, she'd fix them with her basilisk stare and say the bodies weren't going anywhere.

"Talk of the devil." Bev shielded her eyes against the light as a torch-wielding silhouette scuttled in from the right. She added a sotto voce: "'bout bloody time."

"You sure, boss?" Mac was squinting too.

The nearer the figure got the less it looked Doc-shaped. "Maybe not."

"Wotcha, sarge." An unsmiling Danny Rees cut the beam. "Sorry you got lumbered." Danny boy was not looking his best. Pound to a penny he'd barfed.

"No sweat." Actually bets were off. It was barely detectable but she'd caught a whiff of vomit. Yep. The not so shiny shoes bore tell-tale traces. "What we got?"

He swallowed. "Christ, sarge. How could anybody do that? What a mess." She'd a certain amount of sympathy but he'd see worse. It went with the territory.

"Here to find out, Danny. So…?"

"I had a word with the couple who called it in? They're in the cottage just down the lane." He jabbed a thumb over his shoulder. "They've got coffee on the go if you…"

"Sod the coffee, Danny. Did either of them say or see anything helpful?"

He glanced at the ground. "Not really."

No then. "What else?"

"I got a list of names from the pub landlord. Locals who were in there last night. Thought we could chase them in the morning."

"Any motors left in the pub car park, lad?" Nice one, Mac. 'Cause Haines sure hadn't walked here. Might have had a chauffeur though.

"I'll check." Tad shamefaced at the omission but at least he hadn't tried brazening it out.

"'Kay," Bev said. "And?"

He waved the heavy-duty torch. "We had a scout round, trying to see where he gained access. Nothing obvious, sarge, but loads of places where it's possible, gaps in hedges, bust fences, that kind of thing. Darren's still out there with uniform trying to narrow it down. Again, we'll get a better idea in the morning, bit more light."

She glanced at her watch. Almost one a m. They could start knocking a few doors later, too. Foxton was no heaving metropolis but it was possible someone had been curtain twitching.

"Sergeant Morriss." A slightly breathless Overdale. She'd eschewed the customary Harris tweed and scuffed brogues for baggy jeans and well-worn trainers. And she'd need them.

"Doc." Tight-lipped nod.

"Late. No excuse. I fell back to sleep. Sorry." The candour took the wind out of Bev's sails but more than that the woman looked pretty rough. Her moon face had an unhealthy sheen; the eyes were red-rimmed, looked sore.

"Bev?" Four heads turned when Chris Baxter called softly. "One of the guys found this." He held a scrap of paper between gloved fingers. "Suicide note."

"I very much doubt it." Making up for lost time, Overdale's professional gaze was already scanning what was left of Haines. "From what I can see the body would have been dead long before a train hit it."

17

It was more what the pathologist hadn't seen. "There wasn't enough blood, boss," Bev told Knight and the rest of the squad. "Overdale says if Haines had been alive when he was hit the tracks would've been awash, ground would've been soaked." The pathologist had talked carotids and jugular spouting like the Trevi fountain. But only if Haines's heart had been pumping. Given the train's impact, there'd been more than enough gore around anyway for Bev's liking. As for the severed head… it wasn't a thought to hold. Bloody thing had already given her nightmares, and she'd only had four hours' kip. Knight had put the early brief back an hour, it was just gone nine now. Maybe she was wrong, but the squad seemed animated by the news of Haines's demise. For sure, no one was shedding any tears.

The DCI still appeared to be taking it in. "So likeliest scenario is Haines was dead before the train hit him?"

Bev and Mac exchanged glances: you could say that. "Best guess is he was murdered someplace else… there's no forensic so far to dispute that. The killer drives the body to Foxton and…" She'd painted part of the picture, rest was best left to the imagination.

Knight nodded. "Does Overdale have any idea how he was killed?"

With the state the body was in? Get real. She settled for a diplomatic: "Nothing obvious, boss. Post mortem might throw up something." Blood tests, too, assuming he had enough left in his veins. "She checked the wrists for ligature marks. Nothing doing." Difficult to check the neck. Bev swallowed, shuddered again. "If he was restrained, the killer took the rope or whatever with him." FSI had checked and checked again: nothing doing. New batch of uniforms and detectives had been out at Foxton since first light, checking for tyre tracks, talking to villagers.

Knight finally stopped pacing. "There's absolutely no doubt about this, is there, sergeant? He was murdered?" Bev raised an eyebrow. Was there a punch line?

"What, like you mean Haines might've got a mate to put him out of his misery?" It came from Mac, but Knight had asked for it. Bev couldn't have put it better herself. Going by the curve on Powell's lip, he appreciated it, too. The DI propped against his favourite wall looked as fresh as the proverbial. Wonder why?

Knight threw Mac a cool: "Are you trying to be funny, Tyler?"

Mac didn't look amused. Like Bev he'd been up half the night and was still firing on more cylinders than Knight appeared to be. "The pathologist couldn't have been clearer. Haines was already dead when the train hit him. End of. I can't see your problem."

"What about the letter?" Knight asked. Coupla lines of type on a bit of paper? A copy was pinned on the whiteboard behind. Bev knew it by heart, wasn't difficult. *God forgive me. I can't take any more. Suffer the little children...*

She drew fire from her partner. "It could've been written by anyone, boss. Killer who tries faking someone's death's more than capable of faking a suicide note." He wasn't as smart as he thought, though. Overdale sussed Haines hadn't topped himself before she'd even set foot on the crime scene.

Knight shook his head. "So a man whose face has been all over the papers, who was in effect named prime suspect in Josh Banks's murder, walks out of here without a stain and a few hours later is found decapitated on a railway line."

That was the size of it and that was Knight's problem. Bev narrowed her eyes, seeing now why he was preoccupied, clutching at dead straws. So much media shit was going to hit the police fan, Highgate was going to smell like a sewage plant. And if the recent leaks were anything to go by, it wouldn't be long before the press got a sniff.

"OK, listen up." Maybe a case of when the going gets tough. Suddenly galvanised, Knight straightened up, sharpened his act, started issuing tasks. Officers were assigned to check Haines's movements, trace and interview friends, family, drinking cronies, neighbours, anyone who could shed light on the man's life.

Knight gazed over the heads of the squad, could almost have been talking to himself. "It's just possible that Haines's death isn't connected with Josh Banks's murder. Obviously it could be a motive but not the only one. Let's not get fixated. Haines was no contender for a good citizen award. Man with his past must've made enemies along the way. This could be someone settling an old score. It's an angle needs serious checking." He landed it on two DCs who looked less than overjoyed. "Take this on board, everyone: Haines's murder gets the same treatment, same priority as any other murder inquiry."

Course it would. Death of a sleazy perv was on a par with a ten-year-old kid's, wasn't it? Pensive, Bev started doodling on her pad. Knight wanted a quick collar, on the off-chance the Haines's development could be kept under wraps. Dream on, mate.

"It's likely there'll be overlap with Operation Swift. We'll hold joint briefs but the Haines murder needs a separate senior investigator. Sergeant?"

She squinted. Doodle looked like a turd. Grimacing, she pencilled in rising steam. Given Josh's killer was still out there, no one on the squad was going to bust a gut over a slimeball.

"Sergeant Morriss?"

"Boss?" Hell had she missed?

"The Haines murder? I want an SIO. Deputy. OK?"

Like she had a choice. "Sure thing, boss." She glanced down. Holy shit.

Within an hour the faeces started flying. Bev was shifting a bit of paperwork in her office before heading out to Foxton again when the phone rang.

"Paul Curran here, Bev. Is it true what they're saying about Roland Haines?" The press officer's customary smooth delivery held an edge. She'd bet his pink flush was on the rise.

Pen poised over a pad of A4, she aimed for casual. "Who's they and what are they saying?"

"I've had a couple of reporters on wanting confirmation Roland Haines is dead."

"Where they from?" Local hopefully. It might give the police a few hours' grace before the big guns started firing.

Sounded as if Curran was rifling a notebook. "Toby Priest from the *Birmingham News* and some woman off the *Mercury*. Didn't catch the name."

Bev blew out her cheeks. Wondered how'd they got on to it so quick? It didn't have to mean another hole in the Highgate sieve. There was a hell of a lot of ongoing police activity in the village. It was possible a punter had tipped them off. "What did you tell them?"

"Said it was news to me." Was that a baby crying in the background? "I'm on call this weekend. I'm at home at the mo, Bev. Is it true?"

"Train ploughed over him at Foxton last night. We're treating it as murder." She heard a low whistle on the line.

"The last bit's not for release. Not yet anyway."

"No surprise there. I'd best come in. They'll be after a statement at the very least."

"Nah. It's…" Suit yourself. He'd hung up. Prob'ly best. Hopefully Curran'd be able to keep the pack off her back.

"So, sergeant, is this another instance of the police failing to do their job properly?"

Bev could happily smack the smirk off Toby Priest's superior mug except her sweaty fists were balled in her lap. They'd lain there five minutes, getting tighter, moister. Keep the pack off her back? This was back against the brickwork time. Little wonder Lancelot had been so happy to pass the poisoned-buck-chalice.

Struggling to keep a civil tongue, Bev lapsed into police speak. "I don't think *any* of us here could have foreseen this tragic event, Mr Priest. I'm sure we *all* agree Mr Haines's death is regrettable." The emphases were deliberate. Considering recent coverage, the press claiming exclusive rights to the moral high ground was rich to say the least. Predictably several eyebrows rose, a few hacks cleared their throats. Bev, making a conscious effort not to shift in her chair, cut a glance to the back where Mac leant against the wall keeping a watching brief. His downturned mouth said it all.

Beside her, a casually-dressed Paul Curran was making notes. Four hours on from his phone call and they were attempting to present a united front from behind a desk in a conference room at the nick. Bev's bum was sticking to the plastic. Whether it was down to the sun streaming through the windows or the grilling from the press she'd be hard pushed to call. The press officer's hope that a bland news release would keep the media happy had proved as misguided as an Exocet with Tourette's. Soon as the nationals and the broadcasting outfits got wind of it, Curran suggested the least worse course would be to hold a news conference. Get it over with in one fell swoop. Glancing round now, Bev wasn't so sure. There was something in the air, and not just the dust motes sinking slowly in a shaft of light.

Toby Priest, small, dark and dangerous, lifted a languorous hand. "So you don't think it an oversight, then, sergeant?" The question, though woolly and casually posed, contained pointed criticism, however tacit. Shutters clicked as she lifted her head. Curran tapped a nervous foot.

Bev reached for water, registered a slight tremble in her fingers, had second thoughts about lifting the glass. She'd no need to be clairvoyant to see where Priest was going with this. "Oversight?"

"Not to offer Mr Haines police protection?"

Bang on. She stiffened. Far as the media should be concerned Haines's death was still under investigation, accident, suicide. The police hadn't breathed a word about foul play. She feigned ignorance. "Not with you, Mr…"

"I understand Haines was dead before the train hit him." Priest wasn't the only one with inside track judging by reactions around him. Or lack of. "In my book, that makes it murder."

Out of the corner of her eye, she glimpsed Curran scribbling frantically. OK. She was on her own then. "Where do you buy your books, Mr Priest?" Icily polite, but the stress was on *buy* this time.

He studied his nails. "Is it true?" The little bastard knew. He was enjoying this.

"As I said…"

"No, sergeant." Priest glared. "You've said nothing… worth listening to. Was Roland Haines murdered? It's an easy question. Yes or no?"

She felt a tap on the shoulder. Curran nodded at a note he'd pushed in front of her.

"I'm not at lib…" She pulled the note closer.

"Do me a favour sergeant. At least stop trying to fob us off." She frowned as she read the words. Priest was still banging on. "You might not be at liberty, but Haines's killer is. And Josh Banks's. That's the truth. And as I said, isn't it another instance of pol…"

"Enough." She raised both palms, waited for pin-drop silence. "Believe me, this line of questioning would seriously jeopardise our inquiry."

"Never heard that one before." The reporter sitting next to Priest stifled a yawn. She'd seen the guy's face recently, couldn't figure out where.

"No bullshit." She leaned forward. "I'm dead serious." That was new. A cop telling it like it is. She ran a steady gaze over every journalist's face. "I'm asking each of you to hold back. Soon as it's safe, I'll personally release the information and co-operate every way I can."

"Easy for you to say," Priest muttered.

Three, four second pause to add gravitas. "I'm giving you my word, Mr Priest."

He shrugged, but at least zipped it. Bev took a few less contentious questions from the floor, repeated an appeal for anyone who'd seen Haines to come forward, then the gathering broke up in desultory fashion. As she drained the glass of now tepid water, she spotted the guy who'd sat next to Priest in conversation with Mac at the back. What was that about then?

And where'd she seen the guy before? It was recent if she recalled right.

"Pitched it well, Bev. Nice one." Curran smiled, pocketing a pen and his phone.

She gathered her papers, smiled back. "Thanks for your help, mate." It had been his call: the note suggesting taking a candid line. Much as it grieved her to admit it, she'd been struggling to hold her own back there. Unlike Powell she was no media tart; her natural instinct dealing with the press was to clam up or, being Bev, rise to the bait. At least the latest tactic had silenced them for a while. "Think it'll work?"

"Maybe." He waggled a hand. "Could go either way."

No chance then.

18

Sleeves neatly rolled back, DCI Knight perched on the edge of a desk, fine hair on his muscled forearms glistening in the evening sunlight. He'd just brought the squad up to speed on where the Josh Banks inquiry lay. Strongest lead by miles was the fact they now had a name and address for the lad who'd tipped them off about the red motor. Ironically, Brett Sullivan still wasn't answering his mobile. Sumi Gosh and another DC had dropped by the teenager's house in Balsall Heath. According to his mother, he was staying at a mate's. She didn't know where but he was due back first thing. It was to be hoped he'd have something useful to add. Eggs, basket and all that.

"OK, sergeant…" Knight shoved a hand in his pocket. "What've you got for us?"

It was Bev's unaccustomed turn in the senior investigator hot spot. Thank God she'd not missed the start of the late brief. She and Mac had run a couple of reds haring back from an afternoon in Foxton. They'd spent most of the time liaising with FSI guys, directing a small inquiry team and dodging daft questions from nosy residents. Take away the police activity and the village resembled something out of *The Archers* with Bev and Mac playing walk-on roles. She hoped she'd got rid of the cow shit on her shoes.

A tad self-conscious, she made her way to the murder board, turned to face the troops and registered Byford's presence at the back of the room. The guv must've made a late appearance and was now leaning against the wall keeping a watching brief. Tucking her hair behind her ears, she glanced at the latest visuals pinned on the board. Apart from Haines's creepy mug shot, there were six or seven pictures of the crime scene including close-ups of the embankment, the railway line and surrounding foliage.

Pointing to an image she said: "Chris reckons this is probably where they got down to the track." Chris Baxter, crime scene manager. "Car, van, whatever, could've been parked here." Handy passing place alongside a stile. "Likely this is the field they cut across." She indicated a gap in the hedge, trampled undergrowth. It was a shame Daisy and her cow pals couldn't talk. Even greater shame there'd been no rain for a fortnight, it meant no footprints or tyre impressions. "Where the grass is flattened here?" Squinting, her finger hovered over another ten by eight. Even standing as close as this, the twin trails weren't easy to distinguish. "Chris thinks it may be where Haines's heels caught as he was dragged down the slope."

"Haines was what?" Knight scratched his jaw. "Ten, eleven stone?" An obvious question.

"Ten and a half," Bev said. Sixty-six kilos. Dead weight either way.

"How far from the lane to where the body was dumped?" Powell asked.

"Hundred and twenty metres give or take." Which meant a killer with broad shoulders or helping hands.

Knight frowned. "And no one saw *anything*?" Like it was her fault.

"Nada." House-to-house and pub-to-parish-hall had drawn blanks. Press coverage might prompt a passing motorist to come forward. But Dag Lane wasn't exactly Spaghetti Junction. "On the plus side… forensics lifted a few strands of blue cotton from the hedge." No one cheered. Everyone knew fibres were less than useless without a comparison. And that assumed they'd been deposited by the killer. "Fly in the ointment?" Bev tapped her top lip. "Local kids use the area as a playground."

"So much for today's brats being glued to Playstations," Powell muttered. The DI was all heart.

More to the point, where'd Haines been glued? Inside or out? They'd uncovered nothing on the guy's movements since his release. And it wasn't for want of trying. A couple of DCs were still out there on the case.

"What about Haines's known associates?" Knight nodded at an officer near the window. It was open but not far enough, room was like a sauna.

"Hand you over there, gaffer." Bev already knew the top lines. Darren New who'd run the checks had kept her informed throughout the day. "Dazza?" Credit where due and all that; he'd put in the leg work in the local area. Not that there'd be any gold stars. The cronies and KAs he'd tracked down hadn't come up with the goods. As he talked the squad through it she headed back to her seat, cutting the guv a covert glance en route. God knows why he'd smiled at her. She'd not exactly covered herself in glory.

If she was being dead cynical, he was probably in need of a friend. The Highgate grapevine had it that Byford had been sitting in on interviews conducted by Knight in connection with the evidence allegedly planted in Haines's bedsit. Informal, not recorded, it wasn't up there with the Spanish inquisition. But it was no way to win mates. The uniforms who'd found the child's sock were royally pissed off to the extent they'd consulted Police Federation lawyers. A couple of crime scene investigators who'd also been questioned had complained to their boss, who'd be taking it up with one of the big chiefs. With dark clouds of suspicion and unsubstantiated rumours floating round, the nick was not a happy place. If push came to shove, the troops would close ranks and Knight would find himself out in the current heatwave.

"Tell you this, gaffer," Darren was saying. "Feelings are running high out there again." Quarry Bank. Now no one was in custody for Josh's murder.

"Some right hotheads on that estate," Mac said. He'd talked to a few earlier in the week. "Not many, but…"

Knight raised a hand. "I'll have a word, see if uniform can increase patrols." Quick glance at his watch, then he rose, rolled down his sleeves. Maybe he had a hot date. Not that hot. He started dishing out tasks to his team.

Bev observed, didn't envy the guy. His workload was onerous without the extra pressure. Querying a fellow cop's professional conduct was a shit job. But in this instance, did someone really have to do it? She still felt her theory about the woman informant was pretty sound. Her call had deliberately led them to Haines's door. What if she'd gone through it and laid the trail herself? Knight hadn't discounted the idea but seemed to favour the bent cop route. Far as Bev was concerned it was a fine line between favour and fixation. Which was why she'd tasked two more DCs with digging into Haines's past. Any journo worth his or her salt, she reckoned, would already be in there with excavators. And that would give Knight even more grounds for believing Highgate had a mole. Mind, on that front he probably had a point; signs pointed to it being an inside job. Rumour had it that Byford had offered, or been asked, to trace the leak. Big of him.

She glanced round to see if Paul Curran had slipped in late, made a mental note to thank the guy next time she saw him. So far the press had held back from using the tip-off about Haines being murdered, though the reports she'd read had highlighted the fact that a man who'd threatened one minute to sue the cops had been found dead the next. She sniffed.

Toss up which was worse, really. Wrinkling her nose, she glanced down, clocked half a sodding cow pat on her right Doc. Mouth tight she swore under her breath. Daisy'd better watch out, next time she'd be dead meat.

The beef Masala defeated Bev. She blew out flushed cheeks, shoved the leftovers to one side and fiddled subtly with the button on her waistband.

"Eyes bigger than your belly, boss?" Obviously not subtle enough. Mac, who'd cleaned his plate ages ago, was now slumped in a red velvet banquette ogling hers.

She cut a withering glance at his paunch. "Not something you'd worry about, is it, mate?" He was too busy gazing covetously at the lurid remains to make a comeback. "Feel free." She waved a magnanimous hand, swallowed a burp. "I'm stuffed." Mind, she'd already seen off satays, samosas, pakoras and spring rolls. All beef. Eat your heart out, Daisy.

The impromptu jaunt to K2 wasn't exactly a works outing, just the two of them plus Paul Curran who they'd bumped into on the way out of the nick. The Moseley restaurant had been her call; any later on a Saturday night they'd have been lucky to get a table.

"Room left for another drink, Bev?" Paul smiled.

Banqueting hall. "Cheers."

"Mac?"

"Kushti." He raised an empty Cobra bottle. "Same again." For the fourth time, not that Bev was counting. Mac was decidedly merry, though. She'd a feeling he'd had a spat with his woman. Could explain why he was at a loose end. As for Paul, his missus had apparently taken the kid to see her parents in Gloucester, decided to stay over for the night. In Bev's case Johnny Depp was getting too demanding, she'd decided to cut him some slack. Yeah right.

Said a lot for the demands and vagaries of the job though, didn't it? Saturday night and here she was with a bunch of cops. OK. Slight exaggeration. Two people from work. Not that they'd talked shop much, everyone needed to give it a rest. Paul particularly. When they'd run into him in the corridor, he'd confided that the gaffer had given him a bollocking. Knight hadn't gone so far as to blame the guy for the leaks, but Paul was convinced Lancelot regarded him as the prime suspect. It was pretty obvious he was upset, needed to chill. Even Mac had picked up on it, urged them all to move on to non-work topics. Probably why there'd been a few silences.

Mind, when the small talk got round to kids Bev had kept mum. She'd managed a few simpering smiles and gushing 'ahs' when Paul showed her the baby pics in his wallet. The photos of Mac's two lads she'd seen before; didn't stop him shoving them in her face though. At that point she'd left them to it, nipped out for a fag. And wished she could escape the pictures in her mind's eye, Josh's and…

Mellower after throwing wine down her neck, she watched Paul beckon the waiter, engage in some friendly banter. Lips pursed, she gave him an unwitting once-over. Ginger wasn't her thing but in this light he really wasn't a bad-looking guy. She smiled, told herself to pack it in. For all his pleasant easy manner, she doubted he was anyone's pushover. From what she'd witnessed, he was able to stand up for himself. And from what he'd said, he'd bloody well need to.

Mac leaned forward, slurred not quite in her ear. "He's spoken for, boss."

She rolled her eyes. He was asking for a good slap, but she knew it was the Cobra talking.

"No, it's my shout, Mike." Byford grabbed the pint glasses and weaved his way to the bar, acknowledging nods from one or two regulars. The Prince was racing green tiles and dark wood panelling, horse brasses and dimpled bronze table tops. Its clientele was mostly old-timers who drank there largely because it was known as a police pub. With the Bill around the wrinklies were less likely to get a load of lip and worse, courtesy of the local yobs. Look the wrong man or woman in the eye in some dives round here and next minute you'd be picking glass out of your face.

The landlord, Charlie, was already pulling the Guinness as Byford approached. Dumpy, chinless and follically challenged, he put Byford in mind of Ian Hislop, apart from the earrings, eagle tattoos and Black Country accent. Without fail, when he saw the superintendent Charlie came out with one of two lines of patter. The big man made a private bet with himself which it would be this time.

"Mr B! Are the bad guys still…"

"… keeping me busy? You bet, Charlie." Actually it was Byford's wager, and he'd won. Eschewing further intellectual jousting, the big man reached for a menu – tacky cracked brown plastic – leant an elbow on the bar and glanced back at Powell. The DI had his nose in the local rag, sports pages it looked like to Byford. It must be three or four years since just the two of them had gone for a drink. Powell had issued this invite. It wasn't how Byford had envisaged spending the evening. He'd hoped to catch Bev after the brief, ask her out to dinner, maybe lay his cards on the table. Whether deliberate on her part or not, their paths hadn't crossed. From his office window, he'd watched her leave with Mac and Paul Curran in tow. The joshing and body language suggested they were making a night of it. Mike's oh-so casual 'fancy a jar, guv' had caught him at a weak moment, perhaps. Anything was preferable to another night in front of *The X-Factor*.

"There y'go, Mr B."

"Ta, Charlie. Keep the change."

Byford had found it harder to divine why a young, good-looking bloke like Powell hadn't anything better to do with his downtime. Talk so far had centred on the case, but he suspected the DI had an unwritten agenda.

"Cheers, guv." Powell jettisoned the paper on the bench, sank an inch or two of the black stuff, wiped froth from his top lip with the back of his hand. "Hungry?" he asked.

Mouth turned down, Byford shook his head. Not in here he wasn't. The menu was greasier than a deep fat fryer.

Powell shrugged. "Saw you with the menu."

"That's why you're a detective." Byford winked. Powell twitched a lip in what could've been a smile. Then maybe saw the remark as an opening.

"Ask me... you're the sharpest detective round here, guv." Staring into his Guinness, the DI missed Byford's arched eyebrow. "Just like you to know... I'm really sorry you're going." The eyebrow was on the rise again. This was so not Powell. Was he being straight or was it a case of thinking flattery would get him anywhere? Like a reference, or a rung up the ladder?

"Appreciate it, Mike." He clinked glasses with the DI then inserted his tongue firmly in his cheek. "Still, you know what they say? No one's indispensable. Always someone around ready and able to step into the boss's shoes. And I believe promotion's a good thing. Everyone needs something to aim for... even police officers." Byford laughed. Not at his feeble quip, more the emotions that had crossed Mike's face. Bev always said Powell was easier to read than a primer.

Smiling, the DI lifted his glance. "Exactly what I told Bev... concentrate on your career for a change, girl."

Byford had a mouthful of stout and almost choked. "Sorry about that. It went the wrong way."

"I could see that."

Byford certainly hadn't. Powell's remark was out so out of left field, it could have been winging its way from Jupiter. Oblivious, Powell ploughed on. "Like I was saying... even without openings coming up at work, Bev needs to push herself forward. She's been treading water too long. You saw how she handled that brief. With a bit more positive rope, if she put her mind to it she could easily make inspector."

Easily? Could she? With a disciplinary record like a music library? Or was he being unfair? "You reckon?"

"I'd certainly put in a good word for her." He raised his glass. "Like you would for me, eh, guv?" he dropped in casually.

Byford barely took it on board. He was dwelling on the years gone by when Powell wouldn't give Bev the time of day, wouldn't even call her by her first name. "Changed your tune, haven't you, Mike?"

"Bev's OK." He met the guv's gaze.

Byford narrowed his eyes. Was the blond blushing? Was the sudden turn-round more than professional? Far as he knew, Powell lived alone, had no family to speak of and received rumour had it that his wife had run off with a toy girl years ago. He'd brought the occasional arm candy to police socials. If Powell was looking for more, Bev would certainly be a handful. But surely she'd run a mile first? "So what did she say?"

Blank look from Powell.

"Bev. When you offered careers advice."

"Thank you, sir. I'll certainly consider it."

"Told you to sod off then?"

He had the good grace to grin. "Yeah."

They drank in synch, the silence between them easy, Byford's thoughts less so. He'd already dismissed as green-eyed absurdity his notion that Powell might harbour personal designs on Bev, but as to her professional development – the DI could have a point. One that Byford had signally failed to recognise. Or acknowledge. It was easy to pigeonhole her as the lippie maverick on a single-seat plough. But with the right guidance and Bev's unusual blend of instinct and intelligence who knew where she might go? Without even knowing it, maybe he'd held her back. Had he the right to ask her to up sticks now? How selfish was that?

"So what will you do, guv?"

He frowned. "Come again?"

"When you leave us? Guy like you isn't going to sit at home twiddling his thumbs. You've got years ahead, haven't you?"

"Haven't really thought about it, Mike." Maybe he'd better get back to the drawing board.

Was Scott's fate sealed the instant he was seized? Had there been the slightest chance he could survive? Escape, even? A moment perhaps when his abductor's attention strayed? Was there a split second when the monster considered not committing the heinous crime? When he was first snatched maybe, if a passer-by had noticed something wrong, alerted the police? A little boy distressed, being dragged into a car, crying for his mother.

The man with the scrapbook tried not to dwell on these thoughts; the speculation was torture: that way madness lay, and the musing was futile. By July fourteenth Scott was dead. It was the day those who knew him began life sentences. Steeling himself to open the book, the man reread the news report in the Leicester Mercury, studied again the photo spread.

Child's body found

It's believed the body discovered by a groundsman at Green Meadow golf club is that of 10-year-old schoolboy Scott Myers. Scott disappeared fifteen days ago while walking home from school in the Highfields district of the city. The disappearance sparked one of the biggest police operations in the county's history. The golf course is near the family home at Hill Top and was searched rigorously by officers and volunteers last weekend. Police refused to comment on the possibility that the body had been overlooked or whether the killer abandoned it there later. They're yet to confirm the identity of the dead child but sources close to the family are in no doubt. Groundsman Bert Saffer said finding Scott's partially buried body was the greatest shock of his life, the saddest sight he'd ever seen.

The family home was deserted earlier today and the police declined to be interviewed.

It's understood Scott's school is to hold a special assembly later in the week in memory of a little boy who was described by every-one who knew him as polite and well-liked.

The paper had obtained a new image of Scott. It was a school photograph, the shoulders of classmates either side just visible. Scott's smile was infectious: a happy time for the little boy? Unwittingly the man smiled back, but not for long. Dry-eyed, dry-mouthed, he had no tears left right now. He'd cried long into the night, dreams when they came unbearable, unspeakable. Eyes briefly closed, he clenched a fist.

Composure almost gained, he studied the distant shot of a police tent surrounded by indistinct figures on the edge of the golf course. The man couldn't begin to imagine what lay inside. No, of course he could. More and more often he had to make conscious efforts to rid his mind of horrific visions. Pity poor Bert Saffer. He'd seen the reality and probably been haunted for the rest of his life. Still, the old groundsman had clearly been OK with having his picture taken. Unlike the police at the crime scene. Two officers had turned their heads from the camera, another shielded his face with a clipboard.

The man bit his lip. Why didn't the police just come clean? Why prolong the agony by not admitting immediately that it was Scott's body? It had been left to reporters to reveal the truth. No matter how much activity was going on behind the scenes, it would be twenty-four hours before detectives officially launched a murder inquiry. Twenty-four hours...

He glanced down at his hand, wondered briefly why the palm was bleeding.

SUNDAY
19

Bev parked the MG alongside the waste ground in Balsall Heath. Apart from the guy in a turban who was having a fag in the newsagent's doorway, the Quarry Bank estate was pretty quiet. Early yet, though; curry smells from close by Balti houses lingered in the air. Reminded her of last night's pig-out, reckoned some of it was still floating round the alimentary canal.

She grabbed her Raybans and stepped out of the car. With the mercury relentlessly rising, she'd finally succumbed to lowering the soft top. Could be a bad move round here; best keep her eyes peeled, not that she was going far. Shouldering her bag, she headed for the spot where Josh's body had been dumped. A handful of other folk must've had similar ideas going by the mini-shrine that had sprung up. Bev thought of the visit as touching base, a sort of secular pilgrimage. Though the Haines murder was theoretically her baby, her main motivation was still a little boy with big glasses and a cheeky grin.

Dropping by now hadn't only been prompted by visions on the way to work. Not that she was hallucinating or anything. Josh's image had stared out from posters plastered all over Moseley and Highgate, presumably further afield as well. Originally intended to tell the public about a missing boy, they now asked for help in finding his killer. Lancelot had ordered the word change. Waste not want not, she supposed. Was a sodding waste though, wasn't it? She aimed a vicious kick at a stone, winced when her big toe took the brunt. Big deal, Beverley. Josh's life had been snuffed out almost before it began. And what was there to show for it? A few cheap bunches of flowers, a garish green teddy, a couple of candles and a Villa scarf. The earth was parched, cracking under the heat. Squatting she took a closer look, wiped a finger under her eye. Must have a speck of dust in it.

She scrabbled in her bag until her fingers closed round the figure. OK, it was stupid, it'd probably get nicked soon as she turned her back. But so far she'd failed to do anything else for the poor little sod. There y'go, Josh, she whispered, then slipped the toy into the folds of the scarf, a Power Ranger with two arms. Tiger, like the one Josh had been clutching when he died, the one still with forensics. She sniffed. Odds of the killer leaving DNA on it were zilch. He'd left naff all anywhere else. More by judgement than luck: she had a feeling the guy they were after left nothing to chance.

Glancing at the flowers, she reckoned the local florist must've had a job lot of chrysanthemums and daisies, gaudy bouquets of the things lay sweating under cellophane shrouds. Reaching out, she read the handwritten messages.

Rest in peace, little Josh. Luv Nanna.

God needed another angel. From the Mackies at number 6.

Big love Josh, from Auntie Wendy.

U'll b in my hart, 4 ever, Joshie. Your loving mum.

Bev raised a bemused eyebrow. Benefit. Doubt. Maybe he would. According to Powell, Stacey now had the twins back living with her at Jubilee Row. The DI had called at the house yesterday ostensibly to tell her Haines was dead, and at the same time establish where she'd been when the guy was getting himself killed. Her account checked out. Powell and Knight were satisfied she wasn't implicated. Likely neither would seriously have entertained the thought but for Stacey's unscheduled appearance at Highgate screaming for five minutes on her own with Haines.

Rising, Bev spotted a couple of sunflowers peeping out from under the daisies. Talk about hiding their light. And they were her favourite. Glancing round, she gently nudged the others aside with her toe. Lucky that, or she'd never have spotted the card.

The letter was on Powell's keyboard when he arrived for work that morning. He'd quickly established that a cleaner had found it near the door in reception and dropped it off on the DI's desk. Great. Mrs Mop's dabs would be all over it. As forensics would find out. The single sheet of A5 plus envelope was in the lab now; DCI Knight was reading a copy. The two men sat across from each other in the senior detective's office. Powell studied the chief's face closely. It gave nothing away, unlike whoever had typed the tip-off.

If you want to know who killed Josh Banks, ask the man who lives at 24 Drake Street, Stirchley. I saw him bundle the boy into his car outside a newsagents in Marston Road on Wednesday afternoon.

Sincerely

A well-wisher.

"Well-wisher?" The DCI sneered, laid the paper on the desk. "Mighta wished us well a damn sight sooner." He smoothed a hand over his bald head.

"Maybe he's been away?" And could've caught the DI's witness appeal on local telly last night. It was the only reason Powell could see why the letter was addressed to him.

"You're assuming it's a he. You're assuming it's genuine and not some time-wasting tosser." He took a sip of espresso. "I'll tell you this for sure: this time round we take nothing for granted."

Powell shrugged. He cut a covetous glance at the boss's personal coffee maker gleaming and steaming on top of the filing cabinet. The DI hadn't even had chance to nip to the canteen for a cup of Nescaff. Getting the original letter off to the lab had taken a while, establishing who lived at the given address had taken another, tasking someone to view the nick's security tapes on the off-chance whoever had delivered the letter had been caught on camera had eaten up more time and by then Knight had been in the building demanding chapter and verse.

Powell watched now as the chief stroked a finger along his top lip. "What do we actually know?"

The intelligence had been gleaned that morning by a solitary DC from a couple of neighbours. Powell had ordered the softly softly approach. If the tip was pukka, the last thing they needed was to let the suspect know they were on to him. The DI glanced at his notes. "Occupants are Eric and Bridie Long. Married, no kids. Lived in the house about seven years." Looking at Knight, he paused for two, three seconds. "Runs a red Vauxhall."

"Red?" Knight's voice was calm. Powell sensed he was itching to go in heavy-handed. Was also aware that after what had happened with Haines, the DCI wouldn't risk another half-cock debacle. "This guy, Long? Has he got form?"

Powell jabbed a thumb over his shoulder. "Tyler's checking now." Mac had been kicking his heels in the incident room waiting for Bev to show. "He'll call soon as he's got anything." A few clicks on the police national computer, it wouldn't take long.

Knight nodded, presumably in approval. "Help yourself to coffee, Mike."

Thank you, God. "Ta, gaffer." Not that he got to drink it.

20

Drake Street, Stirchley was the sort of place you'd go out of your way to avoid. A long way. Powell parked the unmarked police motor just up the road from number twenty-four, peered through the windscreen and told Carol Pemberton he hoped her jabs were up to date. Lips in exaggerated pucker, he sneered: "You'll need a tetanus booster after this."

"Just a little prick…" The DC leant forward to grab her bag. "Isn't it, sir?"

Powell's hand paused on the seat belt release. "You being sarky?"

A curtain of glossy black hair hid her face. "Me?"

He narrowed his eyes, suspected she was getting as lippie as Morriss in her old age. Pembers was a year younger than him. Could easily walk the sergeant's and possibly inspector's exams if she didn't put her kids first. "I do the talking. Got that?"

"Be my guest, sir."

Locking the car, he ran his gaze up and down the narrow street. Even bathed in sunlight the two-up-two-down terraces peppered with satellite dishes were the pits. Rotting window frames and once red brickwork were now shades of dog shit. Long's was probably the worst. Straggly dust-laden weeds sprouted here and there from crumbling mortar and sagging guttering. The Hanging Gardens of Babylon this was not.

He sniffed. "Knew I shouldn't have worn the new suit."

"Glad you've got your priorities right, sir."

"Eric Long you mean? He's not going anywhere." Not with officers positioned at the back of the property as well as two further unmarked police vehicles in the street. Over the top? Maybe. Better safe... Unlike nine-month old Hannah Cox, the daughter of Long's former partner who'd died in squalid circumstances from neglect and abuse back in 1999.

Mac Tyler had passed on information he'd picked up from various websites as well as the PNC's less lurid data. Top lines were: Eric Long aged forty-three had served three years for causing or allowing the death of a child or vulnerable person. Many commentators believed it was murder and Long should have been sent down for life. The victim's grandfather wanted the 'baby-killing bastard put down.'

Powell banged the door with the side of his fist. "Let's see what he's got to say for himself, eh?"

"I reckon she was lying, chief." Mobile nestling under her chin, Bev perched on the MG's bonnet, scrabbling in her bag for a light. The other hand held the card she'd found at Josh's makeshift shrine. Bev thought it likelier now that it had been deliberately concealed, given it looked to have been written by his father, a man Stacey Banks claimed not to have seen hide or hair of since Josh was in nappies.

She heard papers rustling, suspected Knight wasn't listening properly. "Read it again, will you, sergeant?"

Rolling her eyes, she obliged: *Sorry, son. Should of been there for you. The bastard's gonna rot in hell.* The handwriting was scrappy as the grammar. But the message to the killer seemed clear enough. And it wasn't have a nice day.

"Lots of people call kids 'son,'" Knight commented. "Doesn't have to be the father."

"*Should've been there for you*, chief?" She held the lighter at arm's length, tried to spark up; empty, sod it. No response from Knight either. Obviously needed a prompt. "It's not the sort of thing some casual acquaintance comes out with, is it?"

Sounded to Bev like guilt kicking in, several years too late. Mind, for all the cops knew, 'should of been there' could refer to the Wednesday Josh went missing. Maybe on occasions Bobby Wells collected his son from school. They only had Stacey's word he was a feckless father. Maybe he was there for Josh that day, and there'd been a row. What if Wells had a temper and taught Josh a lesson? The wording on the card could be part of an elaborate plot aimed at casting suspicion elsewhere. Bev blew her cheeks out; maybe she watched too much telly.

"You could be reading too much into it, sergeant." Patronising git.

"Sure. 'Cause we're pursuing a shed-load of other leads, aren't we, chief?"

Silence on the line suggested she'd gone too far. Mind, it made up for the sodding church bells ringing in her other ear. He'd not hung up, she could hear breathing. She peeled herself off the bonnet, headed for the newsagents to get a lighter.

"Sorry about that, sergeant, DC Tyler just popped his head round the door. We're bringing someone in for questioning in connection with Josh's death." He told her about the letter left at the nick.

"Fair enough. Can't just drop this though. We need to talk to Stacey..."

"I'll get someone round..."

"Come on, chief, I'm on the doorstep."

"You're on the Haines case, sergeant."

"Overlap, you said it yourself."

If Bobby Wells had nothing to do with Josh's death, he sure had more motive than most to get shot of Roland Haines.

"You can't pin nothing on me."

Even if Eric Long wore more than a string vest and trackie

bottoms, the DI would baulk at approaching the guy with a barge pole let alone drawing pin. Tall and lanky with prematurely grey hair that fell just below hunched shoulders, Long currently slouched in a grubby wingchair, empty cans and full ashtrays lay on the carpet at his knobbly feet. Unwashed, unshaven and unkempt, he was also apparently unable to recall his movements last night let alone last Wednesday afternoon. "Keep me nose clean these days, I do."

Powell was intrigued by Long's response. The DI had kept his cards close to his chest so far giving the guy the impression they regarded him as a potential witness. So was his outburst the knee-jerk reaction of many an old ex-lag? Or a pre-emptive strike from someone up to his neck in shit.

Time to get down and dirty. "See, here's the thing..." Perched on the edge of a lumpy moth-eaten settee Powell shuffled a tad further forward, elbows on knees. "Why would someone tell us they'd seen you in Marston Road if you've never been near the place?"

"How should I know?" The open-mouthed yawn released a wave of rancid breath in Powell's face. The armpit hair was almost as revolting. "Nothing to do with me."

The DI was torn: sit back and risk the Hugo Boss or suffer more halitosis hell. He cut a glance at Pembers who'd bagged the only hard chair in the room and had the added advantage of sitting near the slightly open sash window. Miss Smug was taking notes, not that there'd been many to take. Long hadn't even wanted to let them in. He'd argued the toss on the doorstep until Powell jangled his keys and pointed at the car.

The DI opted to move back a fraction. "You saying our informant's mistaken then?"

"Looks like it, don't it." The grin was gross, grains of rice caught in gaps between crooked teeth slick with saliva. It struck Powell that Long was archetypal Paedo Man. They could be in an episode of *Cracker* here. But Long's act didn't ring true somehow. It was almost as though he was putting it on, enjoying himself.

Powell wasn't playing games. "Let's try again, eh? Last Wednesday afternoon, where were you?"

"Look, copper, I've told you I can't help. End of."

"You still on the register, Long?" Course he was. One of the first things they'd checked.

He curled his lip. "What's this all about? I made a mistake years ago... I paid my dues... so unless you've got..."

"Tell you what I've got. Our informant doesn't just place you at the scene of a crime. He also describes seeing you bundle Josh Banks into a car."

"Well, he's fucking wrong."

"Prove it. Where were you?"

"Where's your wife, Mr Long?" Both men glanced at DC Pemberton who'd asked the question. "Maybe we could ask her." Carol cocked her head.

"Leave her out of this, I don't want her bothered."

"If I were you, I'd be bothered." Powell scratched his jaw. "See, if you were there, we'll prove it. And if you weren't, someone's got it in for you big time, haven't they?"

"Tell you the truth, matey. Either way, I don't give a flying fuck." He reached for a pack of Embassy, slowly eased one out and held it between two tapering fingers that ended in long dirty nails. "Got a light? Save me getting up?"

"You are getting up, sunshine. Right up my nose. Get dressed. You're under arrest."

"Twenty Silk Cut and a lighter, please, mate." The newsagent was sampling his merchandise. Sat on a stool behind the counter, he had his nose in the *Sunday Mercury*. It was the guy she'd seen earlier having a fag in the shop doorway.

Tasty close-up, too. She flashed a smile. His eyes widened; he dropped his glance back to the paper then at Bev again. Classic double-take.

"Don't do you any favours, does it?" Turning the paper round, he laid it on the counter. The finger-pointing was superfluous; the picture was unmissable. A snapper had snatched it at the news conference. Her mouth open, one eye shut, she looked like a Sumo wrestler with special needs.

"Bad angle." She sniffed.

He pursed his lips, gave her the once-over. "Yeah." Even turbaned up, he bore a passing resemblance to Oz Khan. High cheekbones, warm brown eyes, full lips, the denims were tight and a white T-shirt hugged a taut neat frame. For a second or two, she fantasised how he'd look in the buff, lustrous locks flowing over sculpted shoulder blades, down flawless spine till they skirted his... She swallowed, tore her gaze away, reached for a couple of KitKats, caught sight of the picture and grabbed a pack of Polos instead. Sugar free.

"You here on Josh's case?" He handed her the ciggies and lighter.

"Yeah." Josh? First name terms? It wasn't just his physique that took her fancy now. "Knew him, did you?" She slipped the baccy in her bag.

"Nice lad." Mouth tight, he shook his head. "He'd run in here sometimes to get away from the other kids. We'd have a little chat. Footie, Doctor Who, his favourite comics."

Interest more than piqued, she kept her voice level. "Get away? How'd you mean?"

"Some of the bigger kids bullied him... made his life hell..."

"What'd they do?"

"Beat him up, threw stones, nicked stuff. Not cash. Never had two pennies to rub together did Josh. They ran off with his school books, pencils, rubbers... Snatched his glasses twice to my knowledge."

"What?" Glasses like the ones they'd not been able to trace; like the ones he'd been wearing when he disappeared.

He nodded. "He'd come in crying. I'd give him a few sweets, try and cheer him up a bit." Tasty and sensitive; the guy's eyes were brimming. Bev's heart bled for Josh, and she balled her fists. But how come quality intelligence like this hadn't been picked up before? Knight had flooded the area with officers tasked to talk to people like...?

"What's your name, mate?"

"Amrik Singh."

She held out a hand. "Detective Sergeant..."

"Beverley Morriss. Yeah, I read the story." Nice smile.

"These youths – know who they are, where they live?"

"Look, I'm sure it was only kids' stuff. Boys will be..." Then saw her face. "You don't think...?"

"I'd like a word, that's all." It was a big leap from bullying to bumping somebody off. But the violence could've spiralled, got out of hand. More likely the kids might've seen something the day Josh went missing. And at the very least the toerags needed a damn good talking at. Come to think of it... "Did you see Josh last Wednesday, Amrik?"

"Haven't set eyes on him for a couple of weeks. I've been in India."

She glanced round. "So who was looking after the shop?" And may have witnessed something.

"Me dad's brother."

"He here?"

"I can give you his address."

She jotted the details down; best get someone there in case he'd slipped the interview net. "These kids, then?" Pen still poised. "Any names?"

"I'd like to help…" He broke eye contact, fiddled round straightening papers. You didn't have to be Einstein. Big kids often had big brothers and brick shithouse dads. Amrik was scared of reprisals if he blabbed. "We have a lot of trouble in here… shoplifting, abuse, racial attacks."

She could believe it, had a certain amount of sympathy, but a shed-load more for a little boy lying on a slab in the morgue. "Look, Amrik, they're not gonna find out who told us. You've got my word on that."

"Easy for you to say."

She waited till he looked up. "It's not for my benefit, Amrik."

He paused, weighing it up then: "Ringleader's a yob called Brett."

She stiffened. "Brett Sullivan?" The absentee mobile phone owner.

"Yeah, d'you know him?"

"Could say that." But not as well as she was going to. She'd give Darren New a call, get him on the case, soon as. Amrik gave her a couple more names and she handed him her card in case anything came to mind. Thanking him, she hoisted her bag, headed for the door. Her fingers were on the handle when he called. "Er… sergeant? One more thing…"

Tentative. Shy? She'd been spot on: he had given her the glad eye earlier. Hey? Maybe she'd scored?

"Six seventy-six."

Blank look. "Come again?"

He held out a flat palm. "The smokes?"

21

Tetchy, jumpy, Eric Long was itching for a nicotine hit. Tough. Interview Room Three was non-smoking. He was sweating it out in there now with a burly uniform on the door for company. Powell leant against the wall in the corridor outside jotting a few notes, waiting on Knight and Pemberton. The DCI would be in a viewing suite watching as the interview was taped; Pembers would be in on the session, but was fetching the DI coffee first. God knew why she'd made a song and dance about it.

"How's it looking, sir?" Mac, shucking into a denim jacket, ambled Powell's way. "Reckon Long's good for it?"

"Good for sod all." He snarled. Long stank to high heaven, they'd have to fumigate the car. The prospect of sharing confined quarters once more was so not appealing. Wasn't what Mac wanted to hear, though. "Dunno really, Mac. Too soon to call."

"Seen that stuff I left on your desk?" Newspaper reports leading up to and including Long's trial back in 1999.

"Yeah, thanks, mate." Powell still had a nasty taste in his mouth. "Where you off?"

"Balsall Heath. Hooking up with Bev. Got a couple of interviews lined up. Best get off or..."

"Say no more." Guts. Garters. Short. Curlies.

"There you go..." Pembers handed him his drink. "Managed to find this as well."

It looked like a match book, something like that. "What is it?" Puzzled frown.

"Sewing kit."

The frown deepened. "For…?"

"I'd have mentioned it sooner, but…" She gave a careless shrug.

"What?"

"Not much you could do without needle and thread." Smiling, she tapped her bum. "And at least we're not going commando today, are we… sir?"

Light dawned, the DI's face dropped. "Not the…?" Cursing, he gingerly fingered the seat of his pants. Fucking settee. Four hundred and seventy-nine quid suit down the sodding drain. And the story'd be all over the station. Long was gonna die.

"When you're ready, inspector." Nonplussed, arms folded, Knight was staring. "Get the show on the road, shall we?"

Reluctantly wearing the jacket, DI Powell circled the scarred metal table in IR3. The movement was aimed at keeping Eric Long on his toes, too. It wasn't working. Sprawled in a chair, Long's fingers were laced casually just above his crotch. The small windowless room was hot, stuffy and reeked of body odour. It was pretty cramped in there as well. Long had opted for the services of a duty solicitor. The fact that lissom blonde Miranda Ellis was easy on the eye was no compensation for Powell's increasing frustration. It was a recorded interview. Though under arrest, Long hadn't been charged, he was supposed to be helping with inquiries. And it was now half an hour since Pemberton had started running the tapes. Thirty sodding minutes trying to drag from Long where he'd been on the afternoon Josh Banks disappeared. Lip curled, Powell reckoned it was a shame they'd got rid of the rack.

"Why don't you advise your client to co-operate with us, Ms Ellis? Might save us all a bunch of time?"

She tapped a slim gold pen on a yellow legal pad. "He's assured you he was nowhere near Marston Road…"

"Do me a favour, love." Powell loosened the silk tie another three or four inches.

"...and has no idea where it is."

"Not enough. And you know it." Powell made to lean into Long's air space, pulled back at the last moment. He was finding it difficult to mask ragged nerves frayed further by Long's constant leg jangling and leer. "So why don't you say where you were?" Either it risked incriminating him or he was an arsey bastard.

"Can't recall." He picked his teeth, examined the nail. "All you need know..."

"Is why you find this so amusing?"

"It's as funny as a triple hernia." He stared, hard-faced. "This is police harassment. You got nothing on me."

Powell tightened his mouth, balled his fists. Cops are trained to treat everyone with respect and restraint. Long was a challenge on both fronts. The newspaper reports Mac had printed off the web described how Long's former partner's nine-month-old baby died in squalor, smeared in shit and covered in cigarette burns. Hannah Cox's emaciated tiny body had been broken and bruised. Long and his woman had come out with the usual crap of blaming each other. The mother had been given the heavier sentence, and died in prison from a heroin overdose.

"Got any kids, Mr Long?" Not according to neighbours. Powell wanted to rile the bastard.

"No." Sullen.

"D'you drive, Mr Long?" The leg movement ceased momentarily. Powell cut Carol Pemberton a glance, she'd clocked it too.

"Yeah. So?"

"Got a motor?" Red Vauxhall according to the officer who'd made the original inquiries.

Two, three second pause. "Did have."

"Meaning?"

"Got nicked, didn't it?"

"When?"

"Week or so." They'd need to go back to the neighbours, find out when it was last seen in the street.

"Report it to the local cops?"

"Like you lot are gonna find it."

"Insurance company?" He'd need a crime number to claim.

"Not worth pursuing. It was only an old banger."

Uninsured more like. "Handy that. Our informant says…"

"An anonymous letter, inspector?" The solicitor crossed her legs, the black silk skirt showcasing slender thighs. "It's not rock solid, is it?"

"Yeah." Long sat up straight. "So if there's nothing else…"

"Relax, Mr Long. Those inquiries you're not helping with? They're not complete."

Bev sat next to Mac on the grubby settee in Stacey Banks's Mill Street council house. Stacey had tidied herself up a bit; the hair looked clean, there were wafts of fabric conditioner coming off her jogging pants. "So, how long's he been back?" Bobby Wells. Josh's not so absent dad. Bev tapped her fingers waiting for an answer.

Head down, Stacey wasn't making eye contact any time soon. "A while."

Week? Month? Millennium? "Meaning?"

"Couple a years."

"Why'd you lie, Stacey?"

"We don't live together or nothing."

Or Stacey'd lose her benefits, wouldn't she? Bev shook her head. "Helps out with a few bob now and again, does he?"

Stacey nodded. "A bit."

"How did he and Josh get on, love?" Mac asked. Glancing round, Bev noticed a few jars of baby food, a couple of teddies. Powell had mentioned the twins were back.

"They got on… OK." Stacey picked at a loose thread on the armchair.

Talk about damning with faint praise. "OK?" Bev prompted.

"Josh could get a bit touchy. Jealous, like." Glancing up, she gave a wry smile. "Liked to think he was the man of the house. Know what I mean?"

Bev hadn't got a clue. Josh was ten years old for pity's sake. "Where's he living now?"

"Bobby?"

No, Barack Obama. Her brisk nod was sufficient prompt.

"He's got a bedsit in Ada Street, number nine, just off the Moseley Road." Mac was already jotting it down. "I'll tell you this for nothing. He wouldn't lay a finger on Josh."Maybe. But what might Bobby Wells lay on someone he erroneously believed killed his son?

"Did he know Roland Haines was in custody?" Bev asked.

Stacey shrugged. "Who didn't?" Couldn't argue with that, thanks to the press.

"Did you and Bobby talk about Haines?"

"No." Too quick?

"Sure 'bout that?"

"Better things to do."

So'd they. "Mind if I use the loo before we go?"

"Upstairs. Door facing at the top."

Bev wasn't going to do it, but couldn't resist. The bedroom door was ajar. Just a peek, she told herself. The twins were in cots side by side, fast asleep, hands bunched in tiny fists. She reached a trembling finger to stroke a perfect peachy cheek, marvelled at dark eye-lashes so long they looked false. Her own babies would've been getting on for two years old now, if… She swallowed. Don't go there, Beverley. One of the babies farted, the boy in blue. Her lip curved in a million mixed emotions. How life could change in the blink of an eye, or the twist of a blade.

Maybe she wasn't cut out to be a mother. Nice one, Beverley, there were better turns of phrase. Either way, looking down on these two now had done her a favour, helped crystallise her thinking. The pain of loss was too much to bear to risk it again. From now on, she'd concentrate on the career.

Probably.

She cast a final glance from the door. Least no one could accuse her of dithering.

"You coming, boss?" Mobile in hand, Mac stood at the bottom of the stairs. "Daz wants a word."

Several actually. Brett Sullivan hadn't come home. His mother wanted to report him missing.

22

"Reckon he's playing games?" DCI Knight was in Byford's office. They'd both observed Powell's interview with Eric Long, just viewed the tape again. Body language, facial expressions reflected and reinforced the man's slack attitude.

"I don't know." The guv stroked an eyebrow. "And I've even less idea why. But either way, what we've got is pretty flimsy, Lance."

"You don't think we should've brought him in then?" Defensive bordering on prickly.

"All we have are anonymous allegations." Wasn't much more than they'd had against Haines.

"I know, guv, but two sources now have mentioned a red car. If we could trace that." Checks with Long's neighbours had proved inconclusive so far. None could swear to the last time they'd seen him in the Vauxhall. The registration had been circulated to other forces so they could keep an eye out as well.

Byford heard the hope in Knight's voice, or was it despair? The guv rose, walked to the window. He knew the feeling, been there, done that. Wanting a collar so badly, homing in on one thin line, one tiny shred of what might be evidence.

"Worth sending a team out with Long's picture? Marston Road? Streets on the Quarry Bank?" The big man perched on the sill, sun felt warm on his back.

"On it." DCs Rees and Gosh had been despatched.

"What about the lad who rang in?"

"Brett Sullivan. Should've mentioned it, guv. Could be a connection between him and Josh Banks. We only picked it up this morning but a newsagent on Marston Road claims Sullivan and a few of his mates used to bully Josh. Picked on the boy when he came out of school."

"What's Sullivan got to say?"

"Seems he's gone AWOL." Knight relayed what he knew.

"And his mates?"

"Checking now."

"If they were around on the Wednesday..."

Knight didn't need telling. "...it's possible they clocked Long. Yeah. We're chasing that, too."

They needed to do more than chase, they had to possess evidence. Or they'd have to let Long go. Byford sighed, he too had read the newspaper reports Mac had dug out for Powell. The big man had also printed off more material of his own. It lay in his top drawer now inside an old file full of yellow dog-eared cuttings he'd recently retrieved. The treatment meted out to Long's victim was reminiscent of what Baby Fay had suffered. He'd give his right arm to bring both the bastards to justice.

"Want the God's honest truth? I wish it were me as killed him." Bobby Wells on Roland Haines. Try as she might and she wasn't trying hard, Bev couldn't picture Wells on Stacey Banks. A shrimp with a comb-over clambering up a Great White sprang to mind. It wasn't an image on which to dwell. Wells was a short skinny-to-the-point-of-skeletal bloke who talked the talk through gaps in chipped sepia coloured teeth. As for walking the walk, Bev reckoned the little guy would lag behind on two left feet and a wooden leg. Metaphorically speaking.

They'd tracked Wells to a dive that called itself a pub round the corner from his Ada Street maisonette. The owner of the kebab shop below who was also Wells's landlord had pointed them in the right direction. Wells had been sitting on his own in the corner of a deserted dingy bar. Bobby-no-mates was nursing half a bitter shandy, scrawny shoulders hunched over yesterday's much creased copy of the *Racing Post*.

When Bev flashed her ID, Wells had looked ready to do a runner till his darting ratty eyes settled on Mac meandering over carrying drinks: Saint Clements. Two.

Bev sipped hers now. "Friendly that is – wish you'd killed him." It had been Wells's response when questioned about his wording on the card: *the bastard's gonna rot in hell.*

"Scum like Haines need putting down." Wells's hollow cheeks caved in as he sucked furiously on a stubby pencil. "Hanging's too good."

Pur-leeze. Save us. Bev rolled her eyes. Despite Wells's ranting, she reckoned the only danger was in not taking seriously anything else the puny little twit came out with. "You say you never laid eyes on Haines?"

"Seen his picture in the paper." The cheeks were at it again. "Read about him. Makes your skin creep."

"He wasn't convicted."

"Yeah." He sniffed. "No thanks to you lot."

Sunlight poured through the pub's stained glass windows, cast shimmering red and green shadows across cracked mud brown lino. Anywhere else it might've brightened things up. Bev grimaced. No wonder they had the Grotsville Arms to themselves.

"OK, Bobby?" Or maybe not. The call came from a man-mountain who'd just entered and was lumbering towards the bar.

"No sweat, Jimbo." Wells lifted a scrawny white arm.

Bev raised an eyebrow. Jumbo was nearer the mark. The guy's grey hoodie and flapping trackies maybe added to the elephantine impression, but he was seriously big as in morbidly obese. Every podgy finger boasted at least two rings, the heavy link chain round his neck was almost lost in the folds of fat.

"When's the last time you saw Josh, Bobby?" Mac asked, rolling his shirt sleeves.

They waited ten, fifteen seconds while he pinched the bridge of his nose, leaving pale indentations among open pores. "Weekend before he die… was killed."

"Where'd you go?" Mac sank a mouthful of juice.

"Kicked a ball round Canon Hill Park, had some ice cream, fed the ducks, sat in the sun." Wistful half-smile.

Nice. The idyllic picture cut no Colman's with Bev, not when a child dies every ten days in the UK at the hands of a parent. And Bobby Wells, though no father of the year, hadn't been quite as hands-off as Stacey had led the cops to believe.

"Always there for him, were you, Bobby?" Bev said.

Earnest nod. "Tried my best." Dense sod. She'd be less heavy on the sarcasm next time.

"Tricky, that. Not living in the same house."

"That supposed to be funny?"

"You and Josh got on well, did you? No tensions?"

"Course we…" His small eyes narrowed. "Fuck is this? What you saying here?"

She narrowed hers, leaned in closer. "Josh was murdered. It's our job to find out who did it. You have a problem with that, we can always go to the station, continue this little chat there."

"Hey, Bobby. Awright?" Elephant man again. Podgy elbow sprawled on the bar. Butt out, big boy. Bev cut him a withering glance.

"It's cool, ta, mate." Wells had previous, knew the score. It was minor stuff, thieving mostly, shops, warehouses, couple of criminal damage charges. Wasn't the first time he'd been questioned by police, he knew what they were after.

It took about ten minutes. Mac recorded detail as Bev elicited Wells's movements at relevant times, the night Haines was killed, the afternoon Josh disappeared and the early hours when the boy's body was dumped. If the alibis were sound, his name could be crossed off the list. Standard TIE: trace, implicate, eliminate. Or not.

"See," Bev said. "Wasn't difficult, was it, Bobby?"

Trembling slightly, Wells drained the inch or so of drink in his glass then fixed her with a hard stare through watering eyes. "However much you sneer and shitbag – I loved my son. I wasn't always there for him. Should've been around more." He bit a cracked bottom lip. "I was only a kid meself when we had him. Wasn't his fault me and Stacey didn't always hit it off. Last couple a years we'd been getting to know each other. Wasn't easy, I'll admit that. But I'd've done anything for that boy. And some bastard snatched it all away."

Momentarily she caught a shadow of the little boy's likeness in Wells's raddled prematurely-aged features. She sensed the guy was telling the truth, it wasn't dissimilar from Stacey's take on the current father-son relationship. Impassive, she said: "I'm sorry for your loss, Bobby." Meant it, too. And when Wells said he'd do anything for Josh... had he meant that? And had it included murder? She wasn't a betting woman, wouldn't be laying odds, unlike Roland Haines who'd liked a flutter.

"Follow the horses, do you, Bobby?" She cocked her head at the runners and riders he'd been studying in the paper.

"Not against the law is it?"

"Where'd you go to bet?" The same bookies as Haines?

"Here and there. What's it to you?"

Casual shrug. "Just wondered." What was that old saying? Keep your powder dry? They'd check it out. See if he was known to the staff at Ladbroke's. Even better, if the security cameras had captured Haines and Wells on tape at the same time, Wells would also be caught out in a lie. Never laid eyes on the guy, he'd said. It wasn't much to go on. But given they were thrashing about without too many leads, it was better than nothing. No mileage in tipping off Wells.

She nodded at Mac, scraped back the chair. "Not thinking of leaving the country are you, Bobby?"

"Yeah, jetting off to the private condo in Saint Kitts first thing." He scowled, muttered, "Stupid tart" under his breath.

She opened her mouth, thought better of it. It was big talk from a little man. But Wells wasn't Bobby-no-mates. Fatso at the bar was worth bearing in mind. If Wells'd had a big job on recently, he could have used a heavy.

Halfway to the door, she turned back: "Hey, Bobby? Say that again and I'll send the boys round."

"Very mature, boss," Mac muttered. But she did let that go.

"Are charges imminent then, Mr Knight?" *Birmingham News* crime correspondent Toby Priest was on the phone. The DCI was on a short fuse, shortening by the second. Priest's call had been put through by a secretary in the press office who didn't have a clue how to handle the reporter's query.

Knight was struggling to handle the increasingly persistent Priest. "I'll ask again: where did you get your information?" He tightened his mouth. Where was Paul Curran when he was needed?

Only a handful of officers at Highgate, and no support staff, were aware a man was helping with inquiries in connection with Josh Banks's murder. The suspect's name was known to even fewer. The information had been circulated on a need-to-know basis, Knight ordering the clampdown in the

hope of staunching further leaks. That was the thinking…
Seemed like a good idea at the time.

"I never reveal my sources, Mr Knight." Bright, breezy, like:
you should know that. "Is it true?"

Which part? Sighing, Knight ran a hand over his bald head.
Priest was privy to the lot: Eric Long's identity, age, address,
criminal past and uncertain future. If the anonymous
allegations proved well-founded. Priest knew about the well-
wisher's letter too, had even quoted from it. The detective
heard sounds on the line that suggested the reporter was
drumming his fingers on a desk. Impatient? Irritated? Keen
to get to the bottom of it? Snap, Knight thought. This was
no leak, it was Niagara bloody Falls. And whoever was
behind the disclosures was going to be in deep shit. Priest was
chewing now, and still waiting on an answer. Noisy little
masticator.

Knight cleared his throat. "I never comment on rumour
and specula…"

"Wouldn't expect you to. The intelligence is on good
authority."

"Whose?" Knight fired back.

Priest dodged. "The best."

It had to be a cop, didn't it? Knight ran through a mental
list of officers he knew were on the inside track. "As I say, I
don't com…"

"I don't want comment. Story's already written. I'm asking
you to confirm that Eric Long faces charges in the…"

"What!" Jumping to his feet, he strode to the window, flung
it open and was hit by exhaust fumes and hot air.

"…in the morning in connection with the death of Josh
Banks."

"No. He absolutely will not. Print a word of that…"

"Thanks, Mr Knight. You just admitted he's in custody."

"Your informant word's not good enough?"

"Course it…" The tapping stopped. Priest had been forced into an admission too.

"What's the going rate for a tip-off, Priest?" Thirty pieces of silver?

"Going rate?" All innocence.

"No one gives this stuff away, do they?"

"Don't know where you're coming from, Mr Knight. Digging out news, finding stories – it's what I do."

"With a little help from your friends?"

"Anyway." The sniff was dismissive. "These charges…"

Knight kicked the bin. "Ever think of the consequences when you get it wrong?"

Pause for remorse? Maybe he'd hit a nerve and Priest would hang fire, reconsider.

"Yeah, all the time. Do you?"

The DCI's mental list of officers who knew that Eric Long had been brought in for questioning was now on paper. Byford had found it on his desk after the late brief along with an explanatory note from Knight. Holding it between his fingers, he ran his gaze over the names: Ed Keynes the DC who'd questioned Long's neighbours first thing; Powell and Carol Pemberton; PC Tim Bloore who'd kept an eye on Long in the interview room; Mac Tyler; and two uniforms who'd knocked doors later in Drake Street: Ken Gibson and Steve Hawkins.

Byford would have a word, of course. But the seven would be acutely aware they'd come under immediate suspicion if Long's identity got out. He couldn't see any of them risk losing their pension for a few quid. Pensive, he wandered to the water cooler, poured a drink, drained the cup. Likelier, surely, the leak had sprung from someone not officially in the know. Christ. The nick was full of people whose job was finding things out. Even if they didn't always succeed.

Back at the desk, he opened the top drawer, stood looking down on a file. The name written in black ink was fading. His mental image of baby Fay was sharp and in colour, helped by the vivid nightmares that had recently returned with a vengeance. Fay's death was the big man's only unsolved murder and he urged himself not to let it become an obsession again. He'd retrieved the file shortly after Josh Banks went missing and had been adding related material, similarly unresolved cases, almost as if to assuage his sense of guilt. So he could convince himself he wasn't the only cop who'd failed a child.

He glanced at the door, pushed the drawer to. "Come in."

Knight popped his head round. "Not stopping, guv. I'm about to head for home. Just letting you know I'm letting Eric Long go. His wife's downstairs. She's given him an alibi."

"Tight?"

"As a gastric band."

Byford gave a grim smile. "Good night, Lance."

The guv shook his head: gastric band. Sounded straight out of the big book of Bev-isms. Come to think of it… he pulled Knight's list closer. Why wasn't her name on it? If Mac Tyler knew about Long, pound to a penny she would too. He added Knight's name while he was at it.

Scott inquiry police 'baffled'

At a news conference today, Leicester police made a fresh appeal for help in their hunt for the killer of 10-year old schoolboy, Scott Myers. It's more than a month since Scott's partially buried body was discovered on a golf course near his home in Highfields. Scott was last seen alive leaving school in Belle View Drive on 30th June. A post mortem revealed he died from asphyxiation.

Hundreds of people have been interviewed and scores of witness statements taken, but the detective leading the inquiry admitted yesterday they're no further forward in securing an arrest.

Inspector Ted Adams told this newspaper he believes someone is harbouring the murderer. "It's likely someone knows who killed Scott. Maybe a mother suspects her son, a girlfriend her boyfriend, a sister her brother. I'd ask everyone to examine their conscience closely. Any information will be treated in the strictest confidence. I want justice for Scott and the family need to know their son's killer is behind bars."

Scott's death has cast a dark shadow over the small community where he lived with his father Noel and mother Amy. Neighbours say Mrs Myers hasn't been back to the house since her son disappeared. After a brief stay in hospital, it's understood she's living temporarily with her parents in Manchester. Scott's brother Alan and sister Wendy are staying with relatives.

Police refused to confirm that a man held for questioning last week was released without charge.

A picture had been taken at the news conference: Ted Adams was flanked by Scott's father and a young unnamed police officer. They were seated at a shiny black table, only one microphone in shot where there'd been a bank when the story broke. It was the silly season but the media obviously weren't biting. Where was the hook? Unless you were a relative or friend of the family, another police appeal was a non-story. On the wall behind someone had stuck a reminder of what it was all about: a blown up photograph of a smiling Scott. The image was huge, the three men dwarfed by it.

Apt, thought the man with the scrapbook.

Four weeks after the little boy's death and the police were still floundering. Asking people to examine their conscience? All that stuff about strictest confidence? Justice for Scott? Meaningless twaddle. If the cliché had been in currency back then Adams would have appealed to the killer to give the parents closure.

Relaxing a clenched fist, the man told himself to calm down. Peering closer at the news picture, he noted that stress was starting to show: Adams's face was lined, the features drawn. Scott's father looked as if he was on medication. He probably was. It would be a couple of years yet before Noel self-medicated with booze and drugs.

The man's grasp tightened on his glass, three fingers of single malt in a crystal tumbler. As for the mother, she was well out of it. Living with her parents? Only if they ran the psychiatric ward where she'd been sectioned.

MONDAY
23

Monday Monday – so good to me. Yeah right. Bev's Midget had a flat, her hair was shite, the top button hadn't fastened on her favourite linen pants and the spot near her nose looked like a set of traffic lights on green. Apart from that…

"Hunky bleeding dory. Thank you, so much, Mrs Cass." She cut off the Mamas and the Papas in their prime, couldn't be arsed to search for another station, couldn't be arsed to change the tyre either. Standing in the kitchen, she was waiting for Mac to show with a lift. Quick glance at the clock on the cooker showed 7.29 – Parker would be here any time, maybe she should perfect a Lady Penelope impression.

And breakfast? Yeah. Why not? Limbs doing the puppet dangle she grabbed two slices of Mother's Pride from her hidden cache, sniffed cautiously before popping them in the toaster. The cupboard under the sink wasn't the best place to keep bread, but if food fascist Frankie came across sliced white, she'd junk the lot in the bin. Bev could live with the faint smell of Persil. Though why she let the mad Italian hold sway in the kitchen was beyond her. On the other hand, Frankie's chicken parmigiana last night was to die for. She licked her lips. She'd never liked those linen pants much anyway. And look at it: not a cloud in the sky again. Day like today cried out for a loose dress.

Muffled ringtone was going off. She glanced round, eyes creased. Where'd she left it? Course. Shoulder bag. On the hall table. Mac's number on caller display. Her chauffeur must be waiting in the car. She wasn't much cop at talking posh but: "Ay'll be with you in a tick, Parker."

"Now. Get your butt in gear, boss."

Not the time to piss round. Mac didn't often sound urgent. Well, not that urgent. "What is it, mate?"

"Body on the Quarry Bank estate. Uniform's out there. Control wants us to take a look." She sensed there was more but he'd hung up. Grabbing her bag and a denim jacket off the banister she dashed out. The engine was still running and a clearly uneasy Mac tapped the wheel. Keeping a keen gaze on him, she slipped into the passenger seat. "And?"

"They're pretty sure it's Darren New."

The attending officers' doubt was down to the extensive damage. The victim's face was bruised and battered virtually beyond recognition. Stamped on too, impressions of at least one trainer were just detectable in the bloody bone-chipped pulp. And the body had taken a kicking. Though first-aid trained, neither Doug Wallace nor Andy Pound, both police constables, had been able to detect a pulse. It had taken senior paramedic Sheila Gardiner to determine that life hung by a thread. It was when Sheila and her colleague gently moved the victim that the warrant card – warm, creased, blood-stained – was found confirming Darren's identity.

Eyes smarting, Bev held it now. The picture showed a chuffed-looking Daz trying hard not to smile for the camera. He loved being a cop, always said joining CID was the best day of his… The image dissolved. She dashed away hot angry tears with the heel of her hand. Strong emotion wasn't going to nail the bastards who'd done this. Hopefully the three-strong FSI team currently suiting up and checking equipment would provide something more concrete. The usual good-natured banter as they prepared was absent: they'd all knocked about with Darren.

Mac, who'd been parking the motor, joined her, puffing

slightly. "How's he doing, boss?"

She shook her head. "Not good." Standing slightly back from the action, they watched the green-clad paramedics huddled either side of the young detective. Their expressions were difficult to read, hushed voices impossible to hear. Their big concern, according to Doug Wallace, was brain injury. Not if, but how extensive. Little could be done on site to reverse the damage but it was vital to stabilise him and prevent further harm. A neck restraint had been fitted and Darren, tubes and drips everywhere, had been placed on a back board. They'd carried out the endo-tracheal intubation to keep the airways open, now they were working to maintain oxygen supply, control blood pressure. An ambulance, doors open, was parked at the kerb, neurosurgeons at the city's General Hospital were on standby, an ICU bed available. But Darren had to make it there first. And Christ knew how long he'd been lying here before the alarm was raised.

"Who called it in, boss?"

"Paperboy." Thank God kids had surgically attached mobiles these days.

Mac glanced round, a puzzled frown deepening the lines on his face. "What was Dazza doing here?" He lived with his mum in Selly Oak. 'Here' was the parking area for Heathfield House, the low rise block of flats Daz had visited, tracking down the non-existent woman who'd tried framing Roland Haines.

"Fuck do I know," she snapped, reached in her bag for a ciggie, came out with a tissue instead. "Sorry, mate." This wasn't down to Mac.

The land was little more than a patch of tired-looking grass, fast food cartons falling out of overflowing bins, it would only take ten or twelve motors max. Daz's souped-up Mini wasn't among them, she'd already scanned the lot.

144

"No idea why he was here, mate." She blew her nose. "The line of inquiries was at a dead... over." Last time he'd been this way was on another tack, trying to trace Brett Sullivan, talking to the boy's mother. "He sure wasn't on duty." Darren had passed the task back to Bev because today was meant to be a day off. Catching a glimpse of his ruined face, she reckoned his leave would be extended, maybe permanently. "So how come..." Eyes creased, she could have been talking to herself.

"What?" He offered her a bottle of water.

Waving it away, she said: "Why'd he have his warrant card out, Mac? One of the paramedics found it when they moved him."

He turned his mouth down. "Could've fallen out during the attack."

She tried picturing the scene. Nothing else had been found either lying round or in his pockets; no wallet, keys, mobile. Surely Darren wouldn't leave home, or wherever he'd been, without them? Nah. They'd been stolen. Was it a mugging then? Random? Senseless attack? Eyes shining, she turned to Mac. "Maybe he spotted something suspicious, someone up to no good, approached to have a word, took out his card, and..." Faltering, she couldn't stand the thought that he couldn't bear to let it go.

"Boss." He reached out a calming hand, almost placed it on her elbow. "It's all speculation."

"At this stage it's all we've got." She spun round, eyes flashing.

"So let's get on with it, eh?" He nodded at the rear of the flats. "See what that lot has to say for a start." The number of silhouettes at the windows had grown, residents having a good gawp at the action.

"Don't tell me...!" She swallowed, took a deep breath. Mac hadn't had the benefit of Doug's top lines. "Teams are in there now. Others are on house-to-house, and we've got patrols cruising the streets." Soon as control put out the word every available cop on the patch had responded. Like her and Mac – Balsall Heath was on the way to Highgate. The case probably wouldn't be assigned to them though, not with the current workload.

"That should keep the buggers out." Doug Wallace approached mopping his brow, police hat gripped under muscular arm. She spotted the white band of un-tanned skin at his hairline, always thought of it as the cop equivalent of cabbie's elbow. Doug was about her height, but in better shape courtesy of the police boxing team. Not that she envied him the nose. Smoothing damp fair hair, he replaced the hat. "Just heard on the radio, sarge. DI Talbot's on his way."

"Good man." Pete Talbot. Experienced SIO. Safe pair of hands.

Rustling off to the side. The paramedics were on their feet. "We're moving him now." Bev walked to the back of the ambulance watched as they bore the stretcher closer, and seeing for the first time the full extent of Darren's injuries bit down hard on her lip. She kept her gaze on his face until the doors closed, willing him to pull through.

"He's stable now." Sheila Gardiner peeled off the surgical gloves, made to leave then paused briefly. "Try not to worry, love. He'll be in the best hands."

Bev watched the ambulance pull away, blue light flashing but no screeching tyres. She'd wanted to ask if he'd be OK but hadn't trusted her voice not to break. She'd wanted a magic wand to wave but didn't believe in fairies. As for scumbags who could do that to another human being, she wanted to kick shit. Cancel that.

She would kick shit.

24

Death knocks were the pits, but breaking news of the attack to Darren's mum had been a close run thing. Pete Talbot was a damn good detective but not big on people skills; he'd asked Bev to take it on. To be fair, she'd probably have volunteered anyway. Mac had dropped her at the nick so she could pick up a pool car. Back at Highgate now, she was walking down the corridor with Powell, heading for an extra brief Knight had felt compelled to call.

"How'd she take it?" the DI asked. He looked different somehow. Bev couldn't put her finger on it, didn't dwell, either. She still had an image in her head of a frail thin woman in bits.

"Hard." Patty New was a widow, Darren her only child. His pictures were plastered all over the modest semi in Selly Oak. Go figure. Mrs New had ranted, raved, chucked a couple of ornaments, screamed about never wanting him to join the police in the first place. She blamed the cops in general and seemingly Bev in particular for what had happened to the son she doted on. People react in a zillion different ways to bad news. Bev had witnessed similar outbursts before. The woman might come round, might not. Right now Bev was more concerned about Daz coming round from the coma. "I dropped her at the hospital." After finally persuading her to accept a lift. "I suspect she'll have a long wait."

"What's the word on Daz?" Powell asked. Word? The medico she'd nobbled operated in initial-speak; some of it Bev could make out, some of it sounded like a furniture showroom: TBI, RSI, ICP, CT. Asked for a rough translation the doctor had talked about traumatic brain injury, rapid sequence intubation, intra-cranial pressure. The CT was easy. They needed to take a scan to determine how bad the damage was.

"Stable." Bev said. The DI had asked for just the one.

"That's good, right?" Always a guy with a half-full glass.

"Except when the starting point's critical." No comeback for that.

"Done something to your hair?" Talk about a non sequitur.

Frowning, she raked her fingers through the fringe, or what was left of it. She'd forgotten last night's DIY job in the bathroom with a pair of nail scissors. "New look. Like it?" Might as well brazen it out.

"Very you." He winked as he held the door for her. "Spiky."

DCI Knight hadn't shown yet. It was just shy of midday. Hot as high noon though. There was a lot of body heat floating round in a briefing room that was pretty packed but unmistakably subdued. Even if Darren hadn't been a popular guy, he was a cop and that meant family, one of their own.

As Powell swaggered to his patch of wall, the difference in the DI suddenly hit her: he wasn't wearing a suit. Mr Button-Up had swapped the designer gear for chinos and open-necked shirt. Of course. The dodgy settee spring. Pembers's story had had Bev in stitches. Bit like the DI, come to think of it. Shame. She'd missed a trick there, could've worked in a line about bum jokes, or something.

"Wotcha." Still smiling, she slipped into a seat next to Paul Curran near the back. The press officer looked knackered, must've had a hectic morning. Bet the nights were no easier either with a baby.

"Bev." He tapped his forehead. She spotted the local rag rolled under his arm.

"Can I have a quick butcher's?"

"Sure. It's the early edition though, nothing on Darren in it." The media had made up for lost news ground since. Driving through town to and from the hospital, she'd seen the story headlined on billboards, heard it on local radio. Christ, she'd do a telly turn herself if she thought it'd do any good. The more coverage the better.

She frowned. Except when it was the kind the cops didn't want. She zoomed in on a short piece on page one. "Where the frig they get this?"

The head-and-shoulders of Eric Long looked liked a police mug shot. The accompanying story didn't do him any favours either. It was only a few lines – restrained compared with Toby Priest's normal lurid prose – but it named Long, said he came from Stirchley and was being held in connection with the killing of Birmingham schoolboy Josh Banks.

She gave a low whistle. "Seen this, Paul? It's contempt surely?"

Derisive snort. "Probably libellous too, given the guy was released without charge last night."

It was news to her. "Really?"

And Curran apparently. "I know… tell me about it. No one even told me he'd been brought in till this morning."

No chance to tell him anything, even about the baby gloop she'd just spotted on the back of his shirt. The guv was striding in, suit jacket flapping, DCI Knight a few paces behind. What little chat there'd been among the squad, ceased; there was a mass straightening of spines, squaring of shoulders. Bev crossed her legs, and fingers. Maybe Byford leading the way meant he was taking over as senior investigating officer? Lancelot hadn't exactly shone in the post. The hope was shortlived as she watched the guv hive off and bag his customary perch on the windowsill leaving the floor open.

Knight positioned himself in front of the whiteboards, ran his gaze over the squad. "I can't start the brief without saying I know how you all feel about the attack on Darren New." Course he did. "It was vicious, cowardly and almost certainly unprovoked. DI Talbot's heading up the inquiry. He's out there now, he's got a good team. Let's hope we get an early result. DC New was a fine young…"

"Was?" Bev yelled, then shuffled back in the seat. Platitudinous cliché was one thing but: "Get it right for God's sake."

Pin-drop silence for a second or five then Knight articulated clearly: "It was a slip of the tongue, I'm sorry." The quick clench of his jaw meant he didn't like being pulled up but had the sense to realise the squad was on Bev's side. He dug a hand in his trouser pocket. "As I say, Pete Talbot's on the case. I think we need to focus on our own inquiries."

"You don't see a connection then?" Powell asked. Bev noted there was no 'sir'. Looked as if it had registered with Knight, too. It was a reasonable question though: Darren along with other squad members had spent a fair amount of time nosing round the Quarry Bank estate in recent days.

"Obviously it can't be ruled out. But until there's evidence, I want it treated as a separate inquiry. Darren's attack could be down to the level of street crime in that area anyway."

Oh! That's OK then. What a fucking admission.

Bev tried biting her tongue. It didn't work. "So what happened to the extra patrols? Did you get on to uniform?" It was probably below the belt. He'd said he would, but more bobbies out there didn't necessarily mean the assault wouldn't have happened.

This time he hit back. "Don't lay that on me, sergeant. You know as well as anyone, we can't cover every inch of the patch twenty-four-seven. We're overstretched as it is. The regular stuff doesn't stop just because we've got our hands full." Knight waved an arm at the whiteboards, one dominated by a picture of Josh Banks, the other featuring the creepy Roland Haines. "And no one needs reminding we've got two ongoing major inquiries."

"Best get on with it then," Bev muttered. Paul Curran was the only person close enough to hear. She caught the twitch of his lips and a low-profile thumbs-up. But before she forgot...

"One point worth bearing in mind: Darren's girlfriend lives out that way." It was the only interesting snippet she'd picked up driving Mrs New to the hospital. Payoff for persisting in giving her the lift. "His mum assumed he was spending the night with her. So he had reason to be there."

"Is DI Talbot aware...?" Knight didn't finish what he saw was a stupid question. "Right. Operation Swift." The DCI's up-sum lasted twenty minutes. Bev's ankle started doing the rounds after ten. She loathed time-wasting meetings with a passion. Finally he threw it open.

Most officers were following up calls that were coming into the incident room at a rate of knots. Intelligence had to be checked, however dumb it sounded. A couple of lucky DCs were still tracking down owners of red cars, especially those in the area and more especially those that had been caught on CCTV. Bev jotted a few notes, perked up when Carol Pemberton started talking.

"Brett Sullivan's still not turned up, sir." She'd taken over the task from Daz. "I've been out there this morning. His mother's now saying he's taken off before and the school says he's rarely there." It was all too common: a hundred thousand under-eighteens go missing every year in the UK, one every five minutes. Most are runaways, most run back. Carol tucked an errant strand of hair behind her ear. "I get the impression he's a bit of a handful."

Knight nodded. "How long since she saw him?"

"Friday night, so we're into the third day." She opened a slim file on her lap.

"And he's... what... fifteen?"

"Sixteen. I asked for a photograph. Mrs Sullivan gave me this." A blond, blue-eyed Brett looking like butter wouldn't melt in his armpit in a heatwave.

"OK. Work with Paul on a news release. We'd best get it out there."

"What about his mates, Caz?" Bev asked. Amrik Singh had given three names.

"Can't get a thing out of them, sarge. They flatly deny having anything to do with bullying Josh and they certainly aren't prepared to drop Brett Sullivan in the mire."

"Had any of them seen Eric Long in Marston Road?" Byford asked.

"No, sir." She shook her head. "We flashed Long's photo all over the estate as well. Not a bite."

Bite. Bev glanced at her watch. Nearly one o'clock. No wonder her stomach was giving her grief. She'd not eaten since... Shit, she'd not eaten. The Mother's Pride was still in the toaster.

Mother's Pride. She thought of Mrs New and Darren. Stacey Banks and Josh. Somehow couldn't get worked up about a bit of white bread...

25

"Watching dirty movies on the job again?" Bev's voice had an arch you could sleep under. DI Powell spun round to find her leaning casually in his office doorway; her eyebrow was raised too. He'd been squatting on the floor in front of a monitor squinting at the screen, and very nearly lost his balance. And cool. "Button it, Morriss."

Rising carefully, he smoothed his hair, sat in the swivel chair. "If you've got nothing better to do than…"

"Actually, I have." Couple of possible leads had come up. "Tony Freeman? Newbie DC? Young guy with the bum fluff?"

Powell raised his palms. "Whatever you do in your own…"

"That is so funny not." She sniffed, strolled in, perched on a corner of his desk. "Anyway… I asked him to do a bit of digging into Roland Haines's murky past." Murky past? She couldn't believe she'd said that. "He's come up with a couple of people he thinks are worth follow-up interviews." Face to face as opposed to on the phone where all the subtle nuances and significant expressions were out of sight at the end of a line.

"So?" The DI dunked a digestive into a mug of coffee.

"Means a half-day in Bristol. Knight's OK with it. Wants me to check you don't have a problem."

"I'd rather you don't take Tyler." With Bev off the patch, he'd not want to lose Tyler as well. Mac's rank didn't reflect his experience.

"Thought you might say that." She helped herself to a biscuit. "Danny Rees could tag along. He could do with learning from the master."

"Who'd you say he's going with?" He gave a crooked smile.

She winked, took a bite then pointed a toe at the monitor. "What's the movie then?"

"Security camera tape from the front of the nick." He was digging around in his drink with a spoon. "Hoped we might get lucky with shots of whoever dropped the anonymous letter."

"The one that dumped Eric Long in the shit?"

"Yeah."

"And?"

"Sure did." He hit the remote. "Whoever just about covers it." Got that right – the shapeless strutting figure on the screen gave no clue: male, female, young, old, thin, fat, black, white, hermaphrodite, take your pick. Baggy jogging pants were combined with a hooded parka; the baseball cap peeking out was just for luck, or taking the piss.

"See what you mean – or not." She dipped her biscuit into his mug. "What you make of all that business then?"

"The letter or Long?"

She gave a half-shoulder shrug. "Either, both, whatever."

"Letter's probably someone playing silly buggers. As for Long, I reckon he was dicking us around. His missus put us right. She said when Long was supposed to have been bundling Josh in a car in Balsall Heath, they'd both been in Stirchley playing bingo.

"A. She would say that…" She reached for another biscuit.

"Sod off." He snatched away the pack.

Suit yourself. "…B. Why didn't he tell us himself? And C. His name wasn't just picked out of a hat." With well-wishers like that who needs enemies?

"Yeah well. A. They won some jackpot; had a pic proving it. B. I genuinely think Long enjoyed playing us for idiots. And C. It's possible some nasty sod remembered the court case, thought they'd have a stir. We're not gonna know because the letter's cleaner than a squeaky clean thing."

She turned her mouth down. Didn't buy the stirrer theory but had her own case to concentrate on. She jumped to her feet. "Anyway, you OK with me going to Bristol tomorrow? I'm aiming on heading off first thing."

"Sure."

She gave a mock salute. "Catch you later."

"You in tonight?"

Her hand stilled on the door. "Tonight?"

"I'm viewing a house round the corner from your place about eight. Time I lived a bit nearer the nick." Shifty eyes; nervous laugh. "Thought if you fancied a drink..."

My God. She'd not seen that coming. Her response must've been down to shock. "Yeah, why not?"

Mind, she jumped a mile when the door swung open. How long had the guv been standing there?

"Knew I'd find you here. Skiving again?"

DC Danny Rees glanced up from a plate of canteen lasagne that put Bev in mind of squashed innards. He gave a tentative smile. "Sarge?" He'd nicked Bev's favourite seat by the window. Good job she wasn't stopping. "How's it going?" he asked.

"Couldn't be better, Daniel. It's your lucky day." She raised a can of Red Bull, took a swig. "Well, tomorrow is as it happens. You're coming to Bristol with me."

"You driving?" Had he gone pale all of a sudden?

"No. I'm getting Scottie to beam us down. Problem?" What had he heard? Had Mac been talking? Or had the Highgate funny men told him her nickname: Jeremy. As in Clarkson.

"Absolutely not. I'm sure it'll be good experience." Creep. "So what's in Bristol, sarge?"

He ate while she briefed him on why they were going,

nodded as she told him to liaise with Tony Freeman on the information he'd already come up with then see what further background Danny could find on the two men they'd be interviewing. Neil Proctor was Robbie Sachs's natural father. Clive Sachs was the kid's uncle. Both had sounded off big time when the case against Roland Haines had been thrown out.

"Sounds good, sarge." He waved his fork. "I'll just finish this and get on the case."

"Don't know how you can eat that stuff, it looks like road-kill. See you in the car park. Half seven, OK ?"

He swallowed. "Can't wait."

She spotted Sumi Gosh on the way out, dropped by to say hello. Their relationship had taken a knock recently. Against her better judgement, Bev had given sanctuary to Sumi's cousin a few months back after someone had used the girl as a human punchbag. It seemed to Bev the father might've had a hand in it and she'd become embroiled in a family split. She arrived home one night to find cousin Fareeda had flown the nest, or had her wings clipped permanently. The only indication the girl was alive was a series of postcards purportedly from Fareeda to Sumi. They were still arriving, about once a month; Bev's fear was that anyone could be writing them.

"Sumi." She flashed a smile.

Brief glance up from a copy of *Heat*. "Sarge."

"How's things?"

"Fine. You?"

"Mustn't grumble."

What was this? They'd been good mates at one time. Now they were skirting round like ballroom dancers on thin ice. Trouble was, Fareeda's circumstances had brought them too close. Bev reckoned the girl had been pregnant and it wasn't just her old man's hand that had been involved. Either way, she knew about the dirty linen in the skeleton cupboard and it pissed Sumi off. It was a tad harsh when Bev had only done the decent thing, but that was the way it went when you let people in – and not just to your home. As long as it didn't affect their working relationship, she could live with it.

Yeah right. Look at how Bev and the guv got on. House on fire. Or what?

Byford swirled a teabag round in his mug. Mint tea. The irritable bowel was playing up again. Irritable something. He'd spent the afternoon working through printouts, police reports, witness statements. As for making inroads? The in-pile on his left was still higher than the out-pile on his right. Both stacks represented a massive amount of people-hours, officers, support staff, a shed-load of resources, and what was the current state of play? Grimacing, he sipped the bitter liquid, feared Operation Swift was grounded. It certainly wasn't taking off. More than that, he was aware some members of the team were disillusioned, disappointed with Knight, that a few felt the supposed high-flyer wasn't living up to his billing. He'd heard the name Lancer-less was being bandied about. Not in the guv's earshot, or he'd have reprimanded the clowns responsible. But it illustrated the point.

The detective flexed his arms high over his head, hoped to iron out a kink in his spine. He winced. It hadn't. Blood flow would be better. He stood, strolled to the window, breathed in the less than fresh air. Sticky, stifling, steamy seemingly for weeks, the weather could do with a break as well as the inquiry – and Knight.

Pensive, he swirled the tea round the mug. Delicate was the word. Definitely tricky. Internal politics, personality clashes, they got in the way of the work. Was there a grain of truth in how the DCI was coping? The case was complex, large scale. Was it getting out of hand? More specifically, Knight's hands.

Already the top floor was badgering Byford to take over the DCI's reins. With no sign of an arrest and cognisant of the bad press, the brass wanted to deflect further criticism by being seen to take decisive action. Phil Masters, Assistant Chief Constable Operations, had called Byford in that morning. What was it he'd said? Come on, Bill. This could be your last big case. Good to go out with a bang, eh?

There was a hesitant tap on the door. "Come in." Byford smiled wryly at the timing.

"Could you run your eye over this, Mr Byford?" Paul Curran approached with presumably a news release in hand. "It needs issuing and the DCI's not around, sir."

Byford skimmed the piece, a Crimestoppers appeal, nothing to do with the current major inquiries. The press office, he guessed, had to juggle all sort of balls. "Keeping you busy upstairs, Paul?"

"Feet don't touch some days, Mr Byford. I like it that way though."

"When's Bernie back with us?"

"November, December, I think."

The chit-chat petered out. Curran glanced round the office while the big man finished reading the release. "This is fine."

"Cheers, Mr Byford. I'll get out of your hair."

He waited until Curran was at the door. "Any thoughts on the leak, Paul?"

Slight hesitation. He turned, flush-faced. "Maybe."

The big man cocked his head. "Like to share?"

The flush deepened; Curran couldn't seem to look the guv in the eye. "If you don't mind, sir, I'd rather keep it to myself... for a while. Until I'm certain... it's not fair to blacken anyone's name."

If Byford didn't know better, he'd say he was in the press officer's sights. Except Curran was still incapable of making eye contact. Why was he so nervous? And had that press release really needed the green light from a senior officer? Curious. Comical more like. The guy couldn't get out of the office fast enough. As Curran opened the door, Byford glimpsed Bev walking past talking into a mobile. The big man tightened his lips. Hoped she'd enjoy her cosy drink with Mike Powell tonight. Bothered?

He picked up the kettle, wandered out to fetch water. Definitely needed more mint tea.

Brett Sullivan was parched. And very nearly skint. The cash he'd thieved from his mum's purse hadn't lasted long. Hands in the pockets of his combats he wandered along the sea front, taking in the sights, specially the birds, the ones falling out of bikinis. Beach was full of bouncing boobs and wobbly bums. Might take a dip later, he'd need to rob a few quid first. He'd already earmarked a couple of open bags lying round, ripe for the picking. Worst came to the worst, he'd have to go shopping again. Well, when he said shopping…

Yeah, coming here had been a smart move. Brighton was dead cool. Right now it was baking, too. Sun was beating down on the back of his neck. Not that he was complaining. If he didn't get a better offer, he'd be sleeping in the open tonight. Leaning his elbows on the metal railing, he scoped out the beach. Spot down there would suit him just fine. As he said, smart move…

Unlike the cock-up with the cops. Glowering, he kicked sand through the bars. How dumb could you get? By not withholding his mobile number, he'd as good as given it to them on a plate. And they'd been sniffing round home: he'd phoned his mum from a call box. Mind, it wasn't just the Bill he wanted to avoid. If Brett had seen the driver of the red motor that Josh Banks was stupid enough to get in, it was likely he had been eyeballed by the guy behind the wheel. Way Brett saw it, the cops wanted him to sing, the driver wanted him to shut it. Either way sticking round Balsall Heath had been a no-brainer.

Pushing himself up from the railing, he sauntered further along the front. His mouth watered at the smells: candy floss and fish and chips, hot dogs and frying onions. His mate Matt's mum had cooked a mean roast. Brett had stayed with them a couple of nights, nice place ten-minute walk from the sea. Miserable cow had chucked him out this morning, caught him with his fingers in her handbag. He sighed. Who cared? Sleeping under the stars'd be cool. Anywhere was better than Birmingham. What with the filth and some nutter on the lookout, the heat was on there an' all.

26

Why'd they have to keep hospitals so flaming hot? Bev had only been inside the place five minutes and was in meltdown. She was about to drown in a slimy pool of her own body fluids, if the dehydration didn't do for her first, or the heatstroke or the spontaneous combustion... or... or. Get a grip woman. She'd only dropped by on the way home, wanting to snatch a word with a medico, knew damn well the flights of fantasy were meant to take her mind off the reality.

That in effect, what the attractive young woman in front of her had said was Darren might not make it through the night. Bev and Doctor Cathy Sugar stood facing each other in a narrow corridor just off the intensive care unit: dove grey décor, stark overhead lights, wishy-washy murals on the walls. Doctor Sugar's earlier initial-speak had been aimed perhaps at blunting the message, but the harsh truth was still buried in the bunch of letters. CSF had been added to the list since Bev dropped Mrs New first thing. Sounded less serious, somehow, than cerebrospinal fluid. Either way it had been detected by the MRI: magnetic resonance imaging. That was the big boy's version of a CT: it could detect subtle changes in the brain. Cathy Sugar's big talk had scared Bev more: the intracerebral haematoma, the hypoxia, the ventriculostomy.

What it boiled down to was: Darren had suffered a depressed skull fracture, there was bleeding into the brain and nowhere for it to go which meant a decrease in oxygen to the surrounding tissues. The surgery they'd performed was aimed at relieving the pressure. There were no guarantees.

"And when he comes round, doc?" Not *if* – that was tempting fate.

Cathy Sugar ran a hand through her chin-length jet black bob, paused for a few seconds, holding Bev's anxious gaze. Their eyes were almost the same striking shade of blue, but the doctor's ivory skin and full red lips put Bev in mind of Sleeping Beauty. Ms Sugar was clearly working out what to say and how to say it. Come on, doc, spit it out…

"You have to under…" And was dodging the issue.

"When he comes round, doc…" Bev knew her eyes were brimming.

"If he regains consciousness." Another brief pause then: "The next few hours are critical."

"Please… give me an idea." Sounded like she was begging.

The doctor gave a resigned OK-you-asked-for-it sigh. "The brain damage could be permanent. He could suffer memory loss, impaired senses, inability to communicate, depression, personality changes…"

Bev raised a palm. The words confirmed those she'd boned up on a couple of medical websites. They didn't cover possible post-operative complications: seizures, CSF leaks, infections – and multiple organ failure. "Thanks doc, I appreciate it."

"You were very close, yes?"

"Are." She felt a tear roll down her cheek. "Are very close." For a brief period Darren had been her DC; they were good mates, had a laugh. She teased him about coming from the Andrex puppy school of policing, all that boundless enthusiasm, but a bit wet behind the ears.

"Trust me. We're doing everything we can." The warm smile appeared sincere. "As I say… it all hinges on the next few hours. Now if you'll excuse me…"

Reaching out more than a hand, Bev asked if she could see him. "Just a quick look, doc." There was no need to say more.

162

Cathy Sugar knew why Bev didn't want to wait a while.

Sympathetic shake of the head. "I'm sorry, sergeant, I don't think…" Maybe it was the look in Bev's eyes, the raw emotion in her voice. The doctor wavered another few seconds then: "Stay where you are. I'll just check."

Arms folded, Bev paced the corridor a couple of times, the heat no longer bothering her. Her mind was fixed on a set of initials neither she nor the doctor had voiced: PVS.

Was a persistent vegetative state worse than dying? Bev closed her eyes: Dear God, please let him…

"OK, sergeant." Doctor Sugar beckoned from the end of the corridor. "Come with me."

She was allowed only a glimpse from the door, saw what could have been an alabaster statue lying in state. A statue with tubes and drains, hooked up to drips, everything bathed in a sickly glow from a bank of monitoring equipment. There was nothing of Darren there – they'd even shaved his Tom Cruise hair. He'd kill them when he found out. Stifling a sob, Bev bit down hard on her fist. She felt the doctor's hand on her arm, for once didn't flinch.

"We should have a better idea tomorrow, sergeant, if…"

He makes it that long. "It's Bev." She scrabbled in her bag, pulled out a card. "Anything changes. Please. Get someone to call me."

"For sure." She took the card, glanced up. "You're shivering, Bev. Are you cold?"

An hour later Bev was chilling out with a medicinal Pinot. She was ensconced in a corner of a Moseley wine bar waiting for Powell's return with a refill. Novel experience on both counts: the company and the fact he was getting a round in.

When he'd dropped by Baldwin Street she'd been in the middle of swapping the flat on the MG for a tyre that'd get her and Danny to Bristol first thing. Slaving over a hot jack, she'd swivelled round at the sound of his voice, found him looming, hands in pockets, sage smirk on face. "Needs a bit more welly, that." Pontificating wasn't in it. Thank you, Kwikfit man.

She'd toyed between doing the feminist bit or telling him to bugger off. Immediately handed over the spanner, with a: "Hey. Why not pat my pretty little head 'fore I go swoon on the chaise longue?" She'd needed a minute anyway to dab on lippie and slip into clean jeans.

Still smiling at his retort about patting her bum if she didn't watch the lip, she sipped the last of the wine and scoped out the place. It wasn't likely there'd be anyone here she knew. It was all a bit grunge-meets-Goth, loads of kohl and cleavage. And that was just the lady men. Not. The cool clientele of The Cross was getting younger, though. Or maybe it was her getting... Perish the thought. Grimacing, she recalled the grey hair she'd pulled out that morning.

"Got wind?" Powell winked as he handed her a glass. Maybe she'd overdone the grimace.

"Gonna buy it then?" He'd stumped up for peanuts too; she helped herself to a pack.

"Buy?" Puzzled frown.

Tearing the cellophane with her teeth, she said: "The house you were viewing? Tudor Road wasn't it?"

"Nah. It was right out of the ark. And it stank of cat pee. Needs too much work."

Fair enough. The job didn't leave much time for DIY make-overs. Last thing she'd fancy after spending a shift wading through body parts would be slapping paint on a wall. Especially red.

Wasn't all bad news though. Powell had mentioned bumping into Pete Talbot on the way out of the nick that evening. The DI leading the inquiry into Darren's attack had seemed fairly happy with the way it was going. In return she'd given Powell an edited version of her hospital visit.

"Pete reckons he's got a witness then?" Upending the pack, she peered in.

"Maybe. Maybe two." He wiped a finger round his top lip. "Man and a woman. They live in the flats, something to do with the tenants' association."

Heathfield House. She recalled the silhouettes this morning. Like something out of that James Stewart movie, *Rear Window?* "Why the maybes?"

He slumped back, legs spread. "Last few weeks they've put in thirty, forty complaints to the nick. Pete got someone to check the logs. They're gunning for a gang of yobs who're running wild, think it's their turf."

"Kind with letters after their name?" ASBO, ABC. She tore open the other pack, poured a generous portion into her palm. Wine was going to her head. No bad thing, maybe it'd drown out some of the crap up there.

"Anti-social, aggressive, abusive. If they're not tanked-up, they're off their face on crack or whatever. A lot of the locals are scared to say anything in case they get a mouthful of fist." Or shit through the letterbox, brick through the window, knife through the neck. Not surprising people didn't want to make a stand. Have-a-go heroes were a dying breed, literally. They risked either ending up dead or putting up a defence in court. "Uniform've been out there shed-loads but you know what the place is like..."

Rat runs, back alleys, side streets. And the yobs would have an early warning system. Like urban sodding meerkats without the ah factor. God, she'd like to punch their lights out.

"So is Pete thinking the witnesses aren't kosher?" She ran a salty finger round the rim of her glass.

"Not saying that exactly. But they're both desperate to get

the scum off their patch. It's not like they actually saw the boot going in. But the youths had been hanging round as per."

"Is he bringing them in for questioning?"

"He's keeping tabs." Surveillance. The rope theory. As in, give them enough, it could turn into a noose. Pete definitely needed more to go on than what could be the dodgy say-so of disgruntled residents. She knew he was releasing pictures to the media showing the full extent of Darren's injuries. Perhaps surprisingly, Mrs New had given permission for the shock tactics. Bev was in two minds about it.

Powell leant across to pick up a menu from the next table. "Heard about Overdale?"

"Go on." Bev hadn't seen the pathologist since their not so brief encounter on the railway line at Foxton.

"She collapsed at work last week. In hospital having tests now."

Bev turned her mouth down, recalled thinking the woman hadn't looked so hot at Haines's crime scene.

"Some bloke from Walsall's covering for her." Could be why they still hadn't had the tox results from Josh Banks or Roland Haines. Overdale maybe wouldn't have been chasing the lab and it'd take a while for the new guy to get up to speed. Powell handed her the menu. "How do you think the guv's looking, Bev?"

Where'd that come from? And why the casual slip? She kept her head down. "Hadn't thought about it. Why?"

"Just wondered." Yeah right. Obviously something on his mind. She kept silent. He'd share if he wanted. "One or two of the guys think he's looking a bit… stressed?"

"We eating then?" She wasn't going to get into that. By one or two Powell probably meant the whole station was gabbing. Were they right? Was there cause for concern? Given she'd barely looked Byford in the eye since the stupid crack about a leaving collection she was hardly in a position to judge. And now wasn't the time to speculate. It was definitely going on the back burner though. "The burgers are good."

The food was handy for mopping up the booze. Probably should have ordered pudding. And cheese. And coffee. Black. Soon as they steered away from work-related topics, talk flowed like the wine. And liqueurs. They touched on classic films and latest books, politics and people. For a guy whose cultural height she'd earlier have described as a lap dancing pole, Powell had sharp insights and opinions. Once he'd dropped the macho act, he was good company, and for a blond he'd always been quite tasty. Better than all that, he could actually make her laugh. Talk about seeing someone in a new light. She'd had no time for the view before. Mind, she was well pissed.

"Good job we walked, Mike." They were halfway back to Bev's place. Gone eleven, the sky was navy with a zillion stars, traffic was light, pavements pedestrian-heavy.

"Call that a walk?" Powell reached out to steady her. She didn't pull away; he left his arm where it was. She needed the crutch, there was no more to it than that. The drinking too much had been deliberate. It wasn't clever, she knew that, too. She could have called a halt, was aware when she'd had enough. But sometimes, if only for a few hours, the edges needed blunting, painful images softening: Darren, Josh, Byford, babies.

"Sod it." The key slipped from her fingers. "Where's it gone?"

Powell bent to retrieve it. Which meant releasing her waist. He caught her but she teetered slightly, toppled towards him. She could have turned her face, could have closed her lips. Powell avoided the kiss. Laughing, he pulled away. "Come on, Bev. You'll regret this in the morning."

Maybe she would. Moving closer, she placed her hands on his cheeks, gazed into his eyes. "Just a kiss, Mike." A moment's light relief from the emotional baggage and dark thoughts. "Nothing heavy."

"Thank God for that." He gave her cheek an affectionate peck. "Thought you were after my body." Smiling, he held the door as she staggered in. "Night, Bev, catch you tomorrow... again."

Had he just patted her bum?

Around two a m Bev's Angus beef burger threatened an unwelcome return. The couple hours' restless tossing and turning had no doubt added to the internal churning. The sultry heat wasn't helping. Even with the window wide open, and a Dylan t-shirt that barely covered her butt, the room was like a sauna in the tropics. It was hot and she was bothered, and not by hitting on Powell. Heart hammering, sweat pouring, scalp prickling, it was a full blown barf alert. Swinging her legs to the floor, a foot got tangled in the duvet long since kicked off the bed. The ensuing hopalong tussle almost sent her flying in the dash to the bathroom. "Bollocks."

It was a bit rich blaming it on the burgers when she'd drunk her own body weight in alcohol.

Either way it was a false alarm. Calming breaths and cold water did the trick. Still holding her wrists under the tap, she stared into the mirror. Dripping hair, panda eyes, spot was on the way out, though. Could be worse.

What was it Powell had said: Come on, Bev. You'll regret this in the morning. She raised an eyebrow. Damn right she would, but only the self-induced hangover. OK, the move on Powell could've been subtler, but they were both adults, and it wouldn't have gone further than a kiss. She wasn't that bladdered. Anyway she'd checked Tudor Road; there wasn't so much as a garden gnome on sale. The DI may have had his eye on something, but it wasn't the property market. So why pussyfoot around?

Holding on to the sink, she leaned into the mirror. If recent experience had taught her anything, it was Life's too short, Beverley. And she wasn't talking stuffing mushrooms, her thoughts were on higher life forms. Regrets? No.

She was with Edith Piaf. Even better, make that Robbie Williams. He was still alive.

When the phone rang around five-ish, Bev's immediate thought was Darren. Mind racing, heart thumping, she picked up the handset, praying it wasn't the news she'd been half-expecting.

"Bev Morriss." Sharp. Peremptory. Perched on the edge of the bed now, breath bated.

"Sorry, sarge. Control here. We've got a sus death. Uniform in attendance. Requesting CID attendance. It's out Stirchley way. Can you…?"

"No problem." Thank you God. Bev reached for a pen. It wasn't Darren, it would almost be a pleasure. "Fire away."

TUESDAY
27

Eric Long was found lying in a bath of his own blood with slit wrists. A black-handled knife close by on the chequered floor was an obvious giveaway. Suicide. Open and shut. Dead cert. Except his wife didn't buy it. Or didn't want to. It was a hell of a purchase. Bridie Long's terrified screaming had woken neighbours who'd alerted the police. Mrs Long was currently in the care of the woman next door. After an initial examination, the uniformed constables who'd responded to the triple-nine realised they were out of their depth. One of them was now briefing Bev in the dim narrow hallway of the terraced house in Stirchley.

"It's a bloodbath, sarge." The way Colin Duckworth had been rubbing his hands put Bev in mind of Lady Macbeth. His ghoulish observation was probably spot-on. Not that she could confirm it. She'd yet to enter the crime scene. There were enough bodies up there already – not counting the stiff. The new pathologist was apparently doing his thing, the FSI team waiting to do its, apart from the forensic officer who'd have been recording every detail from the word go: stills and video. The DCI would be joining the party soon. Bev had called Knight at home knowing he'd want to attend: the name Eric Long not so much ringing a bell as sending out shockwaves. Was Long's suicide genuine or did they have another Roland Haines on their hands? Grappling with that idea knocked Alka-Seltzer on the head as a hangover cure.

"Literally," Duckworth said. "A bloody bloodbath."

"Colin, leave it out." Gags she could live without.

"I'm not kidding, sarge. It's like an abattoir." She cut him a withering glance, registered not relish as she'd first thought but revulsion. The guy looked as sick as she'd felt earlier. Sweat ran off one of his chins and the flabby flesh was white.

"Get some fresh air, eh, Col?" Last thing they needed was a pool of vomit muddying the waters. "See if anyone out there needs a hand." When she'd arrived it had seemed there were more police vehicles parked up than private motors. She'd had to leave the MG in the next street. The flashing blues had attracted a few gawpers: couple of women in curlers and dressing gowns, an old bloke with pyjama bottoms flapping under a raincoat. Could explain why the press was out in force, too. Preferably it was down to one of the not-so-busy-bodies outside calling a few news desks in the hope of a tip-off fee or getting their mug on the telly. As opposed to a leaking cop on the make.

Bev glanced at her watch, just coming up to six. Should have enough time. She picked her way to the foot of the stairs along one of the duckboards FSI had laid in the hall. "Chris?" she hollered. "If you need me, I'll be next door."

If Bridie Long had seen a ghost she couldn't look any worse. In fact a ghost would probably be an easier option given the haunted expressions currently running across her gaunt features. The woman's complexion resembled creased parchment and the mauve smudges were like eyeshadow that had missed the lids. Her hunched sparrow-like frame seemed lost in the corner of a huge leather settee as she stared sightlessly into the middle distance through pale blue pink-rimmed eyes. Bev knew she'd be replaying the death scene in her head. It was a silent movie even though the thin dry lips moved constantly, or maybe there was a soundtrack only she could hear.

"Mrs Long?" She certainly wasn't listening to Bev. Closing the door with her bum, Bev headed further in to the stuffy over-furnished room. The drab sepia-and-sludge décor co-ordinated with Bridie Long's frumpy shapeless frock. Bev had to step over a fat comatose cat sprawled full-length across the carpet. It woke with a start, hissed and lashed out with a paw. Black or not, the sodding thing was lucky it missed.

"Mrs Long? I'm a police officer. Detective Sergeant Morriss. Bev Morriss." She reached out a hand, wasn't surprised it went unnoticed or ignored. The attending officers had told her without irony that the woman was on a knife-edge, close to losing it big time. Bev perched on the nearest armchair, elbows on knees. "Mrs Long, I'm sorry for your loss. But I need to ask you a few questions." She'd been tasked by Knight during the brief phone call to see what she could elicit before the woman lost it completely.

"I can't... stop... seeing... the blood... it's there all the..." She clawed the crepe-like skin of her neck. It hurt just to watch.

"Please, Mrs Long. I want to help but you must talk to me. Can you tell me what happened last night? What time you found your husband? What you did then?" They'd not been able to work it out. If she was at home when the deed was done, why hadn't she heard something? Acted to stop it.

She glanced at Bev for the first time. "I was at a friend's. Left here about nine." The voice was a flat, lifeless drone.

"A friend's?" The prompt wasn't taken, Bev let it go for the moment. "What time did you get back?"

"Late." She itched to take the woman's hand from her neck.

"How late?"

"We'd had a barney. I was riled. I stormed off then thought it best to get back." Male? Did Bridie have a bit on the side?

"What time?"

"'Bout half four."

"Half four?" Must've been a hell of a row. And a damn good mate.

Mrs Long had clearly picked up the inflection. "I found a text from some fancy woman on his phone. Told him two could play at that game. Just wanted to teach him a lesson." She ran a finger under her eye. "Childish I know." She could say that again. Sounded like love-struck teenagers, rather than middle-aged marrieds. Eric Long was what? Early forties; she looked late fifties. Maybe he liked older women. Had liked.

"I'm going to make a few notes, OK?" Bev slipped a hand into her bag. Wasn't ideal. It cut down eye contact and observation but needs must. She wrote: woman, text, mobile. They'd need detail, but it could wait a while; initial interview was generally surface-scratching stuff. Hopefully Mac would show before too long. "So you got home and…?"

"Made a cuppa tea. Thought I'd take one up."

"Before then? The front door? Was it locked? Were there any signs of a forced entry?" It was delicate ground; she was groping in the dark, hedging bets. She knew Bridie Long was absolutely adamant her husband hadn't topped himself. Given what had happened to Roland Haines, she could be right. But until the evidence signposted the way, every path had to be covered. Conclusions needed reaching, not jumping to.

"No." She was doing that thing with the lips again; maybe the dentures needed a tweak. "Nothing."

"What about the kitchen? Notice an extra cup? Glass?" Had Eric Long known the putative killer, invited him in for a drink?

"Might've. I'm not sure." She shook thin, badly cut salt and pepper hair. "Can't seem to think straight."

Next question wasn't going to help. "What about the bathroom? When did you go in?"

"Soon's I saw Eric wasn't in bed."

"Had the bed been slept in?" Might help narrow the time-frame.

"It was a bit rumpled, but…" She shrugged. Straightening the sheets was probably a novel concept.

"So you went into the bathroom…?"

"It was the smell." She slapped a hand to her mouth and there was nothing melodramatic about the gesture. "It's coming back now. There was this weird foul smell. I stepped inside… slipped in the…"

"Was the light on?" How much had she seen, how long had there been to take it in? She'd not be allowed back any time soon for sure.

"I wish to God it hadn't been." She shuddered visibly. "I could only've stood there seconds, but the sight'll be with me forever."

Join the club, thought Bev. Cops had a mental montage of shit memories. Byford called it the little bits of hell on his pillow. She paused while the woman composed herself. "Mrs Long. I know it's not easy, but… was your husband… depressed… did he have any financial problems, emotional worries… anything going on you're aware of?"

Who hit the stroppy switch? Eyes narrowed, tongue sharpened. "You've got a fucking nerve. Emotional worries? Something going on?" Hands scrabbled in a cheap white vinyl bag for a pack of Embassy. "How 'bout the cops dragging him in for questioning over a kid's murder he had sod all to do with. How 'bout getting his face in the paper? How 'bout having strangers shout abuse in the street. That do you, will it?" Her hands shook so much she couldn't strike a light. "Emotional worries? You having a laugh?"

Bev took the matches, helped her spark up, in need of enlightenment herself. Was Eric Long depressed enough to commit suicide or what? "I'm not quite with you…?"

She spat out a fleck of tobacco. "Course you're not. It was you lot tried stitching him up. Sure he was hacked off about that. Had every reason an' all. But I'll tell you this: no way did he kill himself. Christ. We'd just won a few thousand at bingo. We were planning to take a trip to Blackpool this weekend... have a break..." She bit her fist.

"Who knew about the win, Mrs Long?" Grope, grope. If it was murder, could the motive be robbery?

"Loads of people. Everyone who was at the Gala on Wednesday afternoon. When you lot said he was in Balsall Heath."

She took another note, then: "Did your husband have any enemies, Mrs Long? Had he rowed with anyone recently?"

"Apart from your mates, y'mean?" Another spit, no tobacco this time. "Told you, he took a load of stick over that piece in the paper. And whose fault was that, eh? My Eric didn't deserve it. Good man, he was... good man..." She broke down then. The collapse wasn't total, but it'd be a while before she'd be in a fit state to answer more questions. "...good man... good man, he was."

Bev curled a lip. Pass the sodding string quartet. Whatever Long was, he was no saint.

She could've been talking to herself but she thanked the woman, repeated her condolences and took her leave. As she stepped over it, the bloody cat hissed again. But it was Bridie Long's listless mantra that still played as Bev closed the door. Good man he was... good man...

28

Who was the vision of lust and loveliness? The tastiest bloke Bev had set eyes on in a long time was emerging from the Longs' front door. Dark hair in floppy curtains, glowing skin, square-jawed. He sure ticked the babe boxes. And here she was hopping round on the pavement, half in half out of a white forensic suit. Shit. She probably looked like a Home Pride flour grader.

"You must be Sergeant Morriss?" Great teeth. Tick that box, too. "I'm Joe King."

"Joking?" Dense wasn't a good look, but he'd caught her on the hop. "Sorry, I…?"

"Doctor King?" At least he tried masking the smile. "Pathologist?" She liked the cleft chin: very Kirk Douglas. "I'm looking after things until Gillian Overdale's back in the saddle."

"Great." No rush, Gill. Take your time. "Good to meet you." The hand she stuck out was clammy. His was cool, very clean with neat clipped nails. "How is she? Nothing too serious, I hope." Well, maybe just a tad.

"She had a viral infection few weeks back." That's OK then. "But it's damaged the heart. Depends now on how she responds to treatment. She certainly needs to rest up a while."

Bev turned her mouth down. "Sorry to hear that." Overdale was a good pathologist. It was her people skills she needed to work on.

"Anyway, I'm about finished here. Just need another tape from the car." Another tape? Christ, how much was he dictating? He picked up on her concern, smiled. "Don't look so worried, it's not that bad. This tape's dead." Intuitive. Down to earth. What a star.

"Sure thrown you in at the deep end, haven't we?" Mental cringe. What a dummy. "Can't believe I just said that."

"Thank God for that." He laughed. "I'd hate to think puns were your party piece. Anyway, your boss said if I found you down here I should send you up."

"Cheers." Send her up? Given that little exchange? She sure didn't need any help in that department.

Not that bad, Doctor King had said. It was pretty gross far as Bev could see. Framed in the doorway, she took stock of the crime scene. Duckworth had got it right when he'd said blood-bath. Water was drained now but the tidemark was scarlet. Would've been like sitting in a tub of red ink. For a surreal instant it brought to Bev's mind the crazy stunts people pull for *Children in Need.* Except they used baked beans. Either way, charity certainly hadn't begun at home here. The gore wasn't confined to the bath. Blood had spurted all over the walls, floor, ceiling as if a class of nursery kids had been let loose with poster paint.

Knight, also in whites, was kneeling, turned his head, when he noticed Bev. "Sergeant. How was the wife? What did you get?"

Bridie Long was in better shape than her old man. Bev couldn't tear her gaze from what was left of him. Eric Long's rail-thin corpse was somehow propped against the taps; it was all too easy to imagine the bones under the tight white flesh. Bottom inch or so of long grey hair looked as if it'd had a bad dye job, deep wounds were clearly visible along both knobbly wrists. Long's hazel eyes were open, vacant; his face held no trace of emotion. Not a clue to the pain, the sheer

177

bloody terror. Bev shivered.

"Sergeant?" Standing now, Knight's voice brought her thoughts back on track.

"Sorry." She glanced at the DCI, gave him a brief resume of the interview, wound up with: "No depression. No money worries. Bottom line is she's still convinced he wouldn't have done that." Nodded again at the corpse.

"I'm inclined to agree. Morning, Bev." Chris Baxter, crime scene manager, now stood at her shoulder, top sheet of his clipboard covered in diagrams, measurements, detailed notes. "Lads downstairs have checked every door and window in the place. There's no sign of a break-in, nothing anywhere to suggest a struggle."

Bev frowned. Surely that indicated the reverse, that Long had died at his own hand? Chris had registered her doubt. "Look at the wrists, Bev." Shit. That meant a close-up. She picked her way carefully along the walking plates, squatted near the corpse.

"Both main arteries have been severed." Chris: master of the bleeding obvious. "It would have been like releasing valves, waves of blood gushing like geysers."

Thanks, mate. She swallowed rising bile. The incisions were deep gouges, flesh was ragged: whoever perpetrated it had meant business. "Could he have done that?"

"Seriously doubt it. Not with this." Chris waved an evidence bag. "He'd have had a job peeling potatoes with it." Even from where she squatted, she could see the blade was too small, too smooth. Chris scratched his head with a gloved hand. "For that sort of damage we've got to be looking at something big, sharp, serrated. Small saw even."

Except they weren't.

"We're thinking the killer took it with him," Knight said. "Certainly no knife in the house matches the wounds." So the knife left was meant to make them think suicide – again?

Chris nodded. "Position of the body doesn't tally with BSP either." Blood Spatter Pattern. "Joe's with us on all this, by the way." Joe? First names already. "Makes a change, eh, Bev? Having a pathologist who's happy calling it at the crime scene." Overdale rarely ventured further than pronouncing death. And even then, grudgingly. Bev slapped a mental wrist: *give the woman a break.*

"Yeah, but hold on here…" Squatting was a pain, she got to her feet. "Long was clearly no Charles Atlas but even Arnie's not just going to lie there and…?" Realisation dawned. Of course. Long would have been drunk or drugged to the eye-balls. "So thinking is…?"

"Some sort of chemical cosh." Knight rubbed his chin, needed a shave. "Probably not injected. The doc couldn't see any puncture marks." Post mortem might change that view though. "Maybe someone slipped him a Mickey Finn."

Bev narrowed her eyes: what was it Bridie said? "His wife thought there might have been an extra cup or glass in the kitchen." Not that she struck Bev as some sort of domestic goddess.

"We've bagged the lot," Chris said. "And we'll run samples." Blood and urine for tox tests. "You're right about him not struggling though, Bev. No defence marks. Nothing under the nails."

"Has to be someone he knew," Knight said. "What time did you say the wife went out, sergeant?"

"Nine," she answered absently. Killer could be a friend, but what if it wasn't? Who else would Eric Long let into his home? The notion hit Bev out of the blue. It would have to be some-one he thought he could trust. Someone in authority. Someone he'd had recent dealings with. Nah. She shrugged off the idea. Christ. A fair few cops could fit that bill.

29

DCI Knight was in the middle of a quick shave before the brief. He'd not had time earlier but setting the squad an example did no harm; a neat appearance was something most of the men would benefit from in his book. A tap at the door was followed by Byford's head in the gap.

"Come in, sir. Won't keep you a tick." Knight smiled an apology before turning back to the mirror; the calendar it temporarily replaced was propped against the wall. "You heard about the early shout? Eric Long?"

Oh, yes. "No worries." Byford raised a dismissive hand, like many cops he kept an electric razor, spare shirt in the office. In his younger days working big cases, he'd slept at the desk off and on, too. Thank God that was in the past. As for the early shout, Phil Masters had called him at home first thing. The assistant chief constable had summoned the detective superintendent to a meeting on the top floor. Nearly ten a m now, that meeting had just broken up. The big man felt as if he was picking up the pieces.

"You OK, sir?" Knight had caught Byford's reflection, their glances met briefly in the glass. The guv sighed, steeling himself. No way could he make it easy, no amount of spin would soften the blow. "I've been ordered to take over the inquiry, Lance."

Knight spun round, eyes wide, jacket flapping. "What?" Had it been a cutthroat razor he'd have done himself a nasty injury.

Byford raised both palms. "I had no choice in the matter. It's not my decision." He'd argued hard against it. Knew how he'd feel in the same boat. But as Masters had pointed out more than once, the investigation was going nowhere. It needed a sharper operator at the helm. Whichever way you looked at it, it was a slap in the face for the DCI.

"It's not a reflection on your abilities, Lance." Not entirely, though there was an element of that in Masters's thinking. The ACC felt they should've had a collar by now. Masters always wanted miracles.

"What is it then?" Clipped, cool. Grooming complete, he lay the razor on top of the filing cabinet.

"It comes down to experience, Lance. The ACC feels..." Knight listened attentively to the account of how Masters felt. The younger detective clearly realised the decision had been made, there was no percentage fighting it. "As I say, Lance, I'm sorry to be the bearer..."

"It's OK, sir. No hard feelings. You're only following orders." His knuckles were tight, white.

But Knight also looked resigned, maybe there was even a glimmer of relief. Byford wouldn't blame him: if it all went pear-shaped, it wouldn't be the DCI who'd have to carry the can. A similar thought crossed Byford's mind when he'd been landed with the task: a failed investigation would be quite some leaving present.

"That's great. Fantastic. Best news I've had in a long time." Eyes shining, Bev slipped the mobile into her bag. Darren wasn't out of the woods yet but his condition had improved slightly overnight. Her smiling thumbs up to the assembled squad elicited a round of cheers. Good thing there was something to be cheerful about. The brief should've started ten minutes ago. It had already been put back an hour. Again. She grimaced. It was getting to be an occupational hazard for Knight.

She laid her notes on the floor, picked up the coffee she'd grabbed from the machine. Needs must, it was probably better than nothing. Tapping a foot, she glanced round: the team was growing increasingly restless. Room was crowded, heat was high, officer numbers were up, but so was the body count. Like they had time to sit round gabbing.

"Where'd you get to, mate?" She'd wondered where Mac had disappeared. Winking, he tapped the side of his nose. She budged over so he could park his butt. One sniff confirmed her suspicions. Jammy sod had detoured to the canteen. She watched him ease greasy wrappers from a pocket in his jeans. Sauce stains pointed to a bacon sandwich. She curled a lip. Imagine eating that... After the early shout and morning run-round, she could down a cart horse, but there were limits...

"Had mine on the hoof. This is for you, boss."

"Ta, mate." Nice one. Nose wrinkled, she examined the filling. "Tad more ketchup'd be good next..."

"Next time? You'll be lucky."

She flashed a smile: it was rude to talk with a full mouth. They'd already discussed Eric Long's death. She'd given Mac a lift back from Stirchley where he'd been giving uniform a hand knocking doors, interviewing neighbours. No one had come up with anything earth-shattering yet.

"So, boss, what did Danny boy say when you told him you couldn't make Bristol?"

Hard swallow then: "Gutted he was, mate." Once she'd explained to DC Rees what mice and men meant in terms of plans going awry. "Soon perked up though when I said he was taking a pool car. And Carol Pemberton along for the ride." Pembers would be more than a passenger: Danny was still green, but the interviews could turn out crucial. Cancelling them wasn't an option.

Mac nodded. "Pembers'll keep an eye on him."

"Likely be the other way round, mate." Most Highgate males lusted after Carol. Not that Bev minded. Much. She slowed the pace on the sandwich, it was going down a treat but hiccoughs were so not cool.

"You bumped into the new pathologist this morning then?" Mac trying to be casual was like Gordon Brown trying to be funny.

Her hand stilled on its way to her mouth. "Point being?"

He raised both palms: what, little old me, winding up the boss? "I hear he's good on the job." No way was she rising to that one. Mac winked. "Must say he's very easy on the eye."

"Good on you, Mac. Takes guts at your age." She wiped sauce off her chin.

Poor bloke hadn't got a clue. He shifted uneasily. "Guts to...?"

"Come out? Wave goodbye to the closet. Way to go, man."

"Sod off."

"Sod off boss." Screwing the wrappers, her smile soon faded. Bit of banter was harmless enough but where the hell was DCI Knight? Any time soon, some clown would start a chorus of *Why are we wait...?*

"Sorry for the delay." Not Knight. Byford's voice. Bev turned to see him striding to the front, the DCI followed a few paces behind. Knight's expression was difficult to read but he didn't look happy. It took no time to find out why. The guv didn't even wait for the buzz to die down.

"As of now, I'll be heading the inquiry. DCI Knight will act as my deputy." No explanation. Known in the trade as a Tommy Cooper: just like that. If anything the noise level increased a gnat's. Byford raised a hand, waited a couple of seconds. "Just so you know – this has nothing to do with any-one's handling of the case. The decision was taken purely for operational reasons."

Course it was. Operational reasons? It was like giving a football manager a vote of confidence. She cast Knight a covert glance. At least he was holding his head up, taking it on the chin. She bet he felt like shit. Typical of Byford though, not kicking the guy when he was down, actually helping him save face.

"The twice daily briefs will continue. I'll be taking them. When needed, I'll call more. There are three major ongoing inquiries now." He nodded to the third whiteboard already added to the line-up. "The scale's such I can't stress too strongly how vital it is everyone keeps up to speed. If you can't make a brief, make sure you know what came out and what needs covering. I don't spoon-feed anyone. It's every officer's individual responsibility to check logs, read reports, keep on top of developments. Jack?"

"Guv." Office manager and professional Yorkshireman Jack Hainsworth raised a hand.

"I want a bigger room for the squad. More computers. More phones."

"Yeah, but…" He was a professional whinger, depressingly negative.

"No buts. You've got until five tonight. Don't worry about the bean counters. It's sorted. We'll have more support staff starting first thing, too."

"Leave it with me, guv." Hainsworth agreeing almost immediately? That must be a first.

"Right, let's get on with it." Byford hooked his jacket on the back of a chair, rolled his sleeves, reached for a pointer on one of the tables. Bev watched with mixed emotions. How did the big man do it? He didn't have to command respect, it was given him in spades. Already the atmosphere had changed: the squad's body language was more positive, attitudes sharper. God, it was good to have him back, made it harder somehow, knowing he'd be going.

"So what have we got?" Facing the team he stood in front of the boards. "Three murder victims. Josh Banks. Roland Haines. Eric Long. Are they connected? Are we looking for one killer? Or three? Both men were recently outed in the media for crimes against children. Is that significant? Could it be a motive for the killings? Or are there reasons we've yet to establish? These are questions that need answers, lines that need following." Cut. Chase. To. Go for it, guv. He ran his gaze over every officer in the room. "I'm asking for common threads. Anybody?"

She glanced at Knight expecting him to pick up. Suit yourself. "Dodgy suicides, guv," she said. "Got to be something there."

He nodded. "Go on." Byford was probably already on to it, but only three or four officers present had been at the latest crime scene.

Sitting forward, she tucked a strand of hair behind her ears. "Chris bagged a knife out at Long's place this morning. Bathroom floor… there it is. Dead handy, eh? Except the blade wouldn't cut melted butter never mind slice flesh." Over-egging the pudding but they got the picture. "Anyway according to the pathologist, Long could've been sitting there waving a meat cleaver round in each hand singing *I'm a Believer* – the wounds still couldn't have been self-inflicted."

"Nice image. Thanks for sharing, Bev." Byford gave a lop-sided smile. She'd miss that. "And Roland Haines's death?"

Warming to the theme, her blue eyes shone. "Yeah, well. There's a guy who takes himself off to Foxton, lies on the track and waits round for the 23.10 to Euston to take his head off. I don't think so."

"Neither does Gillian Overdale." Byford stroked an eye-brow.

She knew he'd be up to speed. "Exactly."

"And in Haines's case…" Mac was on the same page. "The killer leaves a suicide note lying round just in case we're in any doubt."

"Or he's taking the p…" Whoops. "Sorry, guv." Best curb the language; he didn't like it.

The eye-roll said he'd heard it all before. "Why would he do that?"

It was a feeling more than anything, she tried articulating it. "As suicides they couldn't be more badly executed: amateur doesn't come close. Overdale could tell before setting foot on the crime scene that Haines was dead before he was laid on the track. As for the knife thing this morning, once the mismatch was pointed out it was obvious. So either the killer's dense as a box of fog, or he thinks we're the Keystone cops. Or…" It had only just occurred.

"What?"

"Or maybe he doesn't give a monkey's either way." Not that she thought him careless. Not that. More… what was the word? Yeah. Cavalier. If he was careless they'd have caught the bugger by now.

"We're assuming there's just the one killer." Knight jumped in while she was still struggling. "Could be two perps. The MOs are similar but not identical, same could apply to motives."

Faking suicide? The modern killer's must-have modus operandi? Bev turned her mouth down. It was rare as a hen's orthodontist.

Byford nodded. "Certainly something to consider. We need open minds every step of the way."

OK, what did she know? Thinking about it though, Haines's death had been covered in gruesome detail in the media, conceivably it could've sparked ideas in an equally sick mind.

Little wonder they were releasing only the barest details on Long's death.

"Who's checking backgrounds?" Byford asked.

"Danny Rees and Carol Pemberton are in Bristol this morning looking into Haines," Bev said. "Mac's made a start digging round Eric Long."

Mac lifted a hand. "You wanted threads. What about misdirection, guv? We get a letter fingering Long. And an anonymous caller naming Haines."

"Yeah, and we've had no joy tracing the woman, guv." Bev tapped her teeth with the pen. "And the only prints on the letter were the cleaner's and DI Powell's."

"Malicious intent certainly. But both names have been in the public domain." It didn't automatically follow the killer was behind both tip-offs, they all knew there were crazies out there who loved stirring. "Again we'll bear it in mind. Thanks, Mac."

Byford nodded before deliberately moving to one side of the first whiteboard: Josh Banks's smiling face gazed out. Like everyone else, Byford stared at the picture for five, six seconds. The point was made without a word being spoken. There'd been no reference so far to the little boy's murder. Bev saw colleagues fidget, sensed uneasiness, maybe even a touch of shame among the squad. Sure, checks were ongoing: red cars were being traced, CCTV footage was being chased, the poster campaign had been widened, extended, street interviews were still being carried out, Brett Sullivan's picture was doing the rounds of the media and other forces, but they were still no nearer finding who'd killed Josh.

"We don't even know how he died yet." There was sorrow in Byford's voice, and a sliver of censure? "A mother can't bury her son." Definite censure. He gazed at the squad letting it sink in. "Somebody chase the pathologist. I want the tox results by lunchtime. I don't care who does it, but don't take no for an answer... I won't."

Bev made a few notes as officers gave routine feedback, the guv issued tasks then: "OK, listen up. Mike Powell will stay as deputy SIO on Josh Banks's murder. Bev, you stick as deputy with the Haines case, and DCI Knight? You look after Eric Long. Obviously there'll be grey areas and overlap; that's why I want every officer whenever practical to report developments directly to me. Not an hour later, not ten minutes. Soon as they happen I want to know, right?"

"DI Powell was in over the weekend, that's why he's off today." Bev pursed her lips. Crafty beggar had kept that quiet last night. "As of now," Byford said, "time off in lieu will have to be postponed and I want all leave cancelled. Anyone has a problem with that, you know where I am. Metaphorically the door's always open." He cocked his head. "As always... I expect you to knock."

He lifted his jacket from the chair, swung it over a shoulder and swept out. No one spoke but there were plenty of meaningful glances being exchanged. "One more thing." Byford turned at the door. "Darren New. It may be a bit early but we ought to do something. Get a card signed, send some fruit, chocolate. Whatever. Maybe someone could start a collection?" Bev thought she detected the ghost of a smile. Nah. She must've imagined it. "Perhaps you could do the honours, Bev?" Had she hell.

Family mourns its lost son

The body of murdered schoolboy 10-year-old Scott Myers was laid to rest yesterday at the church of Saint Joseph the Martyr in the Leicester village of Highfields. Parents Noel and Amy Myers and their remaining children Alan and Wendy were surrounded by relatives and friends at the sombre service which took place on the hottest day of the year. Pupils and teachers from Belle View primary school and detectives from Leicester CID were among the mourners. Several children gave readings, and special prayers were said in memory of Scott whose body was found on a golf course near his home five weeks ago. The funeral was the first time Scott's mother has appeared in public since her son disappeared on the way home from school.

Police are still searching for Scott's killer. When asked what progress had been made, a spokesman refused to comment.

Laid to rest? Laid to rest? How fucking stupid was that? A sombre service? What else would it be? All-singing-all-dancing may as well crack a few jokes while we're standing round? As for the hottest day of the year? Who gave a damn? Would bucketing rain have made it any less gut-wrenchingly painful?

Tears blurred his vision; the man with the scrapbook could no longer read the article. The bland meaningless words weren't the target of his blind anger anyway. He knew that well enough. He blinked hard, took three or four calming breaths before he could bring himself to look at the photographs again. He was actually pleased the shots had been taken. Not that the press would have been invited, he was sure. But the snatched pictures were the only record of the occasion. The man had cause to be grateful. He steeled himself again.

Was any sight in the world sadder than a child's coffin?

Strip away the smooth white wood, the shiny brass handles, the flowers fashioned in the shape of a teddy bear, a football. The answer lies within. Was Amy Myers imagining her son in there, torturing herself with those images? It appeared so. The photograph showed a haunted woman, her life wrecked. Hunched between the arms of her husband and another man, she looked incredibly frail and unfocused, as if she were already some place else. The children looked like lost souls, too.

The man closed his eyes, bit down hard on his bottom lip. In one respect the reporter had been right: it was Amy Myers's first public appearance since Scott's death. It was also her last.

Oh, yes. And the police were still searching for Scott's killer.

Laid to rest? He slammed his fist into the wall, slammed it again and again and...

30

"Methadone?" Bev made a note on a scrap of paper, toned down her voice. "Blimey, doc. That's a turn up for the book of proverbs." Despite the casual suggestion to Mac he might like to chase the pathologist, Bev had assigned herself the task. Job had to have some perks didn't it? Prodding the handsome Doctor King was a darn sight more appealing than ploughing through yet more background on Haines and Long. Her desk was already snowed under with printouts, police reports, web archives and the fallout from a pack of Maryland cookies. Apparently the doctor had been on the point of calling Highgate anyway, the tox results had just come in.

Josh Banks had died from asphyxiation following a methadone overdose. Trying to get her head round that now, Bev didn't feel quite so perky. "How would it work, doc?"

"It was probably administered in a drink. Josh would have become drowsy, fallen asleep then eventually stopped breathing. Respiratory arrest we call it. I know it's not much comfort, but death would have been entirely painless. Josh wouldn't have known what was happening."

Josh. She liked that. The little boy wasn't just another number on a file to the doctor. Josh's picture would remain in place on her office wall until they'd nailed his killer. Glancing at it now she ran a mental check on what little she knew about methadone. A synthetic drug, it was used primarily as replacement treatment to wean addicts off heroin and cocaine. Trouble was it could be obtained illegally and no one had any real idea how much was floating round on the street. Abused, it was lethal. Some reports claimed it killed more drug users in the UK each year than heroin. Hard to equate with a little boy who'd only been hooked on Power Rangers.

Bev pursed her lips. "I guess a fair few people can get their hands on it, doc?"

"If you could see me now, sergeant, I'd be holding a piece of string." He could hold anything he liked, he'd still be a sight for sore eyes. "It's mostly associated with treating drug addicts but it's also a widely prescribed painkiller. Mainly for cancer patients, people terminally ill, in chronic pain."

She sighed. That narrowed it down. She made another note: they'd need to check medical centres, doctors' surgeries, drug clinics, see if methadone had been on a burglar's recent shopping list. Assuming whoever used it to kill Josh had needed to lift it. "Why methadone though, doc?" Dumb question. As if he'd know.

"Maybe the killer didn't want to cause Josh pain." Dumb answer. She tried to stifle a snort. Bastard killed the boy, didn't he? "Sorry, sergeant, I didn't really think that through. Maybe I'd better stick to the facts in future, not muscle in on your territory." The voice held the faintest hint of amusement.

No, doc – muscle in, do. Bev fanned her face with a sheaf of papers. God, it was hot in here. Or was it just her? Either way, the downdraught displaced some of the stuff on the desk, revealed a pic of Roland Haines's ugly mug; his creepy eyes stared up at her. She curled a lip. Then froze. What was it Mac said that night at the railway cutting? Haines wouldn't have known what hit him. No, because he was dead already. But surely he had to be sedated first? Like Eric Long had to be out of it before someone took a butcher's knife to his wrists. If methadone was bad enough for Josh...

She strolled to the window, gazed out over the car park. "Doc? Roland Haines? You don't..."

"The thought had occurred. And Eric Long. I'm pushing the lab hard, sergeant."

A looker and on the initiative ball. "Hard as you like, doc." She winced. That so could have been better phrased.

"Trust me…" He fed her the line.

"You're a doctor." And she made him laugh.

"Tell you what, why don't you call me Joe? Anything but Doc. Reminds me of all those westerns: Wyatt Earp, Doc Holliday et al shooting up Dodge City." She had a sudden vision of the guy in cowboy gear with a gun in his pocket. *What is it with you, Beverley?* Mind, the mental picture was a lot more inspiring than the current view of police cars and traffic cones.

"Joe it is then. It'll be my pleasure, d…" Why oh why did the giggle have to sound so girly? Still, he was clearly in no hurry to wind things up and there was no harm in a little wheel-oiling small talk. "And… please… call me…"

"Beverley… I heard. Comes from Old English. Know what it means?"

Intelligent, interesting, informative. Him, she meant. "Got me there, doc."

"No reason you should. Names are a bit of a hobby with me… boring, I know…"

"No." Never: whatever floats your boat. "Go on. Share it with me."

"Beaver stream."

The smile vanished. "Beaver stream." She so wished she hadn't asked.

"Or meadow. Beaver meadow." Was he taking the piss? Enough already.

"Just call me Bev, eh? Must dash." Pulling a face, she ended the call.

"Beaver stream?" Mac was propping up a wall, arms resting

on paunch, legs crossed at the ankle. "What's that all about then?"

She spun round, eyes flashing. "How long you been nebbing it, mate?"

"Just slipped in, boss." He tilted his head. "Door was open."

"So?" She flounced back to her chair. "I was busy."

"That what you call it?" Sotto voce.

"Watch your lip."

"More mileage watching this." He fumbled in a pocket, held aloft a security camera tape. "May I, boss?" Must've known he was pushing his luck. She nodded briskly, not a happy beaver. She watched as he wandered to the player, inserted the tape, hit play.

It showed the inside of a betting shop, lots of punters, a bank of TV monitors. Picture wasn't brilliant, a bit grainy. She rose, moved nearer the screen. "Is it Ladbrokes?" Where Roland Haines had lost a few shirts.

"Try again." Mac had. He was another guy who'd shown a bit of initiative. He told her he'd had no joy at Ladbrokes so he'd been visiting other bookies within a five mile radius, struck gold at Joe Coral's. For gold read Haines and Bobby Wells in shot on the same frame. Wells was on the move and only in profile. Blink and you'd miss it. But it was there. Mac paused the tape. "Bobby lied, boss. Said he'd never set eyes on Roland Haines."

"Bingo. Well done, mate." Sure it wasn't a full house, but it was a line. A line that needed pursuing. Armed with the new knowledge they'd re-interview Bobby Wells, apply a bit more pressure this time. She glanced at her watch: one-fifteen.

"Let's hope it's a photo-finish, eh, boss?" He tapped the side of his nose.

"God, you slay me." She dismissed him with a flap of her

hand. "Car park. Ten minutes. You're driving. Don't be late."

He waited until he was at the door. "The doc, then, boss? Into beavers, is he?"

It took Bev four of those minutes to nip to the loo, dab on lippie, finger-comb her hair and make sure there were no cookie crumbs stuck in her teeth. The guv had said he wanted developments delivered personally. Five minutes would do just fine for a brisk, businesslike, professional presentation. Hovering now on the threshold of Byford's office, she pinched a bit of colour into her cheeks. The door opened while she was pulling a bra strap straight. Classy start.

"Bev?" Pause. "Did you want a word?" The big man's lip curved the merest tad.

"Quick one, guv. Unless you're on the way out?" Didn't look to be – no jacket, keys, files on him.

"No worries." Waving an arm at a chair he walked to his desk. It felt right somehow sitting opposite the big man talking about a case again; talking about anything, come to that. Good job she'd made the effort, his warm grey eyes rarely left her face. She mentioned Mac's tape, making sure he got the credit then relayed the tox results, wrapped it up by saying the labs would hopefully now fast-track the Haines and Long blood samples.

Byford played a red pen through his fingers. "Methadone? Wasn't Haines a user?"

Shit. He was. Should've struck her before. A search team had found heroin at his pad and he'd used a line of Charlie as a sweetener to get a bed for the night out of his stepsister.

"I think he only dabbled, guv."

"Think?" He raised an eyebrow.

"'Kay." Slapped wrist. "Needs checking." Couldn't immediately see where it would get them though.

Laying down the pen, he sat back, fingers laced behind his head. "It's possible he was trying to come off it and was on a methadone treatment programme."

"What?" She frowned. "You saying the perp – who'd already used methadone to kill Josh – bumped Haines off with his own supply that just happened to be lying round?" Killed by a cure. That was novel. It was also a hell of a stretch.

He shrugged. "I never…"

"…rule anything out. I know." She smiled, knew a zillion other things, too. None of them to do with work. She banished the thoughts, needed a clear head. "Don't see how it fits though, guv."

"Truth be told, neither do I." He gave a crooked smile, walked to the window, perched on the sill. She had a sense of déjà vu, but then she'd watched him do it a thousand times. "Neither am I convinced whoever killed Josh also murdered Haines," he said.

"And Eric Long?"

"And Long. We could really do with the tox results."

He ran both hands over his face. The harsh sunlight streaming through the window wasn't doing him any favours. His lines looked a lot deeper than she remembered. The George Clooney resemblance was less striking. Mind, Clooney was looking less himself these days, what with the eye lift. She couldn't see the big man going in for cosmetic surgery somehow. Maybe it was a temporary thing and he was just up against it, like Powell said. If they were still an item, she could ease the… *Stop it, get a grip, woman.*

"At least the test results would help us know what we're dealing with. Until then it's not much more than informed guesswork."

That was guv-speak for pissing in the wind. "Doctor King says he'll push the lab, guv."

He nodded, loosened his tie. "I need a drink." He meant water, headed for the cooler.

While the cat's... Shuffling forward she gave his desk a quick scan. He'd not been marking essays with that red pen. So what had he been up to? No way. Property pages, and he'd circled three, no, four houses. Squinting she read the name of the paper: Westmorland Gazette. Sodding hell.

"Seen enough, Bev?" He was holding the cup to his lips. Seemed to find it amusing.

"You bet." Or not. Standing now, tight-lipped, she glimpsed a file half hidden under a load of other stuff. The Baby Fay case notes. It was a hell of a time since they'd been around, she certainly didn't recall the file being so bulky. If Byford was taking on board all the emotional baggage again, no wonder his eyes had a set of luggage.

Tough. It was his choice. And he'd need suitcases when he headed off into the sunset.

She couldn't believe it. The fucking Lake District.

And to think she'd been working up to say how brilliant it was to work with him again, just like old times. Yeah right. She hoisted her bag, headed for the door.

"You heading out to see Bobby Wells now?"

"Yep."

"Keep me posted."

"Yep."

"And tell Mac – good work."

"Yep."

In the doorway, she finally turned. "Hey guv? I'd like to say how good it is to have you back... I'd like to."

"Hey sergeant?" Granite-faced, he caught up with her in the corridor. "How'd you like to tell Stacey Banks her son's body can be released for burial?"

In the gents five minutes later, Byford plunged his face in a sink of cold water. The Stacey Banks dig had been below the belt but Bev had asked for it. OK, not asked for it. But nosing round his desk, putting two and two together, coming out with a crack like that – what did she expect?

Certainly not the dart he'd shot back. The case was getting to him as much as her. He snatched a handful of paper towels, dried off in front of the mirror. On reflection he regretted the remark. He pictured her blue eyes tearing up, her mouth a tight line. There'd been more than pain and hurt there. For the first time he'd seen contempt directed his way. Maybe dislike.

For a few minutes back in his office he'd sensed a real thaw. He'd watched her talk, her face mirroring every expression. He'd always loved that. Sighing, he ran a comb through his hair. Bev could no more hide her feelings than he could wear his heart on a sleeve. It partly explained the dithering. Christ, they could make the final of the pussyfooting Olympics, on crossed wires.

Just for once he'd come close if not to making a move, at least to dropping a hint, and now where were they? Back to square one would be good. After the last exchange, he'd be lucky to get on the board. For all her famed empathy, Bev hadn't a clue how he felt. With the pressure of the case building, time to tell her was running out.

And she was crap at maths.

Mac held the car door for her. "So what kept you, boss?"

"Just drive, eh, Mac."

He clocked her face and for once did exactly as he'd been told.

31

Paul Curran stood in DCI Knight's office running a fraught hand through sandy hair slick with sweat. A cheap tie was askew and a trainer lace undone. Since returning to Highgate from the Stirchley crime scene, the press officer had apparently done nothing but field calls from a frenzied media clamouring for news on Eric Long's death. "My mother told me there'd be days like this, Mr Knight, but…" Empty palms said it all.

Mine too, thought Knight. He'd been toying with putting in for a transfer. Unlike Curran, the DCI's cool pose and casual demeanour gave nothing away. Leaning back in his swivel chair, he crossed a languid leg. "What are they after this time, Paul?"

"Preferably an interview with the SIO. Statement at the very least. They want confirmation of things I know sod all… sorry, sir… nothing about."

"Like what? Sit down." Curran's nerves were getting on Knight's.

"Like Eric Long didn't kill himself. That it was staged to look that way. That there's a maniac on the loose."

Knight steepled his fingers. It wasn't guesswork. So who the hell was feeding the pack intelligence? The leaks weren't just jeopardising the inquiry, they were partly to blame for what Knight saw as his demotion. And who was supposed to have been tracing the source? Yeah right. Byford. He'd like to know just how far the man now in charge had put himself out.

"We have to keep information back, Paul. Only officers on the inquiry are in the loop. You know we can't release everything."

"For sure, but when I'm not privy to what's going on it makes the job impossible. Hacks are telling me stuff I don't know. I end up looking stupid." The clipped tone and slight flush suggested professional pique. The DCI knew how he felt, but in the nose-out-of-joint stakes it was no contest. Curran needed to get over it.

He picked up a pen. "I'll have a word with the chief, get back to you soon as, OK?"

Curran sighed, clearly resented the casual dismissal. "Cheers." He stood, opened his mouth to speak, appeared to think better of it.

"Was there something else?"

He hesitated briefly then: "No, it's nothing." Head down, he started walking away. Seemed to Knight he was dragging his feet.

"Sure about that, Paul?"

Fingers resting on the door handle, he turned back. The blush deepened, he was reluctant to make eye contact. "Look... it may be nothing... tales out of school and all that... it's just... the leak... I'm hearing a name being bandied about." Clearly uneasy, the guy shuffled from foot to foot.

"Never mind school, let's have a little chat." He beckoned the press officer back to his seat. Knight's indifference was feigned, the DCI was on full alert. He recalled Byford mentioning in passing yesterday that Paul Curran might be on to something but felt it was too early to name names.

Curran perched on the edge of the upright, smoothed then fidgeted with his tie. "I've heard a few of the news guys shooting off. You know what they're like when they've had a drink."

"*I* don't." The remark was pointed.

Curran read the DCI's tacit disapproval. "I don't make a habit of it, Mr Knight. I thought if I was around I might pick something up." Still fiddling with the tie. "Don't get me wrong,

I'm not exactly one of the lads. Handy, sometimes, though…
blending into the background." The laugh was brittle, the
tone bitter.

Knight couldn't give a toss about Curran's public profile.
"How handy?"

More displacement activity. This time he rubbed the back of
his neck, dislodged a few skin cells. Knight felt like wringing it.
"The name keeps coming up, Mr Knight. Not just in the pub,
I've heard it at crime scenes, reporters hanging round killing
time gossiping, banging on…"

"Get on with it, lad." He slung the pen on the desk.

Curran swallowed. "Detective Superintendent Byford."

"What?" He stifled a snort. No wonder he'd fobbed off the
big man. Curran was hardly going to take Byford into his
confidence. "Don't be ridiculous."

He raised both palms. "Don't shoot the messenger, Mr Knight.
I'm only repeating what I've heard. It's all very matey, y'know?
Bill this, Bill that, Bill the other. Could be hacks bigging it up for
all I know. It's just that…" Talk about blood out of stone.

Knight leaned forward. "If you've got something to say, say
it."

"I saw cuttings on Byford's desk. Eric Long."

"So?" Why the hell not?

"Before the guy was killed."

Too much. "You're telling me Byford had something to do
with that man's death?" Knight guffawed.

"No, no, course not. They weren't all about Long. There
was a piece about Roland Haines, several other men I
didn't recognise, that didn't mean much to me." He made eye
contact. "I think the stories were all about crimes involving
kids."

"What are you saying?"

"Hasn't he got a thing about it?"

"Haven't we all?" Byford wasn't the only cop who hated adults who preyed on children. "Your point is?"

"I don't know, Mr Knight. I've tried thinking it through, but…" He shrugged. "Maybe Mr Byford thinks the public needs protecting from people like Haines and Long. However misguided it is – leaking who they are, where they live – maybe he thinks he's going some way towards achieving that."

Knight turned his mouth down. Had he dismissed the idea too soon? "Nah, I can't see it, Paul. He's a senior detective."

"Not for much longer, Mr Knight." He held the DCI's gaze. "He's on his way out. Maybe thinks he's got nothing to lose?"

"Apart from his pension and professional integrity?" Knight shook his head. "This is little more than conjecture and malicious rumour. If it gets out and there's nothing behind it, it'll be your neck on the block." But what if it was true? Was it just possible Byford thought he was acting in the greater good? Or could the detective be on the make and arrogant enough to think he was untouchable? Knight didn't know the man well enough to judge. He needed, as Curran had said, to think this through.

"I know, I know." The press officer raised both palms. "It's why I came to you, Mr Knight. And I'm sure you're right. Shame there's no way of checking calls."

There was. Knight knew that if Byford was ringing from an internal phone, logs would show duration and frequency of calls. If they were suspect, an interceptional tap could be set up that would enable them to listen in. Depending what came out, they could go further and request billing details from Byford's private phone provider. If. Could. Maybe. It'd never get authorised on such flimsy grounds.

Knight picked up his pen. "What exactly have you got, Paul?" He wanted commas and full stops, not just chapter and verse.

"What you doing here? Thought I'd seen the back of you lot." The only part of Bobby Wells that was on show was his aesthetically challenged face. The rest of the guy was hidden behind a front door woodworm wouldn't rent. Cooking smells wafted up from the kebab place below, not the sort to make the mouth water. Wells gave Bev and Mac the once-over then sneered. "You the fat blue line then?" The crack must've been hilarious.

"Sorry, Mr Wells. Didn't quite catch you." Smiling brightly, Bev stepped closer. "Was that a 'Good afternoon, officers. Welcome to my humble abode. How may I help?'"

"Sarky cow." Making to close the door was his second mistake. Bev's foot slipped. The rotting wood split and splintered. "Fuck was that for?" Whinge whinge. He was lucky she wasn't wearing the Docs, the door might've come off the hinge, the dent would certainly be bigger. Mind, her toe wouldn't be throbbing so hard.

"Resisting arrest."

"I'm not."

"You are now. Cuff him, Mac." It was a bluff. They'd nothing to hold him on. Lying wasn't a criminal offence. Hopefully he'd not call it. They could maybe have a sniff round too while they were here, without the need for time-wasting red tape. Mac reaching in a pocket was enough for Wells to change his tune.

"No need for that, love. Course I'll let you in. Fancy a cuppa?" The obsequious smile was gut churning, too little dental work on display.

Disguising the limp, she brushed past him, straight into a stuffy squalid sitting room. Paper peeled off walls that in the current heatwave weren't even damp. What rolls were in situ were vomit-inducing swirls of lurid purples and greens. God knew what was ingrained into the grubby carpet but her feet were sticking to it. As an incentive to get on with the interview, it was up there with a world cruise. Propped on the mantel-piece was a framed photograph of Josh. It was a sobering reminder why they were here, and the only decent thing in the place.

Wells was wringing Uriah Heep hands. The sudden fawn-ing was probably down to the ganja fumes clinging to the upholstery and his granddad shirt. "Like some tea?"

"I'd like the truth."

"Not with you, love." He sank skinny haunches into the sort of settee normally found on a skip, a hand signal suggested they find their own place to squat.

"Drop the love, Mr Wells." She'd already scoped out the least unsavoury seat, perched now on the fraying arm of a wing chair. Mac played sentry at the door. "If you're not with me... how about Roland Haines? When's the last time you and Roly cosied up?"

Nonplus central. His Dopey was better than Walt Disney's. "Dunno what you mean. Never set eyes on the man." Again. It was like a line in a script.

"Sure about that?" Mac asked.

"Hundred and ten per cent."

Not a mathematical genius. She gave a mental eye roll. "What you reckon, Mac?"

"Amazing."

"Extraordinary."

"Absolutely."

"And fucking incredible."

Following the rapid fire with head turns, Wells was in danger of whiplash. Or he could have been auditioning for a remake of *The Exorcist*. "What's going on here?"

"Not here, Mr Wells. Joe Coral's Tenby Street... what date was it, Mac?"

He pulled a notebook from a breast pocket. "Sixteenth June." Turned a few pages. "Twenty-first June. Fourth July." Bev kept a straight face; Mac was making it up on the hoof.

"Told you before…" Wells reached for a baccy tin on the floor. She watched as he rolled a few strands in a liquorice paper. Was the slight tremor in his fingers down to nerves? Or the track marks she'd just spotted on his arms? Glancing at Bev, he moistened the edge of the paper with his tongue. "I like a flutter."

Still processing the fact Wells was a user, she said: "Roland Haines did too."

Shrugging, he sparked up, released smoke trails through both nostrils. God. It was enough to make you swear off the weed for life. "As I say, I wouldn't know about that."

"Got a twin, Wells?"

"Not that I know of." Back to cocky now, he sprawled in the chair, flicked ash on the floor.

She balled a fist. "Yesterday I was not born. You were there with him." To an extent, it was a flyer. The tape showed only that they'd been in the same room.

"Prove it."

Staring at Wells, she held out a hand to the side. "Got the pictures, Mac?"

"Damn, boss. They're back at the nick." Course they were.

"No worries." She jumped to her feet. "Come on, sunshine."

That put the wind up him. Straightening sharpish, he looked scared, panicky almost. "No, please. I don't…"

"Have a choice." She gave a thin smile. "Grab a toothbrush if I were you."

"I met him a couple times. OK." Elbows on knees, he dropped his head.

Better. Even better than she'd anticipated. "For?" Not that she didn't have an idea.

"He could always get hold of... stuff." Haines wasn't his regular supplier, Wells said, just now and then: heroin, cocaine, cannabis. They'd met a few months back in a pub.

"You knew he was being held for questioning in connection with your son's death?" Bev asked.

Wells nodded. "Sorry, love, I need the loo." He flicked the baccy into the empty grate.

Could hardly refuse, but she gave an inward groan. "DC Tyler can hold your hand."

Sodding nuisance. It ruined the flow. She waited until they were outside before taking a quick snoop. Rifled the usual places: in and under cushions, top of shelves, chimney breast. Not even sure what she was looking for. The stash was no surprise and wasn't even hidden. Few baggies, couple of needles behind a plant pot. If nothing else they could take him in on...

"Sarge! In here." Following the stink, she barged through the right door first, found Wells trying to squeeze through the bathroom window. Mac had a firm grip on both ankles, obviously not before taking a kick in the face. Bev grabbed the guy's legs and together they manoeuvred him back. Skinny as he was, he'd never have made it. As for the drop, he'd likely have snapped his neck. How desperate did he have to be?

She shook her head as Wells pulled his clothes straight, ran a hand through his hair. Mac wiped blood from his nose with a wad of loo paper.

"Not looking good, Houdini." She tapped a foot.

"Sod off." Surly, scared.

"You lied through your teeth then tried to do a runner. Why?"

"Because you lot would've had me in. I've been banged up before. Never again. And, please, you've got to believe me, I didn't kill the guy. I swear I'm telling the truth."

And change the habits of a life time? Yeah right.

"When did you last see him?"

"Friday. In the street. He'd just been released."

"Speak to him?"

"No."

"How come you knew we'd just let him go?"

"Must've read it in the paper."

She handed him a skanky toothbrush from a chipped mug. "Best grab a coat too, Mr Wells."

"Why?"

"Resisting arrest." It would do for a start.

Mac chucked bloodstained tissue down the pan. "And assaulting a police officer."

32

"Are you limping, sarge?" DC Danny Rees caught up with Bev in the corridor at Highgate. He'd not long arrived back from Bristol with Carol Pemberton. Bev had spotted their motor pulling into the station car park ten minutes or so ago when she'd been leaning through the office window trying to cool down. It was hotter than the Med out there, sky was bluer, too. Not that Danny or Carol had looked in particularly sunny mood.

"Had an argument with a door." Bev sniffed. Sodding toe was still throbbing, she'd dabbed a bit of witch hazel on it. "Mind, you should see Mac's nose." She gave Danny the gist of the interview, the fact that Wells was now in a police cell. "The guv's gonna have a session with him later." Smiling to herself, she replayed the exchange she'd just had with Byford. After delivering Wells to the custody suite, she'd headed straight for the big man's office and dumped a Gregg's bag on his desk. For you, she'd said. He'd asked if it was his leaving present. She wasn't the only one who did sardonic. No, guv, she'd countered. It's humble pie. I'm sorry. It wasn't often she grovelled to anyone but she'd been well out of order. Apology accepted, sergeant, he'd said, fancy a drink after...?

"Sorry, Danny, come again."

"I said it's a good job somebody's being questioned." Reverie broken, she picked up on his downbeat tone.

"Waste of petrol, was it?"

He held the door for her. "In a way." He seemed reluctant to share what was obviously bugging him, but even so tailed her into the incident room.

"Was or it wasn't, Danny." She made for the central desk, acknowledging nods and raised hands from the half-dozen squad members bashing phones or tapping keyboards. Danny perched on the edge as she leafed through a stack of printouts playing catch-up. "I'm pretty sure neither of the men killed Roland Haines, sarge."

"Fair enough. Needed checking though." After the case collapsed, Clive Sachs and Neil Proctor had slagged off Haines left, right and centre in the media; a series of threats culminated in them turning up at his house one night with a noose. They were clearly spoiling for a fight but Haines wasn't up for it. The Bristol cops reckoned the harassment campaign was why he left town.

"They still hate him," Danny said. "Piss on his grave if they could. But the list of recent movements they gave us seems to stand up. We left a couple more checks with a local DC but I can't see it amounting to much."

"So it was a waste then. Way it goes sometimes, Danny." Glancing up from the paperwork, she gave a half smile. "Most times come to that."

"Not completely though." She put the papers to one side, still couldn't read his expression. "It was a real eye-opener, sarge."

"Having Carol there?" No. There was more to it than that, and not in a good way.

Danny shook his head. "Pembers is great. But it's not what I mean." He cast an uneasy glance over his shoulder. All that studied indifference on display was a giveaway, their tete à tete was attracting attention. Even without it she sensed Danny was having a hard time voicing his concerns.

"Come on." She grabbed her bag. "Coffee. My shout."

Five minutes later she headed towards Danny with a tray. He'd sussed her favourite spot by the window and sat there now shredding a sugar sachet. "Lucky to get a table or what?" she quipped. The canteen was deserted.

"Expecting company, sarge?" He gawped at an array of pasties, pastries, cream slices.

"Comfort food, mate." She winked. "Missed lunch, didn't I?"

"A month's worth?"

"Stock up when you can, Danny." She could always pass some on to human doggie bag Mac. "Help yourself, mate." She tilted her head at the tray, tucked into a Cornish pasty while he picked at sausage roll, clearly building up to something. She gave him a couple of minutes then: "Come on, Danny. Spit it out."

Laying down the fork, he held her gaze. "Not sure I can hack it, sarge."

"The job?" That bad? She pushed the plates away, leaned in closer.

He nodded. "The men we were with today were eaten up with grief. Five years on and they're still raw about what happened to little Robbie. There were pictures of the kid everywhere. They couldn't mention his name without choking up."

She nodded slowly. "Terrible thing, Danny... to lose a child." Under any circumstances. But to murder...?

"I know that now. The pain never stops, does it? Not even if the killer's behind bars. The people left behind have to live with it, don't they? The hurt doesn't go away until the day they die. Sorry, sarge, I'd just never seen it before. It really got to me." Tearing up, he dropped his head. "Pathetic isn't it?"

He meant his reaction. "No it isn't, Danny." She laid a tentative hand over his. "It means you care, means you're a decent human being." It was better than the macho posturing that still went on in the hard men school of policing, but Danny needed to toughen up a tad if he was going to stay

210

the course.

"I didn't have a clue how to talk to them. If Carol hadn't been there…"

"What are you, Danny, twenty-one, twenty-two?" She took her hand away.

"Twenty-four."

"Carol's older, more experienced, been round the block a few times. Don't tell her I said that though for God's sake." She smiled.

He didn't return it. "I was a waste of space, sarge."

"Lighten up, Danny. We're none of us perfect." And it's not just about you.

"What if I'm not cut out to be a cop?"

"Fake it. We all do." She bit her tongue. No point getting snippy, but he was rolling in it a bit. "Policing's no walk in the park. It's tough out there, the pits. The loneliest job in the world, dealing with the shit no one else will touch. Thinking you've seen the worst things human beings can do to another, knowing there are horrors you can't even imagine waiting round the corner."

"Why do it then, sarge?"

"The uniform." The crack prompted a token lip curve. "Every cop has a different reason. You have to find your own, Danny. But the thing that keeps me going? Gets me out of bed in the morning? Thinking, just now and again, I might be making a difference helping to send the sick bastards down: the rapists, the murderers, the child molesters. Someone's got to clear the bad guys off the streets, Danny."

"So what happens when we don't… and they get away with it?"

What was this, *Mastermind?* She shrugged. "Pass."

Leicester Mercury

Scott's murder – suspect held

Leicestershire police say a man's being questioned in connection with the murder of 10-year-old schoolboy Scott Myers. Scott vanished walking home from school on 30 June this year. His body was found fifteen days later on a golf course near his home in the village of Highfields. The discovery sparked one of the biggest police operations ever held in the county. The man, who's not being named *, is understood to have been detained after information received from a member of the public. When asked if charges were imminent a police spokesman refused to comment.   *(Sol Danvers)

The name was written in the same hand as other annotations in the scrapbook. The man had read it before, knew it appeared on later pages too. He shook his head, face contorted with hatred. Sol Danvers: head teacher at Belle View Junior School. The man who'd led prayers for Scott's safe return. The man who'd used such glowing terms to describe the little boy. While all the time…

With hands that shook, he leafed back through the scrapbook searching for the page that displayed Danvers's photograph. He'd not noticed earlier but the teacher bore a passing resemblance to Philip Larkin: the neat hair, the smart suit, the horn-rimmed glasses lent an air of scholarly authority, respectability. Here was a man who could be trusted, it said. Clearly not everyone was convinced. The police might have protected his precious identity, but it was common knowledge in the small community where the Myers family lived that Danvers was the man in custody. Maybe a neighbour or colleague saw police arrive at his house or school, watched him being driven away in the back of a car.

The man didn't care. It was immaterial. Whatever information the cops had been given, the idiots couldn't make it stick. Danvers the Larkin lookalike had walked.

He gave a mirthless laugh. It wasn't just parents who fucked up kids.

33

"How poorly is she?" With a keen eye on the clock, Bev was on the phone to her mum. She knew Emmy wouldn't be calling if Sadie was feeling on top of the world, but no way was Bev dropping everything now. Not when, in a manner of speaking, she'd soon have her hands full with the guv. If she'd known a humble pie offering could lead to a drink invite, maybe she'd have apologised sooner.

"She says she's fine, Bevy, but she's had this cough for weeks now. The doctor wants her to go in for tests, but you know what she's like." Tiny, feisty, stubborn, proud. That was Bev's gran. Or had been. She'd taken a knock in every sense five years back when a yob attacked her, hacked off her hair, left her for dead. She'd seemed more her old self these last few months, but at eighty-plus was no spring chicken. Bev gave a tender smile: more game old bird. Even so...

"I just can't get away, mum." She sniffed her wrist. Hoped she hadn't overdone the DKNY. "Does it have to be tonight?"

"It'd cheer her up no end. Take her out of herself. She'd love to see you, sweetheart."

The smile faded. "I'll pop by over the weekend, OK?" It was unlike Emmy to play the guilt card but Bev already had a full deck. Her workload provided reason and sometimes excuse not to pay family dues. A reminder was something she didn't need.

"That's a real shame, Bevy."

Sadie wasn't exactly at death's door. And it had been months since the big man had come knocking at Bev's. "Really up against it at the mo, mum."

"Fine. I'll tell her you're busy, shall I?" Emmy being snippy. She usually left that to Bev, who much as she loved her mum rarely let her down in the strop-stakes.

"Three unsolved murders," she snapped. "What do you think?"

"Beverley." Rare that. "You really wouldn't want to know what I think."

Open-mouthed, Bev stared at the phone. Emmy had hung up. That was a first. She sank into the seat, pondered for a while, then pushed a few buttons. "Guv…?"

"Better late than never eh?" A tad breathless, Bev slid into the dimpled leather bench opposite Byford. The Feathers was more or less his local so he'd suggested waiting for her there. Not that he'd been idle; she'd just seen him slip pad and pen into his pocket. Bev had been occupied polishing her halo. Dazzlingly bright now, beatification was surely just around the corner. In two hours she'd fitted in a house call to tell Stacey Banks Josh's funeral could go ahead, then dashed to her mum's place where she'd plied her gran with Bristol Cream and brandy liqueurs. Sadie was in better spirits when she left and Bev had picked up Brownie points from her mum into the bargain. The fact her carefully applied slap was now a distant memory and she'd spilt a spot or two of Sadie's sherry down her frock…

"What can I get you, Bev?" …was worth it for that smile.

"Pinot… just for a change."

"You want a small glass then?"

He'd cracked the line before. Smiling anyway, she watched him stroll to the bar. Told herself he wasn't really looking older, was bound to feel the pressure being back on a big case. She sat back, tried to relax. It was a while since she'd been in here with the big man. Couldn't say she'd missed the place.

The Feathers was a bit of an acquired taste: all cheesy chintz and brass bed pans. Still she wasn't here to assess the décor. She smoothed her hair, licked her lips. *It's just a drink, Beverley, just a drink.*

"Ta, guv." She savoured that first sip. "Solved it then?" She aped writing action, reckoned he'd been killing time making case notes, or working on his memoirs.

"I wish." He was on orange juice. "I was just jotting a few ideas. Three victims, Bev, and it's still unclear how many killers we're looking at."

"Tell me about it."

Theories had been thrashed out at the late brief, again inconclusively. Likeliest scenario was still that the faked suicides were down to one perpetrator, but there was a chance Long had been despatched by a killer who'd picked up the idea from press coverage of Haines's death. Not copycat, but similar principle. The media was a possible link in providing motive too. Both victims had been outed recently for crimes against children. The cops knew from Bridie Long that the exposure had provoked hostile public reaction towards her husband. But there were other possibilities. The Longs had recently won a few grand. Killer might have thought he'd find it lying around the place, easy pickings. As for Haines, he'd been dealing hard drugs. It seemed to Bev they were holding bits and pieces of different jigsaws; didn't know what the pictures were, or where Josh Banks's death fitted in.

She took another sip. "What did you make of Bobby Wells?" Byford and DCI Knight had interviewed the guy late afternoon.

"Not a lot." He pursed his lips. "He strikes me as a small time crook. I can't see him as a killer somehow. But we'll run the checks. He's not going anywhere." Not with an assault charge hanging over him. He'd appear before magistrates tomorrow, more than likely be remanded in custody.

"Does he admit to knowing Eric Long?" Bev asked. Wells's attempted runner had pre-empted the line of questioning back at Ada Street.

"He says not."

"Yeah, well, he's a congenital liar. What about the search team at his pad?" The officers had been told to look for methadone among other things.

"Nothing." Byford shook his head. "Anything from the lab on the test results?"

"Sometime tomorrow, hopefully." They were still waiting on confirmation that the replacement drug had played a part in the deaths of Haines and Long. If so, surely it had to follow the same killer had claimed all three lives?

"There is another way we could find out." He pinched the bridge of his nose.

"Go on." A thought had already occurred to her.

"If it is one killer…" He held her gaze. "And if he is eliminating adults who harm children…"

She nodded. "…he's not finished yet."

"I'd say he's barely started." He raised an eyebrow. "And I daresay there are plenty of people out there who'd cheer him to the bitter end. If not give a hand." He drained his glass.

Lynch mob mentality? The remark was out of character; she reckoned he was playing devil's advocate. "You serious?" His expression was unreadable.

He shrugged. "Some people see child killers as scum. That they forfeit the right to life."

Some people. "Yeah but, you…?" She didn't like the way it was going, the tone of his voice, the fact he wouldn't look her in the eye.

"I'm just saying…" He held out empty palms. Saying what? She recalled the case file on his desk. Baby Fay's murder.

217

Knew the grief it had given him over the years, was aware he made annual pilgrimages to her grave, had witnessed him in the grip of recurring nightmares about her torture and death. The file was definitely bulkier than before. Was there related material in there? Other child crimes? *Fuck's sake, Bev. You're questioning the big man's integrity here.* Not for a nanosecond did she think he'd take out the bad guys himself. Never. But someone on the inside was leaking intelligence that enabled others to.

"You OK, Bev?"

She dropped the frown, shook her head, needed to think straight. "Know what, guv? I've got a bitch of a headache." She slid out of the bench. "Reckon I'll hit the road."

She didn't even finish the drink.

The Pinot in the fridge took a hammering when Bev got home. Even before reaching Baldwin Street, she'd virtually dismissed the Byford as mole notion. Ludicrous. Get real, woman. For Christ's sake, he was a senior detective, a decent bloke, the most decent she knew.

Thankfully her housemate was in residence. Having Frankie around meant it was easier to switch off. They'd cobbled together a late supper, ate it on their laps, watching a re-run of *Have I Got News For You*. Frankie had dropped a slice of Mother's Pride on Bev's tray. The message got through without a word being spoken.

It was in the early hours the thoughts wormed their way back into Bev's head. Just how well did she know the guv? He'd been her boss since God was a girl. But he'd distanced himself big time these last six, seven months. Had he felt bitter being taken off operational duties? Anger having an internal inquiry hanging over his head? He'd certainly not shared his feelings with her, they'd barely exchanged a syllable during the limbo period. Was he after revenge? Did he see leaks to the press as a way of hitting back at the way he'd been treated?

Mouth dry, head pounding, she swung her legs out of bed, drained a glass of water on the bedside table. Fact was cops were ideally placed to let information slip. Byford perhaps more than most. He'd be slipping out himself soon enough. After thirty-odd years on what – when he started – was called the force.

When he started... The image was imprinted on her brain but she took the picture from the top drawer anyway. She'd clipped it from an old newspaper, a young Byford in uniform looking like the cat who got the creamery. Her return smile was involuntary. She shook her head. Policing had been the guv's life for God's sake. He'd never let colleagues down, bring the service into disrepute. But, hold on....

Despite the stultifying heat, she froze. The cutting floated to the floor as her hand flopped to her naked thigh. Maybe he felt he'd already overstepped the line. Narrowing her eyes, she saw again that night in December. Scarlet blood seeping into the snow, the sound of cracking bone, Byford grappling with the man who'd attacked her, shadowy figures then stillness and silence.

When the guv saved her life, he'd taken another. Accident or not.

WEDNESDAY
34

"I've just come from IC. I'm really pleased to say he's showing signs of improvement." Bev heard the smile in Doctor Sugar's voice. Great way to start the day. She didn't get to speak to Cathy every time she rang the hospital but always asked if she was around on the off-chance. She liked the woman and was pretty sure they shared a soft spot for Darren. Mind, after last night's feverish imaginations, Bev was almost convinced she needed treatment herself. Byford as bad guy? How likely was that? She'd suspect Sadie was an Al Qaeda sleeper next.

"Top notch, doc. Is he up to visitors then?" Sliding open the middle drawer of her desk, she struggled to extricate the massive get well card. She'd get the few remaining signatures after the brief, try and drop it by this evening.

"Hold your horses." Mock admonition. "He is still unconscious, Bev."

"No worries. I could sit there bombarding him with Stones music and taped messages from Gordon Brown."

"Could set him back if he's a Beatles fan and votes Tory." The doctor laughed. "Seriously, he is off the tubes and performing much better on the GCS." Glasgow Coma Scale. Bev was well-versed in initials now. Cathy had run her through the scale earlier. Patients scored between one and fifteen according to eye, verbal and motor responses. When Darren had been admitted he was barely hitting four. He'd registered eight on the latest tests.

"All them scales – we'll have him playing piano when he comes round, doc."

Audible groan then: "You're wasted in your job. Bye, Bev."

Her smile was still there though.

Bev's faded momentarily. She only wished she could tell Darren the scrotums who attacked him were behind bars.

"Hey Morriss! Have you heard?" DI Powell in sharp suit and silk tie drew up alongside Bev in a corridor at Highgate. Clutching a couple of files she masked a smile, reckoned he'd reverted to type in more ways than one. And he'd overdone the Ralph Lauren aftershave again.

She cocked her head: "Good morning, Bev. How goes it?"

"Yeah yeah." A friendly smile and flapping hand dispensed with social niceties and the doorstep near miss in one – for the DI – surprisingly subtle fell swoop. She'd half expected a blast of *No Regrets* or *A Kiss is Just a Kiss* from the man who thought PC was something you sent in the post. "Witness phoned in after the telly appeal. A neighbour saw Eric Long letting some bloke into the house the night he was killed."

She gave a low whistle. "Description?" Falling into step they headed for the briefing room.

"Not bad." He ran a hand through his hair. "Car's on the way to bring him back here. We'll line up one of the artists. Get them to work on an e-fit. Could be a break."

About bloody time. She held up crossed fingers, turned the gesture into a wave as she clocked Mac ambling towards them.

"Talking of break," Powell said. "What the fuck happened to you?"

Mac lifted his hand, winced as it grazed his nose. It wasn't broken but swollen fit to burst. "He's had a nose job." Bev quipped.

"Get your money back if I were you, Tyler." Powell held the door, gave a knowing smirk as she passed. "Bet he regrets it. Don't you, Morriss?"

She glanced over her shoulder. "Non."

"So when are we expecting this witness, Mike?" The guv stood centre stage caught in a shaft of sunlight. He'd jettisoned the jacket five minutes back and was now rolling his sleeves. Bev was in a light cotton shift dress and still feeling the heat. Byford would be the last cop to count chickens but it was easy to see he found the lead from Drake Street encouraging. More than that: she reckoned it had perked up what had been a lacklustre brief and a downbeat squad desperate for movement.

Powell's Rolex glinted in the light. "Forty minutes or so, guv."

Byford nodded. "Liaise with Paul Curran, will you? We need to get it out there fast." If the image was halfway decent, they'd release it to the media before the metaphorical ink was dry.

"He's heading out to some photo shoot in Handsworth." DCI Knight piped up. "Neighbourhood policing, I think he said."

It'd take a while for the visual to be pieced together and a cynic might say neighbourhood policing and Handsworth was an oxymoron. "Should be back just in time then, thanks, Lance."

The DCI failed to return the guv's fleeting smile. Bev pursed her lips. Was Lancelot still piqued? Listening with half an ear, she made a few notes as the big man recapped where the inquiry stood. Nothing substantial had changed since their run-through in the pub last night. With hindsight her sharp exit had definitely been too hasty. Not getting offered a replay was something she probably would regret.

"Right, anyone have anything else?" Byford slipped a hand in his pocket.

"One of the motors picked up on CCTV?" Sumi Gosh had been chasing and checking. "Turns out it was stolen, sir."

And still missing. "I've only just found out." Good job she made that clear: the guv looked as if he was about to have a go.

"OK. Circulate details." Other forces would keep an eye out too. Probably no connection but elimination was a big part of any inquiry.

Mac raised a finger. "I've got an address for Alfie Cox, guv." Some of his digging had paid off. "He's the grandfather of..."

"Hannah Cox." Byford nodded. "The child of Eric Long's former partner." Bev did a mental double-take. Talk about being on the ball. "Go on."

"He was pretty vocal when Long got sent down," Mac elaborated. "Said he should've got a much longer sentence."

Byford raised an eyebrow. "If I recall correctly, he said Long should've been put down." Spot on again. He'd certainly been doing his homework. "Cox must be getting on a bit now. But if you think he's worth an interview..."

Bev crossed her legs. Don't get too excited, guv. Anyone would think suspects were coming out of their ears.

"What about those test results, Bev?" Byford asked.

"Left a message first thing, guv. He'll get back to me soon as." The pathologist had been on a call out to Wednesbury. Some bloke found beaten to death in a back alley. Thank God it wasn't their baby. One thing they weren't short of was victims.

Grieving mother in death crash

Tragedy has again struck the family of murdered schoolboy Scott Myers. Mrs Amy Myers, the boy's 29-year-old mother, was killed in a car crash yesterday on the M69 near Hinckley. It's believed Mrs Myers's car careered off the motorway at high speed before smashing into a tree. Police have confirmed that no other vehicle was involved but accident investigators spent several hours at the scene.

Witnesses say Mrs Myers appeared to lose control of the car. Her husband, 35-year-old Noel, refused to comment and asked that the family be left alone to grieve in peace. It's understood Mrs Myers had been struggling to come to terms with the loss of her son Scott, who was abducted and murdered in June this year. His killer remains at large.

The Cortina was pictured, its bonnet embedded in the trunk of an oak tree, its bodywork crumpled concertina-like, clumps of wild flowers visible in the foreground. No one could have survived the impact. Moist-eyed, the man with the scrapbook hoped Amy's death had been instant, unlike the last painfully long drawn out months of her life.

He reread the opening words: Tragedy has again struck... His lips puckered. It was a little early for the 'jinxed family' line to be wheeled out. It wasn't long before reporters latched on to it though. Was it Amy's funeral coverage when the tag first appeared? He resisted the temptation to leaf forward through the book. Timing didn't matter, the term was meaningless, totally inappropriate either way. Scott had been killed by evil intent not bad luck.

As for 'struggling to come to terms...' Sighing, he slumped back in the chair: more weasel words. Amy had coped well enough to convince psychiatrists she was ready to be released from hospital, coped well enough to convince her husband she was fit to drive, coped well enough to take only her own life on that desperate last journey.

35

Bev was clearing paperwork before heading out to Alfie Cox's place with Mac. Despite Byford's less than delirious reaction, she thought Cox worth having a look at. What was the saying about revenge being a dish best served cold? How'd they know Cox didn't have a deep freeze factory?

Bev wouldn't say no to a walk-in fridge. Heatwaves were all well and good on holiday; fat chance of that round here. She gave a derisive snort. Best invest in a fan. She reached for a file, pulled out one of the press reports Mac had culled from the last day of Eric Long's trial. A snapper had caught Cox in mid-flow, spewing vitriol. He looked straight out of heavies' academy: bull-necked, bald headed, bared teeth and tattooed. She narrowed her eyes. What would he be now? Mid-fifties. Not exactly over the hill. Heck. Byford was heading towards sixty. Either way a trip to Small Heath was probably one up from bashing the phone or knocking doors. Though some-one was…"Come in."

"Here you go, boss." Mac bummed the wood to, ambled over bearing canteen coffee.

"Cheers, mate."

"Should be champagne. Would be if I'd known." No wind-up, voice was genuine.

"Known what?"

He parked his backside on a chair. "I bumped into one of DI Talbot's men in the queue. Ivan?" Usually he followed it up with 'the terrible' but the gleam in Mac's eyes meant he wasn't pissing round. The news was good. "They've made an arrest." Darren's attack. Peter Talbot was SIO. "Youth from the Quarry

Bank estate. On the way in now."

She punched the air, huge beam on her face. "Fan-fucking-tastic."

"Not all, boss." Milking it, he took a sip of coffee. She'd land him one if he didn't spit it out. "The boy's mum dobbed him in. Called this morning. Ivan reckons once they start the questioning he'll drop his mates in the shit an' all."

Thrilled to bits, she paced the office as he gave her the gist: the woman had found bloodstained clothes in her son's bedroom earlier in the week. He'd fobbed her off with some lame excuse. She knew he was no angel but what mother wants to think the worst of her son? Then last night she'd seen Darren's picture splashed all over the front page. Just thinking about it brought tears to Bev's eye. Releasing it had been a close call. Pete had taken quite a bit of stick over the decision. Obviously the shock value had paid off.

"Wasn't just that," Mac said. "She checked his mobile first thing. There's actually footage. Darren lying at the back of the flats. She knew her lad ran with a bad crowd but had no idea they were capable of that." Mindless violence.

"Tough love then," she said. "Not before time."

"Even so, Bev... takes a mother courage, that."

"Yeah." She sniffed. "Shame it doesn't run in the family."

Mac drained his cup, lobbed it binwards. "All set then, boss?" Pointing, she raised an eyebrow. He found the target this time. They were at the door when the phone rang.

"Doctor King. Thanks for getting back. Just one tick." She shielded the mouthpiece, told Mac to meet her at the car in five.

"Private consultation, boss?" Smirking, he crept out.

"Sorry about that, Joe." Shared interests and all that, she'd looked up the meaning of Joe. Reckoned it couldn't be any worse than beaver stream. She'd nearly died laughing. He who will enlarge. Each to their own interpretation but she'd not be sharing hers right now.

"Results were on the desk when I got back, Bev. As you suspected, lethal doses of methadone present in both blood samples. Odds are you're looking for one killer."

No real surprise. Not a bunch of help either. She sighed. "Couldn't give us his name, inside leg measurement could you, doc?"

"'Fraid not." He laughed. "Your colleagues in Wednesbury are desperate for a name, too."

She frowned then realised where he was coming from. "Your stiff this morning?" Mouth open, eyes screwed: *tell me I didn't say that, God?*

"Sorry?"

"Technical term, doc. Corpse. Cadaver. Carcass. Corpus delicti."

"Quite." She heard throat-clearing noises. "Anyway the body's a John Doe. Late sixties, early seventies probably. If he carried identity, it had gone by the time your people arrived."

"If?"

"Feeling was he might have been homeless."

"And he was just set upon in the street?" Poor old sod.

"Looks that way. They couldn't see robbery as a motive." If the Wednesbury cops were that desperate for an ID they'd have to release a death picture. "It's to be hoped he's reported missing," King said.

"Why's that?"

"Taking photographs isn't an option." He paused. "When there's no face."

Arms folded, ankles crossed, face deadpan, Mac lounged against the motor, peeled himself off as Bev approached. "Pass it then, boss?"

Frowning, she paused, hand on passenger door. "Pass what?"

"The medical."

She flared a nostril. "You need to work on that one, mate."

"Hey, boss." Head tilted. A patrol car was pulling into the car park. A youth sat in the back flanked by two uniforms: dark hair, pale skin, obligatory scowl. A grim-looking Pete Talbot stared ahead through the windscreen.

Bev's fists were tight balls. "Let's get out of here." Mac took one look at her face, opened his door. No wonder he'd waited al fresco. The car was like a blast furnace. She winced as flesh met hot leather, scrabbled in her bag for Raybans. They drove in silence for a while. Mac broke it. "Was it methadone?"

"Haines and Long." She nodded. "The guv knows." She'd popped into Byford's office to pass on the findings. He'd task two more officers with checks at doctors' surgeries, health clinics, drug treatment centres. Like a lot of plod work, it was a long shot.

"Open your window, mate." Even if it was cold out there, her blood would still be boiling.

36

Alfie Cox was unrecognisable from the press pictures. Tight-lipped, his wife Marjorie listened in silence then led Bev and Mac in to a neat Edwardian villa in Elm Road. The front sitting room was equally neat though too small for the fussy wallpaper. Roses don't always grow on you. It was immediately apparent why the wife had done the honours: Cox was in no fit state. He was slumped at an awkward angle in an over-stuffed armchair close to an electric fire that blasted heat from all four bars. Grey cardigan and slacks hung loosely from his frail frame. He wasn't just sick. He had the jaundiced paper-thin skin of a dying man, a look in clouded amber eyes that said he knew it.

"It's the police, Alfie." Marjorie Cox was in rude health by comparison. Bev would have knocked the floral pinny and sturdy shoes on the head but the woman's figure was enviably trim, face still pretty. Why the hell hadn't she opened her mouth earlier, said how ill her old man was?

"Detective Sergeant Bev Morriss, Mr Cox." His thin fingers were cold to the touch. "This is DC Tyler."

"Come in... sit down... I won't get up..." Cox was short of breath as well as time. His tone was amicable. "Why are you here? It's not about the tax disc, is it?"

Bev and Mac exchanged glances. Whose brilliant idea was it to turn up unannounced?

"I'll tell you why they're here." Marjorie Cox's flushed cheeks weren't down to the temperature. Fuming, she tapped a foot. "They want to know if you killed Eric Long." *Why not mince your words, love?* Bev hadn't been that blunt on the doorstep; Mrs Cox was sharp, sharp enough to intuit what hadn't been said. She cut Bev a glance. "Well, go on. Fire away. Bear in mind he's not set foot out the house for three months. And he's on oxygen most the time. And he sleeps down here cause he can't manage the stairs. And he weighs less than eight stone. And he's got less…" The anger was coming off her in waves. In a weird way she seemed to enjoy having someone to vent it at.

"I'm sorry." Bev raised both palms. "We'd no idea…"

"You can say that again," she sneered. "Coming here with your stupid questions, raking it all up."

"Mrs Cox," Mac said. "We're only…" Doing our job.

"Don't give me that bullshit." She moved towards them, jabbing a finger. "If you'd been doing your job properly that bastard wouldn't have got away with murder."

"Marjorie… love…" The words petered out, Cox's body wracked by a coughing fit.

She swept a hand in his direction. "My husband's guilty all right… convinced it was his fault our granddaughter died. He believes he could have saved her, should have known what was going on." Her violet eyes glittered as she took a deep breath. "He blames himself and it's been eating him up ever since. The cancer's killing him now." A single tear ran down her cheek. "But you know what…? He's been dead inside for years. Eric Long as good as murdered Alfie, too."

"He's not dead yet." Harsh. But Cox was bent double sobbing. "He needs you." And Bev didn't appreciate the lecture. "We'll see ourselves out."

Her parting shot reached them when they were in the hall. "I'm glad Long's dead. Glad someone killed him. If I'd known where he was, I'd have done it myself."

"Think she would have, boss?" Mac turned the ignition, checked the mirror. Bev glimpsed Marjorie Cox arms tightly crossed watching impassive from the sitting room window as the car pulled away.

"No, but nothing surprises me these days." What was it Byford said the other night? People think child killers forfeit the right to life. Mrs Cox was certainly in that category but Bev didn't see her having the strength or stomach to slit Long's wrists. Was it a crime any woman would commit? Either way, she'd already crossed Cox's wife off her mental list. "You hungry, mate?"

"Nah."

"I take it back. That's fucking amazing."

"I'm starving."

Her lip twitched, then struck by a sudden thought, she frowned. "Have the Coxes got other kids?" Who might now be big strapping blokes.

"No, I checked."

Good-oh. "Hit Subway, shall we?"

"Thought you'd never ask."

Powell popped his head round the incident room door, spotted Byford chatting to a group of detectives and walked across. "There you are, guv. Wondered where you'd got to. Have a look at this."

The e-fit was the result of a two-hour collaboration between a police artist and Long's Drake Street neighbour, Timmy Bass. Powell had sat in on the session for a while, questioning the man further on what he'd seen. The visitor, average height and weight, dressed in dark clothes had arrived on foot around ten o'clock. After a brief conversation, Long had let him in to the house. No raised voices, no sign of reluctance on Long's part. Bass had thought nothing of it until seeing the witness appeal on *Midlands Today*.

Byford studied the image then gave a wry smile. "I s'pose his mother might recognise him."

"Not brill, is it." The image was pretty bland: man in his thirties maybe, round face, short fairish hair, no distinguishing features. "Think it's worth issuing anyway?" It was a toss-up whether keeping the story in front of the public outweighed a possible tidal wave of useless calls from time wasters.

"We've got extra hands. May as well." The half dozen new support staff would lighten whatever load came in.

"Ta, guv. I'll nip it up now."

"I'll walk with you." Byford wanted a quiet word, knew with Powell it wouldn't go any further. "Have you got a minute, Mike. My office?" Byford entered first, they stood just inside. When he'd told the squad his door was always open, he meant when he was at his desk. "I have a feeling someone's been snooping round in here."

Powell glanced round as if expecting some nosy git to be hiding in a corner. "You sure, guv?"

"Virtually."

"Anything missing?" Powell loosened his tie.

Byford shook his head. "Just a sense stuff's been shifted… papers… files…" He'd found a drawer open a whisper. Or maybe it hadn't been closed properly. As he'd told the DI, it was a feeling more than anything. "You've not sussed anything similar?"

"No, deffo." And he would. Powell kept his desk pristine, not so much as a bent paper clip out of place. Bev swore the DI used a ruler to line up everything that wasn't nailed down. There was no point asking if anyone had been grubbing round hers, it was barely visible under the paperwork most of the time. "Any idea what they were after, guv?"

"Search me." He shrugged. "You've not heard any talk round the station?" Course not, he'd have mentioned something. "Be aware of it anyway, Mike. Just in case. Forewarned and all that."

"Sure, guv. I'll keep an eye out here too." His office was a few doors down.

Byford nodded at the e-fit in Powell's hand. "Best get that up to Paul." Alone in his office, the big man crossed to the window. Almost called Powell back to tell him Curran was in the car park. He watched the press officer stroll towards the back entrance, turn to wave at the woman who'd dropped him off. Probably his wife, there was a baby seat in the back of the Volvo. The big man gave a wry smile: wouldn't have missed fatherhood for the world but more days of dirty nappies and broken nights he could live without. A thought came from nowhere: *what about Bev?* Would she be happy to forego the pleasure? His snort said it all. And who was he kidding? The thought hadn't come out of the blue. The woman was under his skin whether he liked it or not. Turning, he shook his head. He had more immediate issues to focus on right now.

He walked back to the desk, tapped his fingers on the surface. Had he been right not to tell Powell everything? He'd told the truth that nothing had been taken. He was almost sure an item had been left. Biting his lip, he took the baby Fay file from the top drawer. He'd added cuttings to it over the years, lost count of the number. But for the life of him he couldn't remember including this. Eyes creased, he held the clipping, skimmed the story. He recalled the case of course, didn't have to be a cop to remember it. The horrific murder of seven-year-old Jamie Black in 1982 had, as was the media's wont, shocked the nation. It prompted predictable calls for the return of the death penalty, three or four hacks brought out books off the back of it.

But Jamie's murder didn't fit the pattern of the cold cases in the folder. Despite a not guilty plea, Patrick Woolly had been caught, convicted and sent down for life.

Unless… Byford reached for the phone.

37

Bev popped her head round the door of the police press bureau. Ambience was different up here: airy, laid back, definitely not the sharp end. She cut a glance at the far wall which was almost entirely given over to splashy leads and celebrity photo spreads orchestrated by the bureau's veteran boss, Bernie Flowers. Much of the coverage stemmed from his years editing *The Sun*. The collage was eclectic: princesses, politicians, page three, and the odd plod. Bernie's greatest hits – or tits as the Highgate wags put it.

"Wotcha, Paul. Got that e-fit?"

Smiling he glanced up from a keyboard, reached for an envelope at his elbow. "Put a copy aside, soon as you phoned, Bev." She'd seen him earlier in the car park, given him twenty minutes or so to catch his breath.

"Ta, mate." Byford had suggested taking the visual to Drake Street. Doh. Like it wouldn't have occurred? It was one of the reasons she'd lined up a second interview with Long's widow. Hopefully Bridie would be more receptive now, might recall more, too. She was still at the neighbour's house, even though number twenty-four had been given the forensics all clear. Bridie was in no rush to move back.

Paul didn't seem to be in a hurry either. Rolling the chair out, he leaned into it, hands crossed behind his head. "How goes it, Bev?" She had a few minutes to kill and they'd not really chatted since the night of the boozy curry. Perched on the edge of the desk, she told him about Darren, the fact some toerag was banged up. She mentioned the card in her office Paul was welcome to sign. He was a good listener, laughed in

235

all the right places. Seemed easier in his skin up here too, but she wondered if he still worried some cops blamed him for the press leaks. Mud sticks, however groundless. Groundless mud? Mental shrug: she knew what she meant. Fact was he needed that sort of suspicion hanging over him like a hole in the head. He was a new boy still on a probationary period. No way could he lose his job, not with a wife and kid to support. And even if he wasn't in the firing line, he might feel forced to move on. He'd confided all this in K2 that night, but it didn't look as if he was going to bring it up now, and it wasn't her job to probe. She smiled. Actually that was exactly her job.But not with mates.

"Changing the subject, was that your wife…?"

"…I saw you with last night?" He waggled an imaginary cigar, like a Marx brother.

Not another bloody comedian. She rolled her eyes. "In the car park." She'd seen him chatting to a woman at the wheel of his Volvo. He'd gone for another ginger. Had Bev's foot-long Italian melt from Subway not been rapidly solidifying in its wrapper, she might have wandered over just to say hello, show the hand of friendship. Have a nose more like.

"Rachel. Yeah. She needs the car today, taking Rory to the clinic. I dropped by home after Handsworth and she brought me in."

Must be lonely moving to a new place, stuck on your own with a baby day in day out. It'd drive Bev up the wall. "If ever you need a babysitter or fancy a threesome?"

"I'd rephrase that if I were you." His lip curved.

Mouth. Grey cells. Fluster. Blush. She raised a palm. "Just a night out, the three of us. Nothing kink…"

"Say no more." He was pissing himself. "I get the picture."

"Snap." Grabbing the envelope, she mustered a smile, aimed for dignified. "Best get on."

Bridie Long didn't look a whole bunch better second time round; wrinkling her nose squinting at the e-fit didn't help. Neither did the lavender air freshener vying with the smell of old cat. "Could be anyone couldn't it?" Bridie sniffed, thrust the image back at Bev, resumed her customary slump in the armchair. Mac, sitting next to Bev on the settee, intercepted; the woman's glance had been cursory.

"Have another look, Mrs Long," he urged. "If your husband let him into the house, likely they knew each other?"

Glaring, she snatched it out of Mac's hand, fumbled down the side of the cushion, brought out a pair of specs. Vanity? It was a bit late for that. Bev and Mac exchanged eye rolls as she perused it.

"Nah. Never seen him before in me life." It was her final answer. Tight-lipped she passed it back, folded scrawny arms, hard and hostile. Bev tapped tetchy fingers on thigh; anyone would think they were the enemy. Even the cat was casting killer glances from the hearth, flicking its tail. Bev curled a lip, should've brought a brace of police dogs with them.

"The friend you were with, Mrs Long?" she asked. "The night your husband died. We need an address, phone number." Crossing t's and dotting i's, but the movements had to be checked. It was just conceivable she was having a fling with an axe murderer.

"Die?" Jeering contempt and dead wrong. "He didn't die. He was butchered." Her eyes were bloodshot, puffy; thin lips painfully cracked. Emotions were raw, and not just grief. "You bastards are to blame. It's all your bloody fault." Bev's sympathy reserves were on red; she bit her lip. "If your lot hadn't come round slinging accusations, dragging him into the nick, raking all that stuff up in the papers."

Raking all that stuff up. Marjorie Cox had used the same

phrase, damn sight more cause than this woman in Bev's book. She'd not get into a slag-off though. "Your friend's name, Mrs Long? Address?"

"That it? Nothing to say?" She ferreted down the other side of the chair, pulled out a pack of fags. Staring at Bev, she sparked up, spoke through the smoke. "My Eric slaughtered like a pig? And you just sit there."

Bev dug nails into a palm. "I'm sorry for your loss, Mrs Long. We're here to…"

"Sorry." She spat. "Should be ashamed of yourself." Sanctimonious old bitch.

"Tell you what shame is, shall I?" Icy, arctic, calm: she was about to blow.

"Sarge?" Mac recognised the signs.

"Shame's stubbing a fag out on a baby's body, half-starving her to death, breaking her tiny bones…"

"Sarge."

"You don't know that." The defiance wasn't convincing, Bridie Long had visibly paled.

"You're absolutely right, Mrs Long." She nodded genuinely contrite. With enough evidence he'd have got a longer sentence. "Maybe he just turned a blind eye while his woman did."

She dropped her head, lowered her voice. "It was years ago. He served his time, paid his dues."

Bev let it go. Nothing she said would change Bridie's view. The woman was blind in both eyes. There wasn't enough time in the world to pay for what had been done to Hannah. And if there was, Eric Long couldn't afford it.

"OK, mate, give." Bev held out a hand; the other stayed on the steering wheel. They were nearly back at Highgate and Mac had barely opened his mouth, probably down to his jaw being set in concrete. They'd eventually left Drake Street with the needful plus the name of a local man who Bridie claimed had hurled abuse at Eric. They also had Long's mobile so a check could be run on the calls. "Come on, Mac. What's your problem?"

"My problem?" She had a great view of his shoulder.

"You think I was out of order back there?"

He gave a resigned sigh, turned to face her. "We're cops, Bev. It's not our job to sit in judgement on people."

"Bollocks." She smacked a palm on the wheel. Somebody bloody well had to.

He tossed his head. "Oh, the cut and thrust of intellectual argument."

"It's a no-brainer, mate. Get real. We're not Robocops." God, it was getting steamy in here. She lowered the window, let in some air. "You saying we shouldn't have feelings same as other folk? What's that Shakespeare line? If you prick us, do we not bleed?"

"Long certainly did." Casual mutter. He wasn't up for argument.

"If you poison us, do we not die?"

"That too."

"Not funny. Not clever." She glowered. He sank a half bottle of Evian. "You know what I mean, mate. There's no point pretending. I don't feel the same for sleazy pervs and their apologists as I do about innocent kids and vulnerable oldies. Human nature, isn't it?"

"Yeah, but she's just lost her old man. You didn't have to slap her down like that."

She sniffed. "I didn't appreciate the lecture."

"So why give one back?"

"Agree to differ, shall we, mate?" She'd save her sympathy for people who deserved it. Sod the one-size-fits-all school of policing. They drove in silence. Bev ran a mental to-do list while Mac leafed through the local rag. At a red just round the corner from the nick, a headline caught her eye: Murder victim named. Must be the John Doe. She tapped a nail on the story. "What're they saying, mate?"

Mac read: "Police have named a man beaten to death in Wednesbury in the early hours of this morning. The body was discovered by a passer-by in a back alley near the town centre. Officers searching streets nearby found a bloodstained wallet dumped in a bin. Prints match those of the murder victim who's now been identified as sixty-nine year old Cyril Lord. Mr Lord lived in Harper House, Wednesbury. Anyone with information et cetera." He glanced up; nodded at the green light. "Boss?"

"Shit." She put her foot down.

"What's it to you anyway?"

"Just wondered." Harper House rang a bell somewhere but she couldn't fix on it, had to concentrate on finding a space in the car park. Tight but doable; she eased the motor in. "Can you get out that side, mate?"

"No problem. Just one thing, boss…" His hand was on the door. "If you're going to spout Shakespeare to prove a point, don't forget what he said about the quality of mercy not being strained." He tapped the side of his nose. Smart-arse. She pulled a face as he squeezed out, jumped when he popped his head back. "It droppeth as the gentle rain from heaven upon the place beneath. It is twice blessed."

The mock Gielgud was too good. "No shit, Shylock." Her lip twitched.

"Portia actually." He winked. "Get it right."

38

"Thought I'd let you know soon as, Bill." Roy Plover, Detective Superintendent Byford's opposite number in Wednesbury, was on the phone. He'd confirmed what the guv had just discovered himself in a call to a contact in the Home Office. Patrick Woolly had been released on licence at the back end of last year under a new identity: Cyril Lord. "Obviously we'll help in any way, but I'm happy to hand it over."

"Thanks, Roy, we'll liaise shortly. Speak later." Pensive, Byford dropped the phone in its cradle. Coming so close to the murder of Roland Haines and Eric Long, the child killer's death couldn't be coincidence, surely? Woolly hadn't been exposed in the media like Long and Haines, but the difference was easily explained: strict reporting restrictions were in place covering his identity and whereabouts, the media were banned from making an approach, no editor would've touched the story. It narrowed the field. Only a select few would've been aware of Lord's real name and criminal past, a small number within the local police, local authority and probation service. And the killer.

Pursing his lips, Byford reached for the cutting he'd found in the baby Fay file. More than gut instinct told him the same man was responsible for all three murders. Was it possible this was a message from the killer telling him the same?

Alerting the team via e-mail, he brought forward the brief by an hour. Something told him they were going to need an even bigger squad room.

Joe King had been right when he said the cops would have found it impossible to release a death picture. A montage of colour shots from the crime scene currently being tacked to a whiteboard in the briefing room was turning the stomachs of hardened squad members. Seated towards the front, Bev had been registering reactions: pig sick to puke alert. Sodding heat didn't help. She flapped the neck of her dress, desperate to get some air down there. Until now, she'd thought Darren's injuries were about as bad as it gets. Patrick Woolly's face had been virtually obliterated, the hatred behind the attack unimaginable.

Only the two detectives on secondment from Wednesbury appeared anywhere near immune, not surprising given they'd both seen close ups of Woolly in the flesh. They were there to aid Highgate's investigating officers overcome the handicap of not having been at the scene. There was little worse for an SIO than not viewing the body in situ. It was unavoidable in this instance; the squad's involvement only became an issue when Woolly's real identity emerged. Hopefully DC Cheryl Starkie and DS Trevor York would go some way to bridging the gap. Bev had chatted to them briefly, both seemed to know what they were doing.

A well-rounded, late thirties brunette with a Dudley accent, Cheryl was just finishing the display: adding a street map and a photograph of Woolly before the damage. Carol Pemberton and Danny Rees were comparing notes in the corner; Sumi Gosh sat at a desk near the window, sunlight glinting off blue-black waves of hair halfway down her back.

"Eh up. It's the three musketeers." Mac, perched next to Bev, cocked his head. Unsmiling, she glanced back to see Byford, Knight and Powell striding to the front. Grim-faced wasn't in it. The guv slung a couple of files on the desk nearest, flung his jacket over a chair, kicked off without preamble. "I'd say the killer's running rings round us. Three-nil now. How many more before we nail the bastard?" Shouting wasn't his style, nor swearing. Normally.

"Four actually, guv." Bev stared nonchalantly, her circling ankle a more accurate signal of her feelings. "Josh Banks is a victim too." Don't forget it, was the unspoken corollary.

Mac raised a finger, probably drawing fire. "Far be it from me, guv. But why assume the Wednesbury stiff's our baby?"

Byford glared as if it was a dumb question. "Patrick Woolly fits the offender profile." Curt, clipped. "He killed a child for Christ's sake. That more than meets the killer's agenda." What was his problem? Bev couldn't recall seeing the big man so tetchy.

Mac rested folded arms on his paunch. "True, but he wasn't in the papers. He's beaten up in the street. We didn't get a tip-off." He shrugged. "Sounds more like a random attack to me."

Fair points. The tic in the guv's jaw said he didn't agree, or maybe he knew something he wasn't sharing. "So the killer's stopped advertising," he snapped. "Until the evidence says differently, Patrick Woolly's our case."

"Yeah, but, how did the killer know who Cyril Lord was?" Mac persisted. "Privileged information, isn't it, guv?"

Barely perceptible signs to anyone else gave it away: Bev was convinced the guv was holding something back. Maybe had something to do with the leak? What a pisser, not knowing who to trust.

"It's one of the lines of inquiry, Mac," Byford said. "First…" He beckoned DS York to the front to give a rundown on what the Wednesbury cops had done so far. A lanky six-footer, Trevor York was animated but the data he delivered was routine: fingertip search of the back alley, cull of CCTV in neighbouring streets, canvass of passers-by, witness appeal on local radio. The area wasn't residential but a billiard hall round the corner from where Woolly was found in Brewers Lane had an active membership. A couple of DCs were going through the list on the off-chance someone had been in the vicinity. Bev took it all on board while casting covert glances at the guv. Something was bugging him big time. He wasn't just tetchy, he was ill at ease, almost shifty.

"Any ideas on the murder weapon, Trev?" Powell, hands in pockets, leaned against his customary wall. It should have a blue plaque by rights now.

The DS jabbed a thumb over his shoulder. "To do that much damage the pathologist thinks a hammer." Obviously not turned up during the search.

"Forensics?" Knight asked.

"Short supply, guv." York brushed a heavy fringe out of light brown eyes. "No defence wounds. No fibres. Victim was old, he'd been drinking, was probably a bit doddery at the best of times. Best guess is the killer was lying in wait in the dark, lashed out. A single blow would have knocked him to the ground then…" He shrugged. Bev shuddered.

Somebody's mobile chirped.

"Sorry guv." Sumi was half out of her seat. "I'll step outside. Need to take this call."

Byford barely noticed; thanking Trevor, he threw it open. Knight asked what, if anything, was being released to the media.

"Nothing. Not without my clearance. I want to see every word that goes out. Last thing we need are headlines screaming serial killer."

"They're sniffing round already, guv," Powell said. "Curran says he's had Toby Priest on the phone asking if it's true Cyril Lord was out on licence."

Tight mouth then: "Tell Curran to refer all calls to me. We're making no comment at this stage."

Least said soonest… And what was that wartime saying? Careless talk costs lives. Bev sat up straight, eyes creased.

Careless. She'd not considered the killer careless before. Cocky maybe, cavalier even. But now...

"Something on your mind, Morriss?" Powell raised an eyebrow. Gawd, was she that obvious?

"He's getting desperate, isn't he? Reckless. Wasting Woolly on the street was a hell of a risk. What if someone was passing? He could've been caught redhanded."

"Your point?" Byford asked.

"He's losing it. Doesn't care. Taking chances. It's escalating, guv."

He snorted. "And that's useful how?"

"Means he's more likely to make a mistake." Next time. The irony wasn't lost. To catch a killer, they needed him to strike again.

"Guv?" Sumi Gosh re-entered, mobile raised. "Just spoken to Staffordshire police. The stolen motor from Balsall Heath?" The only car clocked on CCTV that hadn't so far been traced. It had now.

39

"Turned up in a country lane in Tamworth, torched." Bev ripped a ring-pull off a can of Red Bull. She and DI Pete Talbot were standing chatting in Interview One's viewing room. The show next door must have attracted a matinée audience too, going by the empty cups and crumpled crisps packets. Typically, Pete had asked if there'd been any progress on Operation Swift. "We're getting it towed over: let FSI loose on what's left." She glugged half the contents of the can, dragged a hand across her mouth. "We're not exactly cracking open the champagne." Warm smile. "Not like you, eh, Pete?"

He gave a modest shrug. The DI towered over Bev, towered over anyone under six-five and not built like a brick shit-house. Gentle Giant? Bollocks. His bulk was intimidating and he wasn't scared to use it on arsey customers. In Ben Lawson's case it hadn't proved necessary. The low-life who'd attacked Darren had spilled so many beans, Pete's team was calling him Heinz.

"Not so big now, is he?" The DI tilted his head at the glass, swigged lemon tea from a thick white mug. He was taking a short break from the interrogation. Bev had dropped by for a nose.

Lawson sat with his feet up, hugging bony knees that poked through ripped denims. Snivel Boy had tears and snot running down his face. The petulant scowl was history, the yob more mindful of his future. According to Pete, he'd dished enough dirt on three mates to cover an opencast mine, never mind his arse. Or thought he had. The little shit couldn't talk his way out of hard evidence like blood traces in the treads of his Nikes.

Bev's palms itched. "Want me to take over, Pete? Read him a bedtime story?"

He laughed. "I want him standing when he gets to court."

Then he'd go down. Lawson and the others. There was already enough forensics to build a case. The team hoped to throw in separate less serious charges as well. All four anti-social gits had been named in calls logged from cowed residents at Heathfield House. Pete reckoned the tenants would be queuing up to give evidence, and not as character witnesses.

She cast Lawson a contemptuous glance. "Has he said why, Pete?" No need to spell it out. Why? was always the big one and, when mindless violence came into the equation, usually the hardest to figure out. Stacey Banks wanted it answered too, she'd asked that day at the station, asked again when she called to give Bev details of Josh's funeral.

"He won't say." Deep crevices appeared when Pete turned his mouth down, the craggy face cried out for Botox. "They were bladdered, egging each other on. They knew he was a cop though. They'd seen him on the estate asking questions."

Fair cop? Is that what it boiled down to? Bev shook her head. Thank God Lawson's mother had come forward. She drained the can, chucked it in a bin. "'Fore I go, can you sign this?" If anyone's name deserved to be on Darren's card, it was Pete's.

Byford watched through the glass, waiting until Bev finished. It was like watching a mime show; he half smiled even though he couldn't make out a word she was saying. Sitting forward, elbows on knees, her eyes shone and rapid hand movements underlined points as she talked. The conversation looked sparkling, animated and one-sided. Darren was a captive audience. Still comatose.

This was the guv's first sight of his officer since the attack. He'd had it in mind to visit before. Not because it was expected of him but because he had time and affection for the young detective. He'd given Darren his CID break, even teamed him with Bev for a while. He'd been told the injuries were bad but seeing the extent was still a shock: the lad was barely recognisable. Still, he was making steady progress according to the nurse Byford had waylaid. The brain swelling had subsided, motor responses were markedly improved. Great news. The big man was glad he'd come. But if he was being completely honest, Darren wasn't the only reason he was here.

Bev was laughing now, reading out messages from the huge get well card everyone at the nick had signed. Byford had brought along a couple of CDs. He'd read somewhere that coma patients may still be able to hear. He gave a wry smile: if it was true, Darren was certainly getting an ear bashing.

"Pete's got the lot banged up, Daz. How brill is that? They'll soon be spending a bunch of time with the queen... if you get my drift? Course you do, don't you, Daz? Hey! And guess what the station clowns call the toerag spilling the beans? You got it: Heinz. No flies on you, Daz. Snivel Boy, I call him.

"Anyway... enough work stuff. Kasabian are playing the NIA in November. My treat, yeah? Grab an Indian after? Got your birthday present sorted, mate. Yeah, I know it's a bit early. But HMV were doing this deal on a *Mission Impossible* box set. Have a Tom Cruise-fest when you come out, eh? Y'know I always take the piss about you looking like Cruise, Daz? Yeah, well, I see it now. You and him could be brothers. Course, you'd be the young good-looking one. Creep creep.

"What's it like in there, Daz? No need to feel lonely, y'know. Everyone's rooting for you, mate. And you should see some of the nurses and doctors, running round after you. Tasty or what? Well, you'll have a butcher's soon enough. Ask me you've had enough time lazing round. We need you back at the nick. I mean, take a look at this…"

Reaching for the card, she glimpsed Byford through the glass. Good of him to show, typical of the guy. "You've got a visitor waiting. I'll get out your hair in a minute, mate." Not that he had hair to get out of, but that was news she wouldn't be breaking.

Family firm collapses

The Leicester building company owned by Noel Myers, whose 10-year-old son was murdered last year, is closing with debts of half a million pounds. Twenty jobs will be lost when Myers & Son ceases trading at the end of the month. The business collapse is seen as the latest blow to hit a family jinxed by tragedy.

Last June, Scott Myers disappeared on the way home from school. His body was found on a golf course near his home in the village of Highfields. Four months later Scott's mother, 29-year-old Amy Myers, was killed when her car ran off a motorway at high speed. Sources close to the family say she never recovered from Scott's murder. An inquest into her death recorded an open verdict. The murderer is still at large.

The family home is now on the market. Mr Myers, pictured leaving the company premises yesterday, refused to comment.

What the fuck was he supposed to say? Yeah. Kid's murdered. Wife's topped herself. Business is buggered. Now I'm losing the house. Happy days, eh? The man raised an ironic toast, swallowed half the contents of a tumbler of Scotch, clenched his teeth as the spirit warmed its way into his gut. How many bottles a day was Noel on by then? In the picture he looked pissed off, not necessarily pissed. It had clearly been snatched, his hand failed to hide an ugly snarl, his hair was mussed, clothes dishevelled.

The man took a sip this time. The cutting was the last in the scrapbook. Shame the house wasn't the last thing Noel lost. With the first drink-drive offence he lost his licence. With the third or fourth he lost his liberty: six months in prison. He'd only avoided a custodial before because he'd pleaded with the court about having two kids and no one to look after them. Court must have decided no one was anyway.

The foster care was only supposed to be temporary. But it

didn't work out that way. Noel left prison in a coffin: cardiac arrest. Well… family was jinxed, wasn't it?

The man laughed out loud, his face wet with tears. He closed the scrapbook, pushed it to one side. The remaining pages contained photographs of people he didn't know. A family he'd never met. Only one face meant anything to him. He gave a rueful smile, finished his drink. He was getting to know her a little now, making up for lost time.

40

Two birds with one stone and all that. After leaving Darren with the guv, Bev had nipped to the cardiology unit to see how Gillian Overdale was doing. The two weren't bosom pals but the pathologist was single and short on family. If Bev were holed up in hospital surrounded by syringe-wielding strangers, she knew she'd welcome a familiar face and a chinwag. So had Overs. They'd had a ball. Well, maybe not a ball…

Still smiling, Bev made her way across the car park. The feel-good factor wasn't entirely down to earning a Brownie badge. The visit to Doctor Death hadn't been wholly altruistic. A casual bit of digging unearthed the juicy worm that early retirement was on the cards for the pathologist. Which meant a potential fulltime opening for he who will enlarge. The meaning of Joe King's name still had her in stitches. Chuckling to herself, she unlocked the Midget.

"What's the joke?"

"What the…" Eyes flashing, she spun round. God knew where the guv had sprung from.

"Sorry, I didn't mean to make you jump." He gave that lop-sided smile. "I'd still love to know what tickled you?"

An image of the big man enlarged flashed before her eyes. "It's a girl thing, guv." The lip curve was involuntary. Why was he hanging around anyway? Did he want a word about Darren? "Good of you to pay the lad a visit. Reckon he…?"

"I came because I knew you'd be here." His face was unreadable, voice soft spoken.

Maybe she'd misheard. "Sorry?"

"We need to talk, Bev." Serious bordering on sombre. She wasn't sure she liked the sound of it. Had she cocked up again? "About the case, guv?"

"That as well."

Paul Curran and Lance Knight were in deep conversation in The Prince; heads bent together over pints of bitter in the back snug. Apart from two old dears in the far corner playing cards the men had the place to themselves. Commentary on some soccer game drifted in from the widescreen TV in the bar. The subject under discussion on the table was the leak, not that it was going anywhere. Much as Knight would have liked to blow the whistle on Byford, it wasn't going to happen. Not on what he had so far.

"A few calls to Toby Priest is neither here nor there, Paul." It certainly wasn't enough to turn the DCI's unofficial snooping through the logs into an authorised tap on Byford's conversations. "I'll keep my ear to the ground but…" He held out empty palms.

"Fair enough, Mr Knight. I just thought it worth passing on." He slurped a mouthful of beer. "Reckon I should try and have a word on the QT with Priest?"

"You'd have to tread carefully." Knight didn't want dragging into some slanging match.

Curran nodded. "I'll see how it goes. Anything from the brief I need to know about?"

"Yeah. News releases. Any statement to the press. Everything's got to go through Byford."

"You're joking?"

"Every word, he said. Last thing we need is the media running with the serial killer angle."

"Great help that is." Curran shook his head, gave a deep sigh. "What if he's not around?"

"Your problem, matey." Knight drained his glass. "And your round."

The Chinese take-out was cold, congealed, virtually intact; the bottle of Pinot more than half full. Byford hadn't touched a drop; Bev had eaten less than him. They sat round the pine table in his kitchen, the first time for months she'd set foot in the house. He'd half expected a flat refusal when he suggested they come here to talk. Also knew she was sharp enough to realise he'd have good reason. He'd told her one of them: finding the Patrick Woolly cutting in the baby Fay file in his drawer. After that they'd lost their appetite for food, needed a clear head.

She ran her fingers through her hair. "You really think the killer left it, guv?"

Either that or he was going mad. He'd rarely felt so isolated during an inquiry, desperately needed someone to talk to he could trust. Not just someone. Not just talk.

"I think he's playing us, Bev. Sending messages."

"Saying?" He wished she wouldn't purse her lips like that. Or cross the thighs. Hot enough in here as it was. He walked to the sink, poured a glass of water. "Roland Haines, Eric Long, Patrick Woolly. What have they in common?" Slaked his thirst.

"They committed crimes against children." She shrugged. "We know that, guv."

"More than that." Why wasn't she seeing it? "They're all instances where the perp didn't get punished – "

Raised palm. "Woolly got life, guv."

"...didn't get punished enough." Keeping his gaze on her face, he walked back to his seat.

She had it in a heartbeat. "With you." Ticking fingers she made his point. "Haines didn't get to court. Long got a derisory sentence. And Woolly's let out with a new identity."

"Exactly. And the killer wants his pound of flesh and then some. He's protecting kids, Bev. More than that, he's avenging them. But his agenda's expanding. He's going after anyone with a record against minors."

She blew her cheeks out on a sigh. "That narrows it down. Not."

"Twenty thousand sex crimes alone every year in the UK." He hadn't checked, knew the figure anyway. "And how far back's he going? Woolly was convicted thirty years ago." Without pointers, the search parameters would be vast.

"'Nother possible factor, guv." She tucked a strand of hair behind her ear. He pointed at the bottle; she nodded. "Way the killer sees it, we've been cocking it up. If he's playing us, maybe it's 'cause he takes us for a bunch of clowns? He's no time for cops. He's showing us how to do the job properly. And in his head that's taking a life for a life."

He poured wine into her glass. "It's taking the law into his own hands. And given the information he seems to have access to... he could be a cop."

"It's not so far-fetched. Christ, guv, I had my doubts about you the other night."

"Thanks." But then maybe it wasn't so surprising given the rumours and lack of trust infiltrating the nick these days. A leak was corrosive in more ways than one.

She explained her thinking, then laughed it off. "Nah, guv." Sip of wine. "The killer's lost a kid close to him, something of that nature. Got to be something personal in it."

Byford nodded. The new line would mean serious plod work: cross-referencing child killers, cold cases, miscarriages of justice; across the country, over the years. He'd ask her to head up a small select team, start first thing. He watched as she sank the wine, stood the glass on the drainer. "I'd best get off, guv. Early shout and all that." She failed to stifle a yawn, stretched both arms over her head.

It was now or never. Steeling himself, he stood, held her gaze. "How about a nightcap?" Bated breath. He saw in her eyes she knew it wasn't what he was really asking. If she turned him down now, so be it. He might lose her, but he was too old to play games, sick of the uncertainty. It was her call: whatever she chose. They could move on together or go their separate ways.

"No ta, guv." She smiled, took his hand in hers. "Never wear anything in bed, me."

Neither did Byford. Later, propped on one elbow, lazy smile in place, Bev ran her gaze over his body, loved the way the moonlight glinted off his skin. It was one of those images she'd capture on that inward eye, cherish for ever. Better than a bunch of daffs any day. Whichever way you looked at it, he was gorgeous: simple as that. He made her laugh, made her happy, made her... The lazy smile morphed to lascivious. And the sex would get even better, less rushed, more relaxed. They'd take it easier next time. Had a lovely ring that: next time. She gave a deep sigh of contentment, closure almost. Being with him this way felt like coming home.

And he wasn't taking off any time soon, he'd told her. His son had sent the newspaper she'd spotted on his desk. Rich lived in Cumbria anyway and wanted his dad's help financing a new house. Byford had been looking over his potential investments. Sure he'd considered it, but how could he up sticks if she was thinking of going for promotion? She chuckled softly. Maybe if they'd spent less time gabbing and more time...? She couldn't tear her gaze from her sleeping partner: the curve of his lips, the broad shoulders, the rise and fall of his chest, the line of thick black hair down...

"I've got my eye on you, young lady." Smiling, he turned to

face her.

She gave a speculative pout. "Is that all?"

This time they did take it easier.

THURSDAY
41

They'd taken it so easy, it was touch and go whether Bev would hit work on time. Ten to eight and she was stuck in traffic and sticky heat on the Highgate Road. At least the forecasters were talking about movement, a band of low pressure allegedly moving in. She tapped the wheel: why was every sodding light against her? Maybe they should have cut out the touchy-feely first thing and just taken off? Nah. Broad smile. Where was the fun in that? It was only nipping home for a shower and change that meant she was in catch-up mode. But hey, it was no problem. Cutting it fine was a small price to pay for an early morning love-fest with the guv.

And the solution was easy.

Hold your horses, girl. It was way too early to shack up. She cocked an eyebrow. Or was it? The big man didn't think so, and he was the boss.

Yeah right. Her grin didn't fit the mirror. She hit the CD player: bit of Cat Stevens this morning, *Father and Son*. What did he call himself now? Yusouf? Whatever. He had the benefit of her backing vocals as she inched the Midget forward. For the first time in a while, she felt energised: the sun was shining, they had a new line of inquiry, the guv wasn't going anywhere. Guv. Why was it so much easier to say than Bill? What's in a name? Chortling – she made a mental note to tell him what was in Joseph: he who will enlarge. William meant strong protector. Might tell him that, as well. Long as he didn't get ideas above his station.

Powell was running a tad late too. He got out of his car just as Bev was locking the MG. She waggled her fingers, threw him a "Wotcha." Headed towards the back stairs.

"Hey, Morriss, where's the fire? I want a word." Her eye-roll was resigned: he had the social skills of a skunk but hey-ho, better the skunk you know… "I hear there's a DI post going in Worcester."

"Oh yeah?" Like she didn't know. She'd just not decided yet whether to submit the completed paperwork. She hiked her bag as they fell into step. "Trying to get rid of me?"

He winked. "Doubt you'd get it." She spotted a shaving nick on his neck, bet it stung when he chucked on the Paco.

"Cheeky sod." Casual sniff.

"You could walk it, Morriss. You know that." Did she balls. "Long as you don't gob off at the interviews." He held the door for her.

"Who says I'm going for it?"

"Your call." He shrugged. "Least the opening's there. New frock, Morriss?"

Silk shift, same shade as her eyes. If Powell had noticed, it must look shit hot. "Yeah. So?"

"Looking good." He gave a mock salute, trooped off to his office, called back. "Wear it on the interview, pet."

The current job was more than enough to keep Bev busy. And the rest of the squad. The early brief had been brisk, business-like. Byford dished out tasks like there was no tomorrow: he'd despatched detectives to all four crime scenes in a concerted effort to canvass more locals. It went further than mopping up house-to-house, it meant stopping, questioning and flashing stills at passers-by and motorists. Though the murders had received mega coverage in the media, it didn't necessarily follow the stories reached everyone. Some watchers switch off mentally when the news is on, or when *The X Factor* isn't. And too many folk round here couldn't read to save their own lives never mind help solve the murders of others. In addition to work in the field, the press exposure was still prompting punters to phone in with what could loosely be called intelligence. Calls had to be answered, assimilated and in some instances acted on. That task was keeping another bunch of officers occupied.

The guv was now closeted with Knight and Powell, reviewing the inquiries and assessing strategies. It was all in the name of accountability. When the brass asked questions, people like the guv had to be able to justify every decision, every thought, every step of the way.

For once, Bev was happy to be back at the ranch. She, Mac, Danny Rees and Carol Pemberton had commandeered a corner of the squad room and were up to their metaphorical epaulettes in checks. Byford had asked her to head up a digging team: crimes against children where – it could be argued – the perp had gone unpunished or got off lightly. It was mostly web-based, but also meant a fair bit of liaising with other forces on the phone. If you asked Bev, they needed a fleet of excavators. Maybe some midnight oil. Definitely a lunch-break.

Even so after four hours solid, she was still decidedly upbeat. Logging off, she rolled back her chair. "I'm grabbing a bite to eat. Get anyone anything?"

"Pack of happy pills." Mac nodded his head at the screen. "Depressing, isn't it, boss? All this… stuff."

"Chin up, mate. Gotta be done."

He raised an eyebrow. "Did Pollyanna win the lottery?"

Something like that. She curled a lip in an exaggerated snarl. "Get on with it, Bozo."

"That's better, boss." He grinned. "I'll have what you're having."

42

"My God, there's actually a cloud in the sky." Mac leaned back in the chair, hands crossed behind his head, paunch straining buttons as per. "I'd forgotten what they look like."

"Not being paid to look at clouds, Tyler." Bev wouldn't say her sunny mood had gone but by seven they were all burned out. Their desks were littered with paper cups, empty cans, sweet papers and KitKat wrappers. They'd do another hour then call it a day. None of the four had said no to a bit of over-time. Unlike the guv, who'd taken an early out after the late brief, some police authority meeting at the Council House. He'd told Bev it had a three-line whip. Mine's got nine, she'd quipped. Her lip twitched at the memory.

"The heat's gone on for ever," Mac muttered, turning to face the screen again. "Be glad to see the back of it, me."

"Moan, moan, whinge… fuck me." Bev froze, her gaze fixed on the monitor, a newspaper front page. Mac, Danny and Pembers were already out of their chairs eager for a butcher's. "Hold on a tick," Bev said. Maybe it was just her. She covered the text with her hands, leaving the picture in view. "Who's that, then?"

They took their time but the chorus was unanimous. "Josh Banks."

"New pic." Pembers tucked her hair behind her ears. "I've not seen him without his glasses before."

"You wouldn't." Bev took her hands away. "It's not Josh."

Three heads leaned in for a closer look. Danny asked first. "So who's Scott Myers?"

"Find out, shall we?"

Byford was in the bedroom, fastening his tie in the mirror. He'd not planned on nipping home, then again he'd not planned on leaving the police authority paperwork on the hall table. He wasn't complaining about the memory lapse. There'd been far more interesting things on his mind this morning, and in other places. He smiled. Thank God she'd said yes to that nightcap. Ironic really. The last time he'd offered the same thing was the night of the attack. She'd not refused, just deferred it twenty-four hours, walked out into the snow and...

Forget it, man. That was then, this is... A ring at the door. He frowned. Wasn't expecting anyone. He dashed downstairs, grabbed his jacket off the newel, shucked into it as he opened the door. Christ, saying he wanted every news release to go through him didn't mean house calls. "Paul?"

"I know this is out of order, Mr Byford, but... please... can we talk?" Hesitant, wary. It was a plea, reinforced by what might be fear in his eyes.

"Can it wait?" Clearly not, or the guy wouldn't be here.

"It won't take long, honest." He didn't look well; flushed, sweating. "I know who's behind the leaks."

Byford checked his watch, had a few minutes in hand. More than that, his curiosity was piqued.

Curran raised a slim file. "It's in here. Believe me... you need to know."

The bare bones of Scott Myers's story didn't take long to unearth: a ten-year-old boy abducted on the way home from school in Leicester thirty years ago, murdered and the killer was never found. Bev and the team were working feverishly to find the flesh, forge a link. She kept telling herself it could all be coincidence. The likeness between Scott and Josh Banks was uncanny. But how did it fit with the murders of Roland Haines, Eric Long and Patrick Woolly?

Glancing across the desk she saw Danny and Carol hunched over screens, tapping keyboards. Mac was on the phone talking to Leicester police, he'd already passed Bev a home number for the detective who'd headed the Myers inquiry. She'd dialled Ted Adams – twice got the engaged tone. Powell and Knight were up to speed, had opted to hang round, the guv's phone had gone to voicemail.

"Mr Adams?" Thank you, God. She was hoping for insight, detail that never made it into the public domain. "DS Bev Morriss, West Midlands police." Adams recalled the case immediately. She'd been expecting an East Midlands accent but this guy's Scottish brogue was so thick she had to ask for a repeat every so often. What was more than clear as the story unfolded was that the unsolved case still haunted the retired detective: for Adams, Scott's murder was the equivalent of Byford's baby Fay: unfinished business.

"I'd have done anything to put the bastard behind bars, lass." No one had even been in the frame going on the reports Bev had read.

"You had a suspect?"

"Closest we came was the lad's head teacher. Sol Danvers. We had him in a couple of times. No forensics though. Wife gave him a cast iron alibi." She sensed a but. "There was talk in the village. Something about the man…"

Sounded slim to Bev. "That it?"

"Instinct's sometimes all you have." Deep sigh. It wasn't enough. She thanked Adams, gave him her number, asked him to call if anything came to mind. Something had: "Shattered the entire family you know, lass. I often wondered what became of the other bairns. They lost a lot more than their wee brother that day."

"They'd be what, early thirties now?" She tapped a pen against her teeth.

"Aye. The little one, Alan, was only just three when it happened. Wendy the girl was a few years older."

"Sarge." Danny Rees, gaze fixed on screen, beckoned her over.

"Got to go, Mr Adams. I'll keep you posted."

The whole team clustered round the desk. The picture on the monitor had been taken at Scott Myers's funeral. Bev frowned, couldn't get her head round it. The grieving father couldn't be Paul Curran, it didn't make sense. She leaned closer, read the caption. It wasn't; it was Noel Myers, arm round his wife, and in the background two kids dressed in black looking like little lost souls: Alan and Wendy. He'd changed the name but Paul Curran couldn't alter the genes: even back then he was the image of his dad.

"They were given up for adoption, sarge." Danny pulled up another page. "Mother was killed in a road crash. Father died of a heart attack in prison."

She felt a chill down the spine, knew with absolute certainty: "He's avenging his brother's murder."

Danny broke what felt like a dubious silence. "How does that fit in with Josh?"

"Don't know yet, Danny." She didn't have the full picture, finer detail could be filled in later. "Curran can't take out Scott's killer: he was never caught. So he's going after the next worst thing. Haines, Long, Woolly."

"Anyone he thinks has got away with crimes against children?" Powell was partly on board.

Eyes creased, she recalled last night's conversation with the guv. *He's no time for cops.* What if he'd started targeting cops too? Her palms tingled. "Where is Curran?"

"Last time I saw him he was looking for Byford," Knight

proffered. "Said he needed a green light on a news release."

Bev kept her voice calm; the racing heart was beyond her control. "Any way of checking the guv's at that police meeting?"

"Sarge?" Mac picked up the hidden urgency.

"It's escalating. He's losing control." She ran both hands through her hair. "Could be he sees the guv as fair game." Glancing round the circle, she saw scepticism.

"Come on, Bev..." Powell remonstrated.

Impatient shake of the head. "Think about it. Even the guv blames himself for not catching a baby killer. Who's to say Curran doesn't see it that way too?"

"He wouldn't know about that case, Bev."

"He does." Knight drew his lips together. "He's seen the file." He related Curran's attempts at casting Byford as the Highgate mole, presumably to deflect suspicion closer to home. "Curran's got no time for Byford. He said..."

"Sarge?" Pemberton interrupted; she'd just finished a call. "The guv isn't at the meeting. He didn't show."

Until he came round Byford had no idea what hit him. Slowly opening his eyes, he winced as waves of pain broke around his skull. Curran sat in the chesterfield opposite, a Scotch in one hand, a Heckler and Koch in his lap. The guy's smile was almost as menacing as the gun.

"Drink, Mr Byford?" The detective shook his head, regretted it instantly. Quickly realised it wasn't an offer. Either way he was in no position to refuse. His hands were cuffed round the back of an upright chair, twine drew blood at his ankles. He watched warily as Curran sprang from the seat, scooped a bottle of Laphraoig from a low table, moved into Byford's peripheral vision. Braced for a blow, he gasped when Curran grabbed his hair, forced his head against the wall, jammed the bottle between his lips. The malt ran down his chin, his neck, mostly it burned the back of his throat. God knew how much he'd drunk but when Curran tipped the bottle, the flow was too great: Byford gagged, spluttered, his eyes streamed.

"Naughty naughty, Mr Byford." Curran took it out, examined the contents. "There was really no need to drink it all at once."

Byford gulped, gagged again. "Why are you doing this?"

Curran walked to the sideboard, selected another bottle. "To make it easier for you, Mr Byford."

"Make what easier?" Words were slurred, vision blurred.

"Shush now." Curran put a finger to his lips. "Have another drink. I promise you won't feel a thing."

It took five minutes for a patrol car to establish Curran's Volvo was parked outside Byford's detached house at Four Oaks. An armed response vehicle was in position out of sight within forty yards. It could be overkill, no one was taking chances. Nine o'clock now. Still light despite louring clouds, Knight favoured waiting for nightfall, arguing darkness would give them the edge.

Bev was on it already. "Let me go in, sir." She sat in the back of an unmarked police motor, Mac alongside, Knight and Powell up front.

The DCI glanced over his shoulder. "No one goes anywhere till we know what we're playing with."

Playing? With the guv's life a possible stake. Byford knew how to handle himself, but if she was on the money Curran had killed three times. Desperate and deadly, he had nothing to lose. She shivered. Partly the drop in temperature, more down to the icy calm she'd forced on herself during the twenty minute drive across town, plea-bargaining with God. Sitting here, watching, waiting, was sending her crazy. "We're not going to know until someone goes in, sir." Still cool, oozing a confidence she struggled to maintain. If Knight thought for a second she was emotionally involved he wouldn't let her anywhere near the place. His face in the mirror was a portrait of indecision.

Strategically stationed police marksmen had established far as possible that upstairs rooms were empty. Downstairs curtains were drawn, a slight gap showed lights on in the living room. "Curran knows me, sir. We get along." Tight fists were clammy with sweat. "I'll talk to him. He'll listen."

More than Knight appeared to be doing.

She cut a glance at the house. What the fuck was going on? "I know the layout," Bev said. "I've got a key."

Pursed lips then: "You'll need a vest." Kevlar.

"I'm kitted out."

"You'll need a wire."

"I have." She'd made sure before leaving Highgate.

Knight sighed, shook his head. "I still think we should…"

"Let her go in." Powell, stating not requesting. She met his eyes in the mirror. "DS Morriss knows what she's doing."

Yes! God. She could kiss the guy. Certainly buy him a drink when this was all over.

Byford had passed out: head slumped to the side, whisky drooled from slack lips.

"Had enough, Mr Byford?" Curran's voice dripped insincerity. For twenty, thirty seconds he stood over the detective, watching, smiling. Satisfied, he raised the bottle to his own mouth, took several slugs before strolling to the settee to retrieve the gun. Ears pricked, he cocked his head. Key in the door? Smiled again. Bev Morriss? She'd certainly been in no hurry to leave last night. Then he cocked the gun.

The smell of booze hit Bev first. For a split second she imagined finding them having a friendly drink. Her nose wrinkled:

no one was that friendly. Padding into the hall, she headed for the only open door.

"Come in, Bev." She stood stock still. How did he know? "Come join the party." Low light. Lush red furnishings. First thing she saw was the gun at Byford's temple, second the empty bottles: her insides turned to ice. "In fact, Bev, you could call it a farewell do." Curran's laugh scared her witless. He wasn't losing it: it had already gone.

"I take it you're wired?" He'd know, of course. She nodded. "That's fine," he said. "Famous last words and all that." She forced a thin smile to humour the mad fucker. He waved her towards an armchair. "Sit down... before you drop."

She walked to it slowly, sat back, apparently unfazed, heart pounding so hard it hurt. She needed to busk it like never before. Even if the alcohol hadn't been spiked, Byford needed a stomach pump fast. Was he even breathing? She couldn't see. "It's not too late, Paul." Conciliatory, cajoling.

He frowned as if considering the option, then: "Oh, I think it is." Toying with her.

She edged forward, elbows on knees, as if getting closer would bridge the gap. "Mitigating circumstances. You could plead extreme provocation. Losing your broth..."

"Lose him?" He spat. "A filthy piece of scum killed him." Her fists clenched when he pressed the barrel into Byford's temple. "And you have no right to talk about Scottie. You never knew him. He's nothing to you."

Neither did you, fuckwit. "No, but I can see he was every-thing to you. I can't pretend to know how you feel. Losing him... your parents... your sister..." His eyes narrowed. Had she hit a chord? "A sympathetic jury will see that, Paul." Like hell they would.

"They won't hear the sob story from me." He switched the gun to his own forehead, pulled an imaginary trigger.

She froze. If he intended killing himself, there was a chance no one would get out of here alive. Curran had nothing to lose, he'd lost it thirty years ago. No. He hadn't. "What about your wife, Paul? Your little boy?"

"You really are thick, aren't you?" He turned the gun again: Byford was back in the firing line.

Get on with it, dumbfuck. Though he'd been sharp enough to get a job that gave access to privileged information, and leak it to the media. "Tell me...?"

"You honestly imagine I could form some sort of relationship after..." He bit his lip. "I thought it was me. Being adopted, feeling unwanted, unloved. I didn't know how I'd lost my real family until..."

She cut the guv a glance; still couldn't detect a sign of life. "Until what, Paul?"

"A scrapbook arrived in the post six months ago from a sister I wasn't aware existed. She tracked me down... told me everything. She needed my help."

For wife, read sister. Rachel. No wonder she'd thought they were alike. "She was pregnant?"

He nodded. "She'd had a pretty shit life, lived on the streets for a while, picked up a habit."

Heroin? "She supplied the methadone?" Made the phone call pointing them to Haines too, presumably.

"Who else? She blamed everything on what happened after Scottie was murdered. We both wanted payback. It was her idea to plant the sock in Haines's pad. I tell you, seeing Rory, watching him grow these last few months..." He bit his knuckles. "I had to do something to protect the little children..."

Home truths time. "You won't be much use to Rory or your sister if you're dead, Paul."

"They'll never suffer again." Smug smile. "They're in a better place. We'll all be together soon. Mum. Dad. Scottie..."

She'd been out of her depth before. This was the deepest ocean. She struggled for words. Curran broke the silence. "Maybe we'll meet up with Josh there, eh? Little Josh started it all really. Seeing his face, it was just like seeing Scottie." His eyes filled with undiluted hatred. "And knowing what I'd missed."

What was he saying? That Josh had been a catalyst for Curran's killing spree? "You murdered Josh?" Her voice was a whisper.

"Don't you ever listen?" He snarled. "I'd never harm a child."

She held placatory palms. "Of course not, Paul. You're their protector. You save them from scum." He calmed fractionally; she breathed again. "Everything you do is to avenge little children, isn't it? I understand that."

Sulky nod.

"Same as Mr Byford there. He's sent down loads of bastards who hurt kids."

"Save it." He snorted. "A child killer's out there now because this prat cocked up."

"And he's never stopped beating himself up over it, Paul. He's a good man."

"Not good enough."

"Paul. Give it up." She stifled a scream as he pressed the barrel harder to Byford's temple.

"Stay away or I'll shoot you first." She'd drawn fire. The gun was aimed at her. She had one last desperate throw of a heavily loaded dice. She sank back in the chair saying, "Then you'll never know who killed Scott, will you?" Her expression, the tone of her voice said she did.

"I hate liars. You get to watch him die for that." Barrel against temple. Finger against trigger.

"Sol Danvers." She screamed. "He's in custody. I swear." Had the name even registered?

His eyes narrowed. "Talk."

She fabricated a pack of lies. Veins fizzing with adrenalin, voice heavy with conviction she told him the vice squad had been keeping tabs on Danvers, he'd been under surveillance for weeks, the net had finally closed, he was in a cell at Highgate. She held his gaze, every fibre of her willing him to buy the story. The guy had doubts, she could see it; but she was scared she'd blown it.

"Give me five minutes with him."

Why did everyone want five fucking minutes with someone? "I'm sure that can be arranged, Paul. Can I release the guv?"

"Do I have your word?"

"On my life. There are people outside who'll take you."

"Wait until I'm out of here." He started walking towards the door. She was out of the seat when she heard the first shot. "I hate liars, Bev."

The bullet hit Byford in the face, a second in the chest. Bev fell to her knees, momentarily stunned. Where did the blood come from? A scarlet pool spread across his shirt, his beautiful face a mass of torn tissue, white bone. She barely reacted when two shots sounded in the street. Could even have been thunder. Except the storm hadn't broken. Not outside. Sobbing, gasping, she ran to him then; cradled him in her arms. "Bill, Bill, don't die, don't leave me." Over and over and over again. Knowing he already had.

Twelve days later

He'd never wanted the panoply of a police funeral, but hundreds had turned out to show respect anyway. His sons had been there too, of course. The Chief Constable had done the eulogy. Bev had sat alone at the back of the church, slipped out first, waited in the Midget, watched through the heavy rain as mourners left. Gentle rain from heaven? Yeah right.

She gave a bitter scowl, lit a cigarette. There were still a couple of black-garbed stragglers bobbing like giant crows among the distant moss-pocked headstones. There was no hurry. The big man wasn't going anywhere. Bev was dead too, inside. Eyes screwed tight, she tried so hard to recall his sleeping figure cast in moonlight, but all she ever saw was his lifeless body bathed in blood. Would he still be here if she hadn't lied? Most cop colleagues thought Curran would've shot the guv anyway. Bev had been there and couldn't say with certainty. It wasn't the hardest thing she had to live with.

She was convinced Curran had a death wish. He'd exited the house waving the gun around; two marksmen took him out. His wish was unfulfilled. Unlike Darren, who was now out of the coma, Curran was in a vegetative state in hospital. It was too early for medicos to say whether the condition would become permanent. Bev hoped for his sake he never came round. He'd discovered his bloodline, turned it into a death line. The hit list had been found at his house along with the scrapbook.

She still thought there was a chance Curran had killed Josh. His twisted weird logic wouldn't see it like that of course. Mad bastard had thought he was sending his sister and nephew to a better place – after smothering them. Why not Josh too? She picked a fleck of tobacco from her lip. If not Curran, who?

She'd heard via Mac on the phone that the red car hadn't thrown out any leads. Brett Sullivan had finally been traced. He'd been all brash swagger as befitted a bully boy: his description of the driver was useless.

Her eyes creased against the smoke. Did every cop have a baby Fay? Was Josh Banks destined to be hers?

She'd track down his murderer if it killed her – assuming she went back to the job.

The rain was easing off, the only remaining crows feathered and raucous. She stubbed out the cigarette, dragged herself from the motor, walked slowly to the fresh mound of earth under which Byford lay next to his wife. She'd considered bringing flowers. A cactus maybe? She'd given him enough of those in the past, her jokey way of saying sorry. Exactly. She'd come empty-handed, heavy-hearted, wearing the blue silk dress. He'd said the cornflower shade matched her eyes. She knelt in the wet mud, lowered her head, stroked the soil, talked to him. Not God. Never again.

How much time passed she didn't know. She was oblivious, too, when the heavens opened. Within seconds rain dripped from her hair, her chin, the thin silk clung to her skin. And for the first time since watching him die, she let the tears fall.

"You don't have to do this alone, Bev."

Furious at the intrusion, she spun round, eyes flashing, ready to let rip. Mike Powell stood over her, his black trench coat soaked, blond hair like a skull cap. He reached out a hand. "Come with me." She opened her mouth to say no; saw the pain in his eyes, the tears running down his pale face. "Let me take you home, Bev."

MORE WITTY, GRITTY BEV MORRISS MYSTERIES FROM MAUREEN CARTER:

WORKING GIRLS

Detective Sergeant Bev Morriss infiltrates Birmingham's vice-land.

ISBN: 9780954763404 **£7.99**

Also available as an ebook.

Dark and gritty... an exciting debut novel...
- Sharon Wheeler, Reviewing the Evidence

DEAD OLD

Elderly women are being attacked, and the killer moves uncomfortably close to home for Bev Morriss.

ISBN: 9780954763466 **£7.99**

Complex, chilling and absorbing...
- Julia Wallis Martin, author of *The Bird Yard* and *A Likeness in Stone*

BABY LOVE

Rape, baby-snatching, murder: all in a day's work for Birmingham's finest. But Bev takes her eye off the ball.

ISBN: 9780955158902 **£7.99**

Carter writes like a longtime veteran... - David Pitt, Booklist (USA)

HARD TIME

Bev Morriss doesn't do fragile and vulnerable, but she's struggling.

ISBN: 9780955158964 **£7.99**

British hard-boiled crime at its best.
- Deadly Pleasures Year's Best Mysteries (USA)

BAD PRESS

Bev Morriss has crossed words with journalist Matt Snow countless times, and can't believe he's a killer.

ISBN: 9780955707834 **£7.99**

If there was any justice... she'd be as famous as Ian Rankin!
- Sharon Wheeler, Reviewing the Evidence

BLOOD MONEY

Bev Morriss is in no mood to play...

ISBN: 9780955707872 **£7.99**

... an energetic and compelling series... that would work on TV - Tangled Web

Meet Bev Morriss again in

CRIMINAL TENDENCIES

**a diverse and wholly engrossing collection of short
stories from some of the best of the UK's crime writers.**

**£1 from every copy sold of this
first-rate collection will go to support the
NATIONAL HEREDITARY
BREAST CANCER HELPLINE**

*She lay on her face, as if asleep. I turned her over and saw the deep
wound on her brow...*
– Reginald Hill, *John Brown's Body*

*...she was shaking badly. Terror was gripping her; the same terror she
previously experienced only in her dreams...*
– Peter James, *12 Bolinbroke Avenue*

*His lips were thin and pale. "She must be following us. She's some sort
of stalker."*
– Sophie Hannah, *The Octopus Nest*

*When he thought he was alone, he squatted down and opened the
briefcase. I was interested to see that it contained an automatic pistol
and piles and piles of banknotes.*
– Andrew Taylor, *Waiting for Mr Right*

*Avengers, that's what we are. We're there to avenge the punters who pay
our wages.*
– Val McDermid, *Sneeze for Danger*

The job was a real peach. Soft, juicy, ripe for plucking.
– Simon Brett, *Work Experience*

ISBN: 978-09557078-5-8   £7.99

THE LATEST FROM CRÈME DE LA CRIME

THE BROKEN TOKEN   **Chris Nickson**
When Richard Nottingham, Constable of Leeds, discovers his former housemaid murdered in a particularly sickening manner, his professional and personal lives move perilously close.

More murders follow, and when answers eventually start to emerge, Nottingham gets more than he bargains for…

ISBN: 9780956056610   **£7.99**

SWORD AND SONG   **Roz Southey**
Musician-sleuth Charles Patterson is called to a suspected murder late one night – and is horrified to find he knows the victim, a young streetgirl.

A chance meeting with an American at an elegant house party raises new questions about the murder – and Patterson's personal life is becoming ever more complicated…

ISBN: 9780956056627   **£7.99**

DEBT OF DISHONOUR   **Mary Andrea Clarke**
London society is outraged when charming, popular Boyce Polp is murdered, apparently by a highwayman. But Miss Georgiana Grey has her own reasons for doubting this version of the tragedy. She uncovers a darker side to Polp, determined that justice will prevail.

ISBN: 9780956056641   **£7.99**

CRIME FICTION FOR ALL TASTES FROM CRÈME DE LA CRIME

by **Linda Regan**:

Behind You!	ISBN: 9780955158926
Passion Killers	ISBN: 9780955158988
Dead Like Her	ISBN: 9780955707889

Regan exhibits enviable control over her characters – Colin Dexter

by **Adrian Magson**:

No Peace for the Wicked	ISBN: 9780954763428
No Help for the Dying	ISBN: 9780954763473
No Sleep for the Dead	ISBN: 9780955158919
No Tears for the Lost	ISBN: 9780955158971
No Kiss for the Devil	ISBN: 9780955707810

Gritty, fast-paced detecting of the traditional kind – The Guardian

by **Penny Deacon**:

A Kind of Puritan	ISBN: 9780954763411
A Thankless Child	ISBN: 9780954763480

a fascinating new author with a hip, noir voice – Mystery Lovers

by **Kaye C Hill**:

Dead Woman's Shoes	ISBN: 9780955158995
The Fall Girl	ISBN: 9780955707896

… a welcome splash of colour and humour – Simon Brett

by **Gordon Ferris**

Truth Dare KILL	ISBN: 9780955158940
The Unquiet Heart	ISBN: 9780955707803

If It Bleeds	Bernie Crosthwaite	ISBN: 9780954763435
A Certain Malice	Felicity Young	ISBN: 9780954763442
Personal Protection	Tracey Shellito	ISBN: 9780954763459
Sins of the Father	David Harrison	ISBN: 9780954763497